Show Me

LAURIE RYAN

Editor: Lois Benedetti

Cover Design and Interior format by The Killion Group
http://thekilliongroupinc.com

DEDICATION

Cancer, in any form, requires courage to stay the course, so it's no surprise that courage plays heavily into my dedication for this story.

To Dave, may he rest in peace, and his wife Sue, for showing me the true meaning of courage.

And to my sister, an ovarian cancer survivor, who is my role model for how to live with courage and dignity and who reminds me to find the simple joys in each and every day.

ACKNOWLEDGEMENTS

The idea for this story came from several different sources. At the time I started writing, we were all grieving over the loss of a dear friend to Mesothelioma, and I needed to better understand the past couple of years. At the same time, someone at a writer's event said something about wanting to read a good ghost story. And thus, an idea was born.

This story was a very emotional journey for me, filled with both despair and healing. I was well into the story and knew my heroine and her diagnosis when my sister was diagnosed with this same cancer. Thankfully, hers was caught at stage one and she is many years cancer free now.

I am grateful to many people for helping to make this story what it is. To Sue and Kathy, for defining strength, to Lois for her unyieldingly positive outlook on life (and her stellar editing skills), to Lavada Dee and Tricia Jones for their unfailing faith in this story.

To my husband and mother, who gave me the time I needed to write this. And to cancer patients everywhere. Always keep hope in your heart. It is, after all, the strongest medicine of all.

1

FIRST CONTACT

Celia Milbourne ran shaky fingers through her dark hair and checked her watch for the third time. Where was he? The file she'd plunked on his desk grabbed her attention like a neon light blinking on and off, never quite out of view. Her file. Her test results. Picking it up, she fanned the pages, then tossed it back onto the desk, thinking about the appointment she'd just come from. The whole discussion with her gynecologist made no sense. How could she be sick? She felt fine.

She thought about what had driven her to make the appointment. The minimal but out-of-character spotting and the feeling that she was on the brink of a bladder infection. Always feeling bloated. Maybe she wasn't quite fine, but she was healthy enough for this to be some sort of colossal mistake.

She sat down in one of the stuffed chairs in front of Dr. Ted's desk, but rose moments later, circling the office where medical diplomas shared wall space with pictures of sailboats. Celia touched the stethoscope on the credenza and stopped to pick up the photo of his wife and his two daughters, the latter both close in age to her own thirty five years.

Nostalgia momentarily dulled her worry. She'd been in this office many times, even had a couple impromptu Chinese take-out dinners as they discussed life or argued solutions to current world problems.

Ted Jameson had been more than just her family doctor for a long time now. First, by filling the gaping hole left after her father's death. Then, he'd become her mentor when she took a job as a pharmaceutical rep. So it was only natural for her to run straight here when the specialist had started spouting words and possibilities that chilled her to the bone. She respected Dr. Ted. He would tell her the truth.

She just wasn't sure she wanted to hear it. A shiver slid down her back, draining any residual strength Celia had left. Her mind swam with results and percentages and possibilities.

The door opened with very little noise, yet Celia jumped, bobbling the family picture before she could place it safely back on the credenza.

"Celia," Dr. Ted said in a voice reserved for, well, just about everyone. He was that kind of doctor.

That calming influence, that happiness to see her was exactly what she needed. Relief shored up her strength, fed it, until her smile was genuine. "Hi."

"This is a nice surprise." He picked up the cup of his favorite coffee, which Celia had placed on his desk, and gave a satisfied sniff, tipping it in her direction. "Thank you. Exactly what I needed. So what brings you here in the middle of the day?"

The smile died as her eyes pointed like a homing beacon to the file. "I need you to interpret—that."

"Sure. Have a seat while I take a look." He sat in one of the comfy seats and opened the file. Still easy. Still relaxed.

Unlike her. Celia's chair felt like a bed of nails. Her hands clutched the arms, then unclutched them as she watched him read. When he sat straighter and frowned, then flipped the page, she was on her feet again, pacing, fighting to keep the ominous sense of dread at bay.

The trap sprung while she was in the corner.

"Come sit down, honey." Dr. Ted took off his glasses and pinched the cartilage between his eyes.

"I-I don't think I want to."

"We need to discuss this," he said, giving the file a little wave.

Her shoes felt like they were made of lead. She took a deep breath and forced one foot in front of the other until she reached the chair. Sitting down wasn't an option, though. Too confining. Everything was about to crash in on her for the second time that day. She needed space to deflect it.

Dr. Ted took a deep breath of his own. "First, your gynecologist was right to be concerned."

Celia started to sweat. Not perspire, like a lady. Sweat. Like she was outside. In Philadelphia. In August. She hugged herself tightly and waited for him to say more. To tell her that "concern" didn't mean what she thought it did. Silence filled the space between them until Celia finally spoke up. "It can't be that bad."

"We won't know for sure until a biopsy is done."

Her eyes widened as she sank onto the chair, no longer caring about confined spaces. The air around her had already closed in. "A biopsy? H-he said that, too."

"I know. And yes, a biopsy. As soon as possible."

"Hold on." She saw his deeply furrowed brows. "It feels like you're not telling me everything. You've never hedged before. Why now?"

He looked at her and the flash of apprehension in his

eyes felt like a clap of thunder over her head. Dr. Ted towered over most people, but rarely intimidated them. Young and old alike were at ease with him, probably due to his friendly demeanor and boyish good looks, even at almost sixty years of age. He was one of the strongest men she knew; in fact, he'd been her rock more times than she could count. Now here he sat, worry evident in his eyes.

Sweat turned to instant chills and Celia shivered, as if a ghost had just walked over her grave.

"Anything I tell you would be pure speculation," he said. "I'd rather wait until after the biopsy. But it's serious, honey. Your lab work is significantly higher than it should be."

"You mean, that CA something or other, right?" she asked.

"Yes. The CA-125. The lower the better, score-wise. Less than 35 is optimal, but even that isn't a clean bill of health. Yours is a 65."

"That doesn't sound good."

"It's not. You shouldn't wait. With your permission, I'd like to make an appointment for you with a gynecological oncologist I know and respect."

Celia flinched as reality chucked a rock straight at her face. He'd used the "O" word. She struggled to compose her thoughts, shaking her head. "It can't be that bad. I'm just having problems with my bladder. It's a simple infection."

"There's also your energy level. You said yourself it was noticeably decreased."

"But an infection—"

"An infection doesn't explain everything. That's why your gynecologist ran the additional tests."

She remembered the blood work, the pelvic exam

and ultrasound she'd endured. Could those tests really be enough to send her to the "O" word?

"So nothing's conclusive yet?" she asked.

"A biopsy is the only way to know for sure, yes. But you should do this right away. The ultrasound showed significant masses on both of your ovaries and you'll need to decide on intervention quickly."

"Wait a minute. You're talking about—" Breath, muscles, everything inside Celia froze, momentarily paralyzed by the possibilities. "It can't be," she said. "I've had all my regular exams. Cancer,"—she whispered the word on a rasping breath—"can't grow that fast. Can it?"

"Some of the more aggressive forms can. This type doesn't generally manifest symptoms until…" He paused. "I'm sure I can get you in to Dr. Mason tomorrow. Janice is right here in Seattle at Fred Hutchinson Cancer Center, highly respected and, in my opinion, the most knowledgeable on the coast. I think you'll like her."

Celia jumped at the only fact that made sense. "Tomorrow? No, I can't. I have to be in Philadelphia tomorrow. I've got a convention in three days. I'm scheduled out on the 9:30a.m. flight to meet up with my team."

"Let your people handle it."

"But I need…"

"You *need* to be here."

Impossible. This was her busy season. She couldn't be here tomorrow. Everything was planned out. She would drop Nicci off at her mother's house early. Thankfully, her nine-year-old never minded time spent at Grandma's. Celia's job allowed them their modest lifestyle, but the related travel meant a big chunk of time away from her daughter. She hated that part of a job in sales.

Damn. Celia's hands cupped her cheeks, then rubbed at the itchy, blotchy hives she could feel surfacing over her neck and chest. She'd never be able to explain this to Nicci. Or to her mother. How could she tell her this after what they'd been through?

Transported several years back, to her father's battle for life, Celia remembered the pain and worry. And the sorrow. Above all, the sorrow. He'd had the "C" word also. And had not lasted long once diagnosed. Her mother's health had nose-dived for long months afterwards. Celia had worried she would lose her only remaining parent to a broken heart.

No, she couldn't tell her mother or her daughter. Not yet. She'd need to know for sure before putting them through that. She leaned back in the chair as the realization hit her. The only way to know for sure was to see the oncologist. Tomorrow. Her shoulders slumped.

"All right. Make the appointment."

Ted Jameson stood, drawing her up with him. As her legs wobbled, he drew her into one of his famous bear hugs. She'd always felt safe there. Until now.

"You're one of my daughters, Celia."

Her eyes brimmed with tears.

"We'll help you fight this."

He slowly released her and she sank down, not trusting herself to stand.

Dr. Jameson patted her shoulder. "I know it's a lot to take in. Wait here. I'll have Marilyn make the appointment." He gripped her shoulder a little bit tighter. "You stay here as long as you need to."

She didn't hear the door close. A pounding had

started, first in her ears, then her head joined the crescendo. The office looked different somehow. More medical. More menacing. The walls were closing in on her.

The door opened again and a whiff of disinfectant set Celia's insides roiling. One hand went to her stomach, the other to her throat as she tasted the bile clawing its way up. She needed air.

She stood, grabbed blindly for her purse, and willed her trembling legs to move, quickly passing the nurse. By the time she got to the front desk, reception was a blur. She had to get out of there.

Seth sat quietly in the corner as Celia's world became a whole lot smaller, a lot more focused, and filled with pain. He hit the arm of the chair in frustration. All he could do was watch. It wasn't his time to intervene yet and just sitting here, powerless, was pure torture.

He left when she left. She stared at the elevator then turned to the stairs. He was outside the building when she burst through the doors and he saw the trapped look in her bright eyes. The word blue didn't do them justice. In actuality, they were more like a kaleidoscope of blue and gray with a hint of green and brown thrown in.

Celia Milbourne was beautiful. Her dark auburn hair flew out behind her in long, thick, layered tresses. The tight skirt of her business suit along with the three-inch heels she wore made it difficult to run. Still, she managed quite a distance before she slowed, finally sitting on a park bench near the canal between Lake Washington and Puget Sound. He saw her head drop to her hands as she began to shake. There was nothing he could do to help her.

Seth crouched in front of her and held out arms that ached to comfort her. She couldn't see him. Not yet. He knew that. He leaned in and placed an invisible kiss on the top of her lowered head, jumping back when she sat up abruptly and looked around. She ran her fingers through her hair.

Had she felt him? She couldn't have.

Could she?

2

REALITY CRASHES THE NORMAL LIFE PARTY

"They think I have cancer." Celia searched the light canopy of trees above her, waiting for some ominous validation. Nothing happened. No lightening, no thunder, no official endorsement from Mother Nature at all. The calmness of the park was undisturbed. The unusual warmth of the fall day didn't suddenly turn wintry. The saltwater scent drifting in off the canal carried no scent of decay. She sniffed the air. Well, no more than normal, at any rate.

Celia expelled a quick, harsh laugh and turned to watch the traffic behind her leap from stoplight to stoplight.

It all seemed pretty damn anti-climactic. Here this huge, possibly devastating thing was happening to her, yet, for everyone else, life goes on. The urge to shout at them, to make them slow down and take notice, was strong. This moment should be as larger-than-life for them as it was for her.

Celia rose from the bench. Her throat ached with the desire to scream. Someone should see that her life had just tanked.

As she slumped back down, Celia's mind collided with the second half of reality. Her life may have more than just tanked.

She worried the silver bracelet-watch her mother had given her, a gift as she'd headed off to college. The delicate roses intertwined to form the band were a reminder of home and her mother's award-winning flowers.

She could picture her now, gray hair pulled into her standard French roll, floral garden gloves on, fretting over some blight or other such thing. A true nurturer. Always caring for something or someone. Celia scratched her throat. *How will I tell her this?*

Blinking through a glassy haze, Celia barely registered how late it was. Damn. She would be overdue to pick up her daughter if she didn't hurry. She headed for the parking garage. Tonight was bridge club and her mother was hosting. The only stipulation to babysitting Nicci this extra day had been that Celia not be late.

She picked up her pace as much as her heels allowed and prayed traffic would, for once, be on her side. Her chances weren't good. Seattle traffic was notoriously backed up in every part of town during the evening rush hour.

As expected, traffic didn't cooperate. Half an hour late, Celia pulled into her mother's driveway a little too fast and the car rocked in annoyance at the shuddering stop. The 1962 convertible, two-seater Mercedes had been her Dad's collector car, sporty and red. It developed into a kind of signature with her clients, too. They seemed to appreciate seeing it roll into their lots and, in fact, she'd plugged many of her company's products while customers admired the Mercedes. She knew all its specs. In fact, it was almost like a partner. An old one, though, that needed shocks. As she waited for the garage door to open, Celia knew she had pushed her father's baby a little too hard today. She looked up and sent a grateful thank you heaven-ward for being able to borrow the car.

Parking, she did a quick make-up fix, praying it would fool her mother into believing nothing had changed in the past few hours. She squinted at herself in the mirror. Did she look pale or was it the power of suggestion? This morning, her skin had looked its normal, autumn fading-tan color.

Celia shrugged to shake off the feeling of impending doom and gave the car a grateful tap as she slid by it toward the stairs. These older homes on Seattle's Capitol Hill were built so close together that expansion was rarely an option. The one-car garage was the bedrock for a smallish two-story home that covered eighty percent of the property. A small deck and her mother's roses claimed the remaining twenty percent.

There'd never been a yard to play in. Then again, none of the neighborhood yards had been much either. Nearby Interlaken Park had been the playground for Celia and her childhood friends, the streets in between, their territory. Celia smiled as she grabbed the railing to climb the stairs. It wobbled. She'd learned a lot about fixing things, both during and after her marriage. Mr. Fix-It, her ex wasn't. Celia set herself a mental reminder to make the railing sturdier for her mother.

Then froze mid-step.

Would she have time?

With that single thought, her heart leapt from its normal, quiet pace to that of a thumping, terrified rabbit. This was the second time today she'd thought about her own mortality. She laid a hand on her stomach. Diseased cells were splitting and multiplying even as she stood here. Would she win this battle? Or would they?

Wow. She was definitely into self-pity today. The familiar itch of hives resurfaced. Celia's chin came up as she clamped a lid on the worst-case scenario box, shoving it to the back of her mind. She wasn't about to become some closet pessimist over mutating cells. Planting what she hoped was a ray-of-sunshine smile on her face, she opened the door and walked inside.

Her mother's kitchen looked like a scene straight out of a 1980's country living magazine. Lacey sheers covered the windows and ivory and rose floral wallpaper muted the effect of the modern appliances. The aroma of cinnamon and baking apples drew Celia to the oven, where Patricia Milbourne, shadowed by a nine year old imp, pulled a pie out to cool. Celia hugged her daughter, tugged on her long, dark-haired ponytail, and leaned over the pie.

"Mmmmm. That looks as good as it smells."

Her mother slapped at imaginary hands. "Hands off. That's for bridge club."

"Ah-h-h," Celia mock-frowned. "Are you sure you couldn't spare just a slice?"

"Mom!" Nicci said.

Looking fondly down at the daughter still wrapped in her arms, Celia corrected herself. "I mean two slices, of course."

"It's for bridge club," Patricia Milbourne said again, with a shoo-shoo wave of her potholder.

Celia turned to Nicci. "I guess that means no."

"Hey, Mom, haven't you forgotten something?"

"Hmmm. What could I have possibly forgotten?"

"Very funny, Mom. Give it up." Nicci held out both her hands expectantly.

Celia slapped them in a low-five kind of way, following through with a wave that floated up above her head. It had become their way of greeting each other. Nicci had insisted on a special handshake instead of a code word for anyone who picked her up from school or daycare. She said that a handshake meant Celia had seen whomever she sent in person, so they must be safe.

"Sorry I'm late, Mom." Celia pecked her mother on the cheek.

"That's all right—" Patricia stopped, hand on hip, and gave Celia one of her long, hard, I-know-something's-wrong stares. "You okay, honey?"

Celia clutched hands that had started to tremble again. She mumbled a fast "fine" and then shamelessly used her daughter as a diversion. "You'd better get your stuff together so we can get going. You know Grandma's got a date."

Nicci giggled as she headed out of the room.

Patricia set her hot pads on the counter and placed a hand on Celia's arm. "Something's wrong. I can see it in your face."

Celia gulped. Damn. She wasn't ready for this conversation. So much for the patch job she'd done in the car. "It's all right. I just have a lot to take care of right now."

Nicci saved her by bounding back in, backpack dragging behind.

"Come on, Babydoll. Let's get out of here and let your grandmother get to playing some cards."

Both girls gave Patricia a hug.

Celia stopped at the door, turning back. "Hey, Mom? It doesn't look like I'll be flying out early tomorrow after all. But I do have some things to do. Could I still drop Nicci off? It'll only be for three or four hours, instead of three or four days."

"Sure." Worry was cemented in deep lines across her mother's forehead. "You know Nicci's always welcome here."

"Except on bridge club night, right?" Impulsively, Celia crossed the kitchen and gave her mother another hug. "Thanks. I couldn't do this without you, you know. You're a godsend. I'll call you later about the time."

She rushed to catch up with her daughter who waited outside, tapping fingers to some IPod beat on the roof of their Ford Escort. It was an old car and had more problems than the Mercedes. But it got her from point A to point B. She looked up at the heavens, giving thanks once again for her mother, who was always happy to let her borrow the Mercedes for her sales calls.

꧁ ꧂

As Celia pulled up to their modest home, her shoulders began to release some of their tension. *Home.* Their neighborhood was mostly two-story, smallish houses with small patches in front that passed for a yard. The pale gray color of her house, with its dusky blue trim, always made her smile. For the first time in her life, she'd picked out colors all on her own. And she loved them.

This wasn't a rich neighborhood. In fact, she couldn't even call it a middle-class one. But it was close. The eclectic mix of families and retired folks, artists and egg-heads, worked well for both Celia and Nicci. Her daughter had plenty of friends to play with and most people kept an eye out for each other. They were within walking distance of groceries, a park, and Nicci's favorite pizza joint. A definite bonus, at least in the eyes of her daughter.

As Celia opened the front door, any sense of tranquility fled when she saw the blinking red light on her answering machine and knew in the pit of her stomach that it was about medical appointments. She chose to do the only thing she could to remain sane.

She ignored it.

While the scent of the soft tacos she made filled the air, the angry light tapped away at the corner of her vision. For the first time, the open design of her main floor irritated her. There was no place to hide.

Celia refused to acknowledge it.

She did the dishes.

And the laundry.

She sorted through her mail.

Tucked Nicci in bed, book in hand, with a stern reminder to read for half an hour only.

Finally, nothing else was left to do and she stood and stared at the red flashes. It took a couple of minutes, but she determined that the annoying bursts came at about one per second. At least, as near as she could tell. "One-one thousand, two-one thousand" wasn't the most accurate time counter.

Once that was resolved, nothing else presented itself in the way of a diversion so she punched the message button.

"Celia, this is Marilyn from Dr. Jameson's office. I'm calling to let you know that Dr. Janice Mason has agreed to see you at eleven o'clock tomorrow. Her office asks that you arrive fifteen minutes early to fill out paperwork and also that you bring your records from the gynecologist. We've contacted them on your behalf and the records will be ready for you to pick up any time after nine in the morning."

The rest of the message was addresses and phone numbers. Celia wrote them down by rote, then sank to the floor. With nothing to hold back the reality any longer, she tapped her stomach with balled fists. She'd worked hard after Nicci's birth to regain her figure and was proud of how nearly-flat and toned it was. A lot of sit-ups had gone into that conditioning. Pressing in the area where she thought her ovaries were, she wondered why she couldn't feel the masses. If they were large, shouldn't she be able to feel them?

Leaning back against the credenza, she realized she was probably going to lose her ovaries. Great. She remembered Nicci's very vocal views about wanting a sister and Celia had left that door open with hopeful intention. She closed her eyes against the twinge of pain, mentally slamming the pregnancy door shut. That wouldn't be happening now. And losing your ovaries meant early menopause, didn't it? Hot flashes and mood swings would be everyday life. What else would happen?

Frowning, she got up and headed for her desk. It was time to gain a measure of control over this spiral her life had become. Celia punched up the internet and paused, her fingers hanging motionless over the keyboard. After an eternity of seconds she typed the words. Ovarian masses. The first hit she got said "How to Tell if an Ovarian Mass is Malignant." She started reading.

Ovarian cancer is a difficult cancer to beat primarily because there are so few symptoms until it is too late. It can feel like a bladder infection. Like pressure in the abdomen, even like indigestion. Thirteen percent of the cases diagnosed are women under the age of forty six.

Great. She was part of the minority.

There are four diagnosed stages. In stage one, the growth is limited to the ovaries. The survival rate is based on five years and is greater than ninety percent.

That didn't sound too bad. She read further.

In stage two, cancer is also found in the uterus, tubes or other pelvic organs. The survival rates decrease significantly at this stage.

Crap. Celia pushed back from the table with shaking hands. Did she really want to read this?

She shook her head and reached for the phone. It was time to find something else to do.

Seth watched as Celia worked. Time, for him, was elusive and difficult to quantify. However, he'd seen Celia in many different situations. There was so much he admired about her, her strength high on the list. When she got down to business, she didn't give up. Her fingers flew, first across the keyboard, then across the legal pad beside her. Back and forth, bouncing from site to site. But she also seemed to know her limitations. And she was right. Small doses would probably be better. He frowned. Reality would invade her life soon enough.

A quick call to her mother, then to her assistant both proved she could hedge with the best of them.

"I just have some things here that I need to deal with," she said to her assistant. "Don't worry, Tana. I'm going to try my best to get there. It'll just be a day later, that's all. Two at the most, I hope. I'll have my cell phone with me. I know you can do this. I trust you."

Her head dropped to her hand as she set the phone down. She sat there, running her fingers through thick hair that shimmered with red highlights. Seth pictured the silky locks in candlelight, with his hands floating through the dark strands, learning the shape of her head. He ached to touch her and even reached out. Celia chose that moment to sit up and he yanked his hand back.

She didn't bother to turn the computer off, just closed the top and stood. He could see the effort it cost to keep her frame upright. She made it to her bedroom, set the alarm, and collapsed onto her bed fully clothed.

Seth nudged a pillow toward her and she hugged it close. He touched her forehead.

"Sleep," he whispered as her eyes closed.

He waited until her breathing slowed, then shifted blankets to cover her, knowing she would be comforted by the oblivion of dreams for the next few hours.

It wasn't much, but it was all he could do. For now.

3

TALK, TALK AND MORE TALK
(WHEN ALL I REALLY WANT TO DO IS
SCREAM!)

Dr. Janice Mason wasn't what Celia had expected. Tiny compared to Celia's above average height, she stood maybe five-foot-one. Her short white hair made her look more like a friendly pixie than a well-respected oncologist. Add to that the jeans and Save-The-Whales T-shirt she wore and Celia didn't quite know what to expect. It was impossible to gauge her age, but Celia thought it might be close to her own thirty-five years.

"I recommend a staging surgery," Dr. Mason said.

One thing was certain. No matter how diminutive the woman was, she had a command of words that chilled souls. And Celia's heart had just been flash-frozen. Surgery?

"Can't we do some sort of needle biopsy?" Celia's voice flat-lined except for the last word, making the question sound more like a plea for mercy than a serious inquiry. She clutched the edges of the portfolio she held open on her lap.

Dr. Mason reached for a model of a woman's

reproductive system, pointing as she described the process. "We would most certainly have to do a second procedure to remove the tumors. The standard protocol, and one which I endorse, is a staging surgery. We go in with the plan to resect any visible tumors and take samples for pathology. Considering the size of the tumors, I suggest removal of both ovaries. As well, we'll take tissue from lymph nodes, abdominal wall, et cetera. A sampling is sent during surgery for frozen section to give us a clearer idea what we're dealing with. Depending on that, it's possible we would need to proceed with a full hysterectomy, which means taking not just the ovaries, tubes, and visible masses, but also the uterus. In addition, we would biopsy the abdominal wall."

Celia's brain almost shut down then and there. She glanced at her notebook and skimmed the long list of questions. Would she lose her hair topped the list. Her own research had frightened her more than Dr. Ted's worry. Depending on the type, the mortality rate for ovarian cancer spanned the spectrum, from full recovery to a fifty-six percent chance of…

Suddenly all her questions seemed fruitless and she snapped the portfolio shut. "You said a staging surgery. Does that refer to the four diagnostic stages of cancer?"

"Yes. This surgery will tell us what stage your cancer is at."

"So the surgery doesn't just remove the cancer. It also determines if any other organs are involved?"

"Correct. It will help us determine the best way to treat you post-operatively."

Knowledge is a weapon. Celia had heard that somewhere. Right now, knowledge didn't exactly feel like a good thing. In fact, at this particular moment, she felt less empowered and more like she was about to throw up.

The doctor continued. "There is some concern that we have more to deal with than just the masses on your ovaries. We'll try to do this by laparoscope, but you may be beyond that. If that's the case, we'll make an incision here." She drew an imaginary line on her own stomach.

Celia cringed. She knew it was called a bikini incision, but... She thought of the skimpy bathing suit she'd just found on the clearance rack at Nordstrom's. *I wonder if they'll take it back?* There was no telling when, or if, she'd ever get to wear it.

Stop it! She reprimanded herself. *Stick to the essentials. Cancer. Surgery. Ovaries.* Celia frowned. "This will send me into menopause, right?"

"Most likely. The level of severity is different with each case. Quite a few get off lightly, symptom-wise."

"What's the surgical recovery period?"

"About six weeks if we have to make an incision. About half that if we can do it laparascopically."

"And chemo?"

Dr. Mason shrugged. ""I prefer my patients have a minimum three-week recovery period. Four is even better. However, we can't determine that until the pathology comes back."

Will I lose my hair? Celia's brain screamed the question. Still, she couldn't ask. It seemed so vain. Instead, she stuck to the facts. "When will surgery be scheduled?"

"We'd like to get going on this quickly. I'll be the primary surgeon, but we'll need to coordinate with the surgeon who'll be assisting. I'm guessing a week, two at the most."

Two weeks, tops. The phrase echoed through Celia's mind as she scratched her neck. Sooner was always worse. "It's all happening so fast."

Dr. Mason placed a warm hand on Celia's arm. "I would suggest focusing on one thing at a time right now. Surgery is the key issue at the moment."

Celia's arms started to tremble and she clutched them to her side. "My whole life is changing." Damn, now her voice had started to quiver.

"Yes."

"I'm just not ready for this."

Dr. Mason pulled up a stool to sit on that looked more like it belonged at a bar than in a physician's office. "Have you told your family yet?"

"No. There's been no time. It was only yesterday..." she gulped.

"Are you married or do you have a significant other?"

"N-no."

"Do you have a good relationship with your family?"

Celia's head bobbed and her frown lifted a little. Her mother was a gentle rock and had taught Celia to be the same. Apparently not well enough by the way she was starting to blubber. "My dad died a few years ago from lung cancer." She gave a bitter laugh. "He never smoked a day in his life."

"I'm sorry," Dr. Mason said. "That's rough."

"Yeah. Tell me about it." Celia sighed. She needed to tell her mother. "This will be very hard on my mom."

She thought of Nicci and felt the panic invade her throat, closing it off. "How—how do I tell my daughter?"

"How old is she?" Dr. Mason asked.

"Nine." Celia's hands combed through her hair. She leaned forward, resting elbows on knees. "I just don't know how I can do this."

"You won't be doing this alone. There's a whole team of physicians, therapists and nursing staff that will help. Counseling is recommended, also. And social services can help you through the decision-making process."

"In the meantime?" Celia knew she sounded like a jilted lover who'd just been told it wasn't her fault. She couldn't seem to help herself.

"We'll get you in touch with someone as soon as possible. Until then, do you belong to a faith you can tap?"

"I always meant to. I just—there never seemed to be enough time."

"You might consider starting with your mother, then. Carrying this burden alone is not recommended. And your mother may be stronger than you think."

She stepped down from the stool and patted Celia's arm. "Why don't you wait here for a few minutes and let me see how long it's going to take to schedule your surgery."

As Dr. Mason left the room, a profound isolation overtook Celia, almost as if she were immersed in a murky pool of still water. She could breathe, but there was nowhere to go and no one to help her. She had cancer. Not that anyone would actually *say* the word to her. The politically correct pre-biopsy word is masses. Growths. Anything but the "C" word. She had not one, but two masses. At least. And no one knew she was sick except Dr. Ted and the oncologist. And her.

Celia felt totally alone.

She closed her eyes and rubbed her arms, rocking

back and forth as the chilly truth began to overwhelm her again. This was pretty crappy timing. The divorce had wiped her out emotionally and financially. Celia had worked hard to bring it all back around and provide a normal life for Nicci. Now it would crumble like paper burned to ash.

The exam room that tried to hide its sterile nature with landscape photography felt cold and Celia shivered as the chill seeped into her bones.

Air stirred, swirling soothingly around her like a comforting embrace. Warmth began to infuse shaking muscles. Celia closed her eyes as she welcomed the heat.

You are not alone.

Her eyes opened slowly and Celia panned the room. It was empty. The door remained firmly closed and there were no windows to explain an accidental draft or wind-tossed words. The words had the sound of an echo, yet she'd heard them. There had been a...familiarity, a comfort to them. Her brows knit together.

Was she talking to herself and didn't even know it? She was alone. That's what her mind told her. Her heart said something entirely different. For this moment, though, for some strange reason, she didn't feel quite so lonely.

"You are not alone."

Seth had whispered the words. How had she heard him?

He shook his head. He had little memory of any time before this and there was a lot he didn't know about his role. He was here to guide Celia, help her weather the storm to come. Instinct told him he had no power to interfere or stop this process for her. Still, he didn't think she should be able to hear him. At least, not for a long time yet.

From the moment he first saw her, he'd been deeply grateful for the opportunity to be here with her, even though his limitations would be all but impossible to bear.

He'd kept watch all last night. As she went from website to website, searching, learning. When she drifted off to sleep he'd listened to her breathe.

This morning, she'd been shaking so hard she chose no makeup and stayed in her sweats. Yet she'd met her mother's worried eyes with unwavering regard when she dropped Nicci off.

"You've got strength in you, Celia Milbourne. And I'll help you find it."

Celia looked outside her bedroom window onto the street. It was Saturday morning and preparations for winter were in full swing around the neighborhood. John across the street checked gutters and downspouts while Mary, his seven months pregnant wife, pulled weeds from flower beds one last time. A couple of the neighborhood kids rode by on their bikes, clearly happy for the weekend reprieve from school and one more day of temperate weather to play in.

Life moved ahead as usual.

For everyone except me.

Celia let the sage-green window covering drop back into place and turned, contemplating the sanctuary she called her bedroom. Filled with light wood colors, autumn sunshine, and femininity, this was where she escaped to when life got to be too much.

She had worked hard for her little house on this quiet

street. The end of her marriage had left her living back at home with a daughter to raise and little money to provide for her. In a back door arrangement, Dan had relinquished custody of Nicole if she would split the equity in their co-owned house with him.

Good old Dan, more focused on himself than anyone else, even his own daughter, it sometimes seemed. He needed more money for his business, he'd said. So she had agreed to sell their house. Nicci was way more precious than paint and wainscoting.

Of course, after that, Dan's business books had become the proof that he was not taking a salary. A good attorney and an unusually sympathetic judge and bam—minimal child support ordered.

She could never thank Dr. Ted enough for getting her through the door at the job she still held—as a pharmaceutical rep for a large international company. It had taken her three years of hard work, living first with her mom, then in a one-bedroom apartment, scrimping pennies, to afford this place. Three long years where she'd been gone almost more than she'd been home. Time she'd missed with her daughter. Time she could never recapture.

Will I get enough time to see her grow up? Celia rubbed her stomach.

Nope. Not going there. Not today. Hopefully not ever. Celia shook her head, squared her shoulders, and went across the hall to her daughter's room.

"Good morning, Babydoll!" Celia raised the blinds as she woke her daughter.

"Mmm." The indistinct mumble came from under the covers.

"Rise and shine. It's Saturday and your father will be here in an hour."

"Can't he come later? I wanna sleep!" The noise still came from the undercover realm, but at least it was coherent this time.

Celia drew back the quilt and saw her tousle-headed daughter clinging to the sheet, a book and flashlight tucked in beside her.

"How late did you stay up?"

Nicci opened eyes filled with that uh-oh-I'm-trapped look. "I dunno."

"Yes, you do, daughter-mine. Now 'fess up!" Celia tickled her until giggles and screams replaced mumbled words.

"—'right, all right! Only 'til two, 'Kay?"

"Two a.m.?" Celia repeated, a mock expression of horror on her face. Fridays were the only night she allowed Nicci to set her own bed time. And how could she complain when the passion her daughter immersed herself in was reading?

One more tickle for good measure, then Celia bounced off the bed. "Well, you'll have to catch up on your sleep at Dad's then, because he's coming in—" she made an exaggerated show of checking the time. "Fifty-five minutes now."

"Arghhh!"

"Come on, kiddo. Up and at 'em. I'll make you some pancakes while you get dressed and pack," Celia said.

"'Kay," Nicci grumbled. But at least she hung her legs over the side of the bed and sat up.

Half an hour later the sweet smell of maple syrup permeated the kitchen. Celia stood behind Nicci as she ate and French-braided her daughter's long, thick, auburn hair, inherited from her and her mother before her. She knew that Dan had no clue what to do with all that hair and the French-braid would last until Nicci came home tomorrow.

Hopefully for once the man would be on time to pick her up. Celia wanted to get this day over with and the sooner, the better.

"I'm going to visit Grandma this afternoon."

"Ah-h-h-h!" Nicci cried, wrenching her hair out of Celia's grasp. "I wanna go!"

Picking up the strands, Celia continued braiding. "Not this time, Babydoll. You were just there yesterday. This is an adult day."

At that, Nicci was quiet and Celia hoped that would be the end of it.

"Hey, why are you home, anyhow?" Nicci asked.

"What do you mean?"

"You're not supposed to be here. You're supposed to be in Philadelphia."

They had looked it up together. Had it only been three days ago? Celia always wanted her daughter to know where she traveled to. She paused. Funny. After calling her boss to tell him she had a medical issue and couldn't go, she'd put the conference completely out of her mind. That was a first.

"I ended up not having to go," she told Nicci.

"Then why do I have to go with Dad? It's not his weekend. He was only taking me because *you* were gonna be gone. I wanna stay home."

"Sorry. Just because I didn't go to Philadelphia doesn't mean I don't have work to do." A small white lie. Something she'd never done to her daughter, not even during the divorce. It just wasn't time to tell her, she rationalized. Not yet.

She needed time.

Her hands shook as she finished the braid.

A short while later, all desire to stay home disappeared from her daughter as Nicci threw herself into her father's arms. With a deep longing, Celia watched them prepare to leave. This disease had tainted everything. Even her ability to view a scene like this. She would always wonder how many more times she would be this privileged.

"You okay, Mom?" Nicci stood in front of her. A glance out the window showed Dan heading to the car, pink backpack in hand.

"Sure, Babydoll. Why?"

"Dunno. You just seem...quiet."

Giving herself a mental shake, Celia smiled and ruffled her daughter's hair. "Just mentally working up my day. Now go. Have fun. You don't want to hang with fuddy-duddy old me when 'The Dad' is waiting, do you?"

Nicci stared for a moment longer, then gave in to the smile curling her lips. "Nope. We're going to the zoo. 'Bye, Mom! Love you!" With that, she flew out the door.

Celia closed the door behind her daughter and turned away, trying to shake of the melancholy. She had a mission to accomplish today and it was time to go.

The garage door was open at her mother's so Celia didn't bother with the front door. She stepped onto the stairs that led into the kitchen and grabbed the handrail. It wobbled and she stopped for a closer look. The railing really was in bad shape. She glanced up at the door behind which her mother most likely puttered at housework, then back at the railing. Some of the rotten wood needed replacing.

"I'll fix this, then I'll talk to Mom." she mumbled, knowing all it did was buy her time.

She cracked open the door. "Hey, Mom!"

"Celia! Hello," Patricia said warmly. "I wasn't expecting you so soon."

"I'm going to pop over to the hardware store and get some stuff to fix this railing. I'll be back in a bit."

"That's fine. I'll have tea ready for us later."

Celia eagerly made the trip to the hardware store and back. After the railing was snug and solid, she took some time to straighten out her father's tools, something she'd talked her mother into keeping after his death, thank goodness. In fact, Celia realized, several tools were still over at her own house.

Eventually, she ran out of things to do in the garage and stood in front of the door into the house.

It was time.

Shrugging her shoulders to relieve the heavy weight that had settled on them, she opened the door. "Mom?"

"In here," Patricia called from the living room, where she was just setting down a tray for tea. "Did you get the railing fixed?"

"Sure did. It's actually useful now." Celia smiled and sat on the sofa next to her mother.

"Who needs a handyman when I've got you around? It amazes me that you learned to do all these things for yourself."

"It was either that or let them rot. You know Danny wasn't very handy this way."

The hint of a shadow crossed Patricia's face, which she valiantly tried to hide by pouring tea for each of them, adding one sugar and a small bit of cream to her own cup. She held the cream out to Celia, who shook her head but plunked two sugars in hers. "Daniel wasn't very good at a lot of things."

"Don't I know it. At least he's wonderful with Nicci

when they are together."

Patricia nodded. "I'll give him credit for that. He has maintained a good relationship with his daughter. And rightfully so."

Well, that's about it for small talk. Celia took a deep breath. Time to get this over with. "Hey, Mom, I need to talk to you."

Patricia opened her mouth to speak, apparently thought better of it, and instead her free hand toyed with the edge of her apron.

"You, uh, know I've been seeing my gynecologist for some issues, right?"

The only concession Patricia Milbourne gave to that knowledge was a nod of her head. Still, she looked like a slinky waiting for the pressure to let up so she could go bouncing off the couch.

"Well, they found some growths on my ovaries."

Her mother's eyes widened. She looked down, running her hand along the floral fabric of the early American style sofa they sat on.

"I'm sorry, Mom. There's just no easy way to tell you."

"Do they—think its cancer?"

Celia hedged. After all, technically, no one wanted to use that word until after biopsies revealed the truth. "They don't know yet."

Her mother smiled and Celia could see a thousand tiny hopes embedded in it. She hated to shut her down. "Mom. You need to understand. The masses are...not small."

"Yes, but—"

"Dr. Mason won't say what it is until the biopsy is done. But we have to be prepared for the worst."

"Have you been to see Ted?"

Celia nodded.

"Well? What did he say?"

"Dr. Ted got me in to see the specialist on a day's notice. This isn't some minor little thing, Mom. I just— don't want you to get your hopes up too high."

Her mother looked down and smoothed the apron across her lap. Once. Twice. A third time. Then she raised her head and wiped furiously at moist eyes. "We can think or do or hope whatever we please, daughter. Don't you forget that. For now, we'll wait. You're right that we need more information before we start coming to conclusions."

She picked up the teapot and refilled both dainty cups, hands shaking only the tiniest amount. "What's the first step?"

Celia took a deep breath. "Surgery."

The teapot rattled as her mother set it down.

"They'll remove the ovaries and take a bunch of biopsies. Anything else, well, they won't know until they get in there." Celia's hand rested on her stomach, as it had so many times in the last three days.

Her mom covered Celia's hand with her own. "When?"

"Next Thursday." Celia watched the emotions weave their way across her mother's face. Most people knew—the sooner they got you in for treatment, the more serious it was. Apparently, her mother remembered that, too. Her hand clenched Celia's in a momentary vise, then let go.

"All right, then. What do we need to do to prepare?"

And that was that. Her mother had switched from worry mode to her customary what-can-I-do-to-help mode. Tears threatened as Celia's heart spilled over with love and respect for this woman who had guided her through all the trials and happiness life brought. She felt infused with love, which her arteries then pumped throughout her body, fortifying her for the ordeal ahead. The fears she had felt in the oncologist's office faded. She was no longer alone. That knowledge felt like a layer of protective armor that would guard against anything harmful.

Taking a long, tension-relieving breath, she followed her mother's lead. "I'm calling my boss later today. He's not too pleased I blew off the Philadelphia show. Tana got overwhelmed and he had to fly out there to help." Celia shrugged her shoulders. "It may put him in a bit of a bind that I need some time off. I need to talk to Jen, too. We'll need her help with Nicci." Celia had been trading favors with her best friend since grade school and it had segued into babysitting for sanity's sake as they each started families.

She got up and started to pace, her voice quivering. "Then...I don't know when or what to tell Nicci."

"Tell her the truth. She can handle it. You did."

"I was an adult when Dad got sick. Nicci's only nine-years-old."

Celia stopped at the window seat that overlooked the garden. Her mother's rose bushes were pruned, with mulch spread around them. All ready for the coming winter. She smiled. The yard was so lovely in the spring. Beautiful award winning flowers in so many different colors. New life emerging after a long, gray winter. Even Nicci enjoyed working in the flowerbeds with her grandmother.

"I don't think I'll tell her anything until after surgery," she said, turning away from the view. "I'd rather have the facts first." *Maybe,* she prayed, *I won't have to tell her.*

"You'll have to tell her something."

"Then I'll explain the surgery, not the condition. Can you keep her while I'm in the hospital?"

"Of course, dear. You know I will."

They spent the next little while ironing out their respective schedules. As Celia gathered her things to leave, she stopped to give her mother a long hug and tears welled again in her eyes. "I'm sorry to have to put you through this again, Mom."

"Me? With all you have to deal with? Don't you worry about me. I'll be just fine." She hugged Celia tighter. "We *all* will be just fine."

"We'll all be just fine." Celia whispered her mother's words like a mantra later, while she waited on the phone. Nicci wouldn't be home until tomorrow afternoon, so she couldn't talk to her until then. Her boss was still in Philadelphia and, while it wasn't the best time to approach him, it probably wasn't going to be a pleasant discussion at any time. So she was on hold at the hotel.

"Yes?" he growled. Not a good sign.

"Hey, Tom, how's it going?"

"Not very bloody well."

Celia winced. When Tom lapsed into the accent of his childhood home, England, he wasn't happy. "What's happened?"

"What's happened? There are too many bloody requests for more information and more bloody samples. Tana's running the booth and I can't keep up with what she's giving out!" He growled again, but this time, Celia heard the mockery in his tone.

She laughed. "I've been telling you for a long time—she's a fireball. It's great for business."

"Yeah, but I had to fly out on the red-eye and she's

been running me so ragged I can't even catch up on my jet lag!"

"Good. I really do wish I were there to help you."

"Me, too." All British pretense disappeared from his voice. "What's up, anyhow? What kept you from doing this convention?"

"I told you. Some medical issues."

"Good? Bad? Resolved?"

Most employers wouldn't dare ask those questions the way confidentiality laws were these days. But Tom was more than just an employer. She counted him among her friends.

"Not good. And not resolved."

The silence on the other end of the phone stretched out until she thought it would break. "What can I do to help," he finally said.

"I have to have surgery."

"When?"

"Thursday."

"That's pretty quick."

"Yeah," she said.

"So it's serious."

"Yep. Female stuff. I'm going to need some recovery time."

"You've got it. Whatever you need."

"I'll know more after my pre-op on Tuesday. Um, Tom? I haven't told Tana yet. Can you keep this to yourself for now?"

"Sure. It's none of her business anyhow."

"Tana's going to have to take over my area for a while, so she has a right to know. I'll get with her before Thursday, if that's all right with you?"

"You've done a lot for this company's reputation, so I trust whatever you set up. Just you get healthy, got it?"

Celia's voice cracked. "I'm going to try. Very hard."

Seth watched her place the phone back in the cradle and sit very still for a long moment. Then, with a big, heaving sigh, she pushed off from the table and wandered into the living room. Celia turned on the television and flipped through the channels. Nothing seemed to interest her because she turned it off and picked up the book she'd been reading, a historical romance novel.

A flash of castles, Victorian-style clothing and horses came to mind. His past? Or maybe a piece of it? The edges of his mouth tugged upward. Her interest in the era could be helpful.

She concentrated on the book, trying to stay focused. Several times she looked off into space, or placed a hand on her stomach. Eventually, though, the story got hold of her and she read page after page without pause.

Well after the midnight hour, Celia fell asleep on the couch with the book still in her hands. Seth waved his hand and the afghan over the back of the couch gently covered her.

Then he settled into the chair to watch...and wait for morning, when he would again see the gentleness in eyes that were a myriad of warm colors destined to melt his heart.

4

OKAY, SO MAYBE TALKING WASN'T SO BAD AFTER ALL

The calmness of late warmth had been supplanted by a fall that seemed to carry a grudge at the delay. October had arrived with a ferocious wind. Not bad enough to kill the power, but reminiscent of the Columbus Day windstorm of 1962.

Inside the hospital, though, there were no seasons. Only routines and schedules. And an odd antiseptic smell no one could possibly consider normal.

Celia wanted to run. As hard and as fast and as far as she could. But the elevator walls held her captive and guards flanked her in the forms of her mother and nine-year-old daughter. She shivered and clutched her small bag tightly to her chest, as if it was the most important thing she owned.

"Cold?" her mother asked.

"No." She answered automatically. She wasn't cold. She was petrified. She'd only been in a hospital once as a patient, for the birth of her daughter. Granted, she'd been there longer than normal because of the complications. But she'd known the outcome. Known she would go home with her beautiful baby girl. This time...

She'd come to terms with the idea that she was losing her ovaries. They really weren't ovaries anymore, anyhow. They were now killing machines, eating away at her life force. And that she might end up with a total hysterectomy.

She could live with that. The real question was whether or not she could live with the answers she would get here. The possibilities terrified her. Would reality be worse?

The elevator doors slid open. Instinctively, Celia took a step backwards. Her sentries held the doors and waited.

Her mother's face was frozen in her we'll-weather-this-storm smile. Nicci, on the other hand, looked decidedly worried. Celia had worked very hard to downplay the reason for surgery, but it hadn't helped that her daughter's good friend had just lost a grandparent. Plus, Celia's own fears may have seeped into her daughter's subconscious mind. This was already way too rough on a nine-year-old.

Placing a hand over her stomach, Celia pictured the cancer and what it was doing. She wanted it gone. For her sake, and for Nicci's. That meant surgery. Giving in to the inevitable, she unwrapped her arms from around her bag, walked out of the elevator and up to the admissions desk.

Seth watched as Celia listened to the clerk drone on about assignment of benefits and personal belongings and all the little details tied to a hospital admission. She had that deer-in-the-headlights look. Her thick auburn hair framed a porcelain face that, he sensed, was close to breaking. Even so, she was beautiful. She sat up straight and listened to the registrar, signing forms. When not busy, her hands seemed to search for non-existent arms to the chair she sat in. Eventually, she settled for tucking them between her legs and the seat. Occasionally, she gave in to the temptation and scratched at the red hives that peppered her neck and chest.

Patient, mother, and daughter were soon ushered into a large hallway with several alcoves sectioned off by curtains. The beige color that permeated everything gave the look of warmth, but did little to mask the sterility of the place.

A young woman, somewhere around Celia's age and wearing brightly patterned scrubs, took the paperwork from the clerk and smiled. "Hi. I'm Doris. I'll be your nurse through surgery and recovery today." Her voice had a mellow quality, a sound that made Celia's shoulders edge down a bit.

Doris glanced at Celia's company. "Mom and daughter, I'm guessing."

"Yes," Celia said. "My mother, Patricia. And Nicci here is my daughter."

Doris spoke directly to Nicci. "We love to have family here to keep our patients in a good mood." She scrunched her face as if giving Nicci the once over. "You will keep her in a good mood, right?"

"Yeah," Nicci answered with a toothy grin. "At least, I'll try."

"Good. Then that's your job. Right now, though, we need to let your mom get changed into her snazzy hospital gear. Do you think you and your grandmother could wait outside the curtain while she does that?"

Nicci puffed up with the importance of being given two tasks. "C'mon, Grandma. We've gotta wait outside." She reached for her grandmother's hand and marched out. By the look of how close her tennis shoes were to the curtain, she had no intention of going any further than she had to.

"A bit of the mothering instinct in that one, isn't there," Doris whispered.

Celia inclined her head. "We take good care of each other."

"Good. She'll help you through your recovery. First, let's start with you telling me what you're here for."

An hour later, Celia had been poked, prodded, and checked out a lifetime's worth. Damn, but she hated needles. And if one more person asked her what procedure she was having, she knew she'd scream. It was their way of making sure the information was accurate and that she was oriented. But the constant reminder drove her nuts.

"You okay, Mom?" Nicci's chair was as close as it could get to Celia's gurney without being underneath it.

"Sure," Celia said, pasting on a smile she prayed Nicci wouldn't see through. "I'm fine."

"You don't look it. You had your mad face on."

"I'm just tired of waiting, that's all." She looked past Nicci to her mother. "I wish it were over."

Nicci patted her hand, careful not to touch the I.V. that was now liberally taped in place. "You'll be just fine."

Nurturing must run in the family. Her daughter was a natural at it. "I know I will, Babydoll." She ruffled Nicci's hair. "Because I have you to take care of me."

At that moment, Doris entered, pulling the curtains back. "It's just about time to go."

Celia saw Nicci's eyes widen and felt her handhold tighten. It bothered the hell out of her that Nicci had to be here for this. Her daughter had refused to stay with Celia's friend Jen today.

"Nicci," Doris continued, "why don't you give your mom a kiss, then I'll walk you and your Grandma down to the waiting room. Does that sound like a plan you're all right with?"

As they left, Dr. Mason walked in. Celia almost didn't recognize her in surgical greens. A much taller, gray-haired man, also in hospital greens, came in behind her.

"Hi, Celia," Dr. Mason said. "How are you feeling?"

"Nervous."

"I know. It doesn't seem natural, does it?

"Not one bit."

"But it is necessary." She acknowledged the man beside her. "This is Dr. Sanders. He'll be assisting me today."

Dr. Sanders held out his hand. "Hello, Celia."

"I'd say it's nice to meet you, Dr. Sanders, but..."

He chuckled. "I get that reaction a lot. That's the price I pay for being semi-retired and not having regular office hours. I see most of my patients right here in pre and post op. So, do you feel ready?"

"No. But I don't really have a choice, do I? I tried to get Dr. Ted to fabricate some excuse for cancelling at my pre-op, but I had no luck."

"Did you bribe him with a good cup of coffee? I hear that's his weakness," Dr. Sanders said.

Celia waved her hands at her temporary bed. "It didn't help."

"It's just as well," Dr. Sanders said, returning to the reason they were there. "I've gone over your records to date and a delay would not be advisable."

Celia gulped. "I know."

"I want to go over the procedure with you one more time," Dr. Mason said. "You understand that our intention is to remove any abnormal growths we find and take tissue for biopsy as needed. Depending on the pathology, you'll be consenting to the possibility of a complete hysterectomy."

Unable to speak, Celia nodded her head. It felt cold in here. She raised her hand, but it shook so badly, she laid it back down again. Janice Mason picked up and held her hand and that little bit of warmth spread throughout Celia's body like a shot of Jack Daniels.

Celia nodded her surgical-capped head and found her voice. "I know. It depends on what you find when you get in there."

"We want to be sure you understand."

"I—ummm, I don't want you to hide the truth, okay? I mean—afterwards."

"I don't—"

Celia held up a hand. "I want to know the truth as you know it."

Dr. Mason studied her for a long moment, then nodded. "No hidden truths. That can all be dealt with later, though. We're off to scrub now. I'll see you in the O.R." She set Celia's hand down and settled a comforting hand on her shoulder. "Relax. You'll be unaware of any passage of time and won't feel a thing."

As the surgeons walked out, Celia hugged herself. Bereft of the warm hand, the cold crept back under her skin. And the shakes were returning.

She was about to lose major parts of her body. Maybe she couldn't see them, but she knew they were there. They had fed her the hormones she'd needed to grow up. They'd given her Nicci. They'd reminded her on a very regular basis that she was a woman. Now, though, they had turned against her.

Celia gripped the side rail of the gurney. For the first time in many years, she prayed. "Please, God. Please let me get through this. Let it be better than they think." Her voice cracked. "Let me live. Nicci is barely nine years old. She needs her mother. And I need to see her grow up."

She lay there, curled up into herself, eyes tightly shut, repeating the same thing over and over again. "Please let me see Nicci grow up."

The sensation of touch wound its way to her brain, as if a hand closed gently over hers. Warmth infused her. Soothed her. The words came out of nowhere. Quiet. Calming. Assured.

Show me.

Celia observed a young child, maybe five or six years old, playing quietly on the floor. The room seemed somehow familiar. She saw the Afghani artifacts, the mosaic rugs from the orient, and the exotic locale photographs. Every flat surface was covered. Walls. Buffets. They all held photographs, but not all were from far reaching places. There were pictures of her parents. And of herself as a young child.

Celia's smile held a thousand memories. This was her grandmother's home. She turned back to the dark-haired child.

Me! This child is me?

Her grandmother came in, followed by a strange man and a young blond boy. The man carried a cardboard box. He set the box down in front of little Celia and she peered over the edge. Inside was a yellow lab puppy, barely weaned.

Maxey!

That was all the time it took for little Celia to fall deeply and madly in love.

Her Maxey. Celia watched the little girl she now remembered throw her arms around the puppy as he slurped sloppy kisses all over her face and arms. The box tumbled over and they rolled on the ground, giggling and licking.

The little boy with the white-blond hair joined them. Funny, Celia didn't recall him and couldn't match a name to the face.

"Hi," he said shyly. "I'm Seth."

"Hi." Little Celia turned to her grandmother.

"Yes." Her grandmother answered the unspoken question written all over the child's face. "The puppy is yours to keep, Celia Louise."

"Yay!" she whooped.

"Whatcha gonna call him?" the boy asked.

The little girl stared at the rambunctious pup for a long time. Finally, all serious and purposeful, she answered.

"Maxey. His name is Maxey."

Celia grinned. Maxey had been her best friend through the end of high school. Her mother had sworn there would never be a dog in their house. Dad had convinced her that their little girl needed a companion. Her mother had relented, but Maxey would stay in the garage. It wasn't long before Maxey slept on Celia's bed. They were inseparable. Maxey had known all of her deepest, darkest secrets and never told a soul. And he always loved her in spite of her mistakes, like the time she let a boy distract her and forgot to feed Maxey until bedtime. No censure. Only another one of his sloppy kisses.

Ah, Maxey. I miss you. Nostalgia pervaded Celia's body like cocoa-warmth on a cold winter's day as she watched the little girl play with her new best friend.

They couldn't see him, but Seth waited with the others for word to come through. Patricia Milbourne sat on the couch, her crocheting untouched on her lap. Worried eyes followed Nicci, who had given up all pretense of playing on the ipad she'd been encouraged to bring and she now paced out to the hall, then retraced her steps. Back and forth, over and over again, peering around the corner each time she reached the edge of the waiting room.

Celia's friend Jen sat in the corner occupying her two small children with crayons and coloring books. Her eyes kept glancing toward the hall as she, too, displayed the restlessness of being forced to wait with no word.

Surgery seemed to be taking a long time. The waiting room had emptied out. The volunteer had been replaced by a sign that indicated anyone present should answer the phone when it rang. They all waited to hear.

They all prayed for good news.

And the more time that passed, the more prevalent the possibility of bad news became in their minds.

Nicci had just returned to the corner when a man in a suit entered the room. Her head whipped around, eyes bright. Then her shoulders slumped with recognition.

It was Dr. Ted.

He went straight to Patricia and reached for her hand. "How's everyone holding up?"

"Waiting isn't much fun," her voice quavered. "Could you—"

As Nicci moved closer, Dr. Ted pulled the girl into his embrace. "I already did. All I could determine was that she's still in surgery." He looked at his watch. "This isn't an unusual amount of time for the procedure she's having done."

"Do you think it could be much longer?" Jen asked from the corner.

"It's hard to tell. It all depends on how much they have to do. How much they need to remove or excise for biopsy."

No one answered. His words should comfort them. The length of time wasn't unusual.

Yet Nicci returned to her pacing.

Patricia settled her hands in her lap in white-knuckle tight prayer mode.

And Jen stared at the clock as if it were a mortal enemy.

Seth knew the reassurance of Dr. Ted's words had faded even before he sat next to Celia's mother. No one and no thing would help, except to know that Celia was safe. That it was over.

At that moment, Dr. Mason stepped into the room. Everyone turned in unison toward the door. She didn't keep them waiting. "Celia came through surgery just fine. They are finishing up and then she'll be moved to recovery."

Patricia hung her head for a long moment, clasping shaking hands together in front of her.

Dr. Ted hugged Nicci tight, a wide grin spreading across his face.

Jen uttered a "thank God" and turned her attention to Nicci, who had started to cry. She drew the girl out of Dr. Ted's arms and sat down with her. Pulling out a Kleenex, Jen wiped Nicci's eyes. She calmed her with words over and over again. "You heard the doctor. Your mom's okay. She came through just fine. Surgery is over with. Now she can heal."

Seth listened and let the words feed the emptiness in his own soul. He knew the truth. This was only the first hurdle of many for Celia.

Nicci got up and went to Dr. Mason. "Can I see my mom, now?"

"Not yet, sweetie. You remember we had to give her something to put her to sleep?"

"Yeah."

"Well, it will take a couple hours for her to wake up from that. After she wakes you can see her."

"Oh. Well, okay. I guess." Nicci went over and slumped into a chair.

Dr. Mason lowered her voice so the children wouldn't hear. "We didn't find anything we weren't expecting."

At Patricia's budding smile, Janice Mason held up a hand. "We didn't find any less, either. We ended up doing a full hysterectomy. The growths had spread to the abdominal cavity. I wish I could give you better news. We removed everything we could see. There is a lot for pathology to look at before we know for sure how extensive the diagnosis is."

"So she will still need chemotherapy?"

"Yes. We would have done chemo even with minimal growths. It's the only way to kill the cancer at the cellular level."

"Will she be all right, Doctor?" Patricia asked.

Seth winced.

"We'll do everything in our power to try to make that happen," Dr. Mason said. "I'm going to change and see a couple of patients, but I'll be back later to check on Celia."

Patricia stood and held out her hand. "Thank you for taking such good care of my daughter."

"You're welcome." Janice Mason nodded to everyone. "Nursing will let you know when she's able to have company. I'll see her later."

After she left, relief was defined in many ways for the group of hopeful friends and relatives. Dr. Ted sighed and excused himself to see some patients also. Patricia picked up her forgotten crocheting and started to work. Jen began gathering up toys and books. Nicci helped her.

And Seth took comfort in all of their actions, letting it relieve his own torment.

The fog started to lift and Celia opened her eyes to bright lights and a world whirling around her. She squinted to shield her eyes and tried to move. It hurt! "Mmm."

The nurse... Doris—that was it—came into view. "Welcome back, Celia."

She felt a hand on her shoulder.

"Don't try to move right now. There's plenty of time for that after you're more alert."

"S-s-s-u-r—"

"Surgery went well. The doctor will be in later to tell you more."

Her tongue felt about three sizes too big. "Nic—"

"Your mom and daughter know you're out of surgery and have talked to Dr. Mason. We can't let them in to see you yet. Just try to rest and let the anesthesia wear off."

Celia felt something placed in her hand.

"That's the call light. If you need anything, just push

the button on the end. I'll be close by."

Then the fog returned and reality disappeared again.

Seth watched her sleep off the stupor of anesthesia. He knew what road she would travel when she woke up. For now, sleep was better.

Sleep would help her heal from the surgery.

Sleep would help her prepare for the future.

When Celia woke, there were no bright lights, only a sluggishness giving way to...pain.

"Welcome back, sleepyhead," Doris said, entering her field of vision.

"Hurts."

"What hurts?"

"Everything." Celia tried to clear her raw throat but the raspy tone wouldn't go away.

Doris's smile was both conciliatory and sympathetic. "I know."

Celia doubted anyone could know how bad this felt.

"Emergency hysterectomy after my twins were born a few years back," Doris said.

"'You do know," Celia said, groaning. "I think I'm going to be sick—"

Doris braced the emesis basin. Each spasm was made worse by the trauma to Celia's abdominal muscles, which were screaming about how much they'd been through. Doris's comforting hands and voice soothed Celia until she was able to relax back against the pillow.

"Full incision?" she croaked.

"Yes, I'm afraid so."

"—hurts like hell."

"It will get easier. I'm setting a small pillow beside you. It helps to hug it when those muscles have to be used. Do you think you could hold down a little juice?"

Just the thought made Celia's insides churn and she reached for the basin again along with the pillow, even though there wasn't much to lose. She'd had nothing to eat or drink since before midnight last night. Hugging the pillow helped, but dry heaves were the worst and Celia slumped back in misery after a particularly gruesome bout of retching.

To add to her gloom, she seemed to be crying without even realizing it. And not your dainty, I'm-unhappy tears. It was an all out flood down her cheeks. She couldn't stop them. Hell, she couldn't even reduce them to a trickle. It was like she'd lost control of her own body.

So she did the only thing she could. She gave in to the agony, trying hard to remember it would be temporary. "This sucks."

Doris placed a cold, wet cloth against Celia's throat. "Some people have a harder time with anesthesia than others."

Celia only heard about half of what the nurse said. The cool cloth felt like a heavenly reprieve and she held it to her throat as if it were a lifeline she'd been tossed. "Ooh, this feels good."

"Yeah." Doris nodded her head. "Do you feel stable for the moment?"

Celia swallowed and felt no warning lump jolt her throat. "I think so."

"Okay. I'll be right back."

The nurse returned shortly with two syringes, which she injected via Celia's I.V.

"What?"

"For the nausea and the pain."

"Sounds good."

"You're going to drift back to sleep now," Doris said. Her voice seemed a long way off.

"Hmm. Nice," Celia said. Then everything dimmed.

When Celia woke again, she was alone in her little recovery alcove. She gulped and felt no imminent nausea attack. Her back hurt, so she tried to shift her weight.

"Ow!" Well, that part hadn't been a figment of her imagination. She had a pretty major incision to heal from by the feel of things.

"Hi," Doris said, entering the room with a small tray.

"Hi. What time is it?"

"About nine p.m."

"Seriously?" Celia rolled her tongue over her teeth. Her mouth felt like she'd eaten paste. Vile smelling paste, at that. She wrinkled her nose.

"I've brought you some juice. Do you think you can keep it down?"

"I hope so."

She handed her a cup with a bendable straw. "Good. If you can keep juice down, then we can move you to your room."

"Are Mom and Nicci still here?" Her voice still sounded like a frog that had not quite completed the transformation to charming prince.

"Your Mom is. Your daughter went home, under protest, with a family friend. I let them in to see you while you slept so she wouldn't worry."

Celia looked up at the tubes for the I.V. and pain pump. She knew she probably had a catheter in and possibly a drain through the incision.

"I have found it's better to let them see that you are

sleeping than to have them imagining something worse."

That made sense. Celia nodded.

"Keep sipping the juice," Doris said. "But not too fast. I'll go get things rolling for your move. I've got just enough time to get you on your way before my shift ends."

"Doris?"

"Yes?"

"Thank you."

"You're welcome. I'm glad I could help."

"Can my mom come in?"

"Not until we get you moved, okay?"

"Sure." Celia sipped juice and closed her eyes, dozing. It took much longer than she expected to get transferred to the med/surg unit. When her mother walked in, the relief brought tears to Celia's eyes. Age didn't matter where pain was concerned and mothers could always make the hurts easier to bear. Especially her mother, who wore a bright, brave smile as she strode into the room.

"How's my girl doing?" she asked, her voice a soft blanket surrounding Celia, taking her back to the days of scraped knees and skinned shins when a mother's words were all that was needed to heal the pain.

"Better now," Celia said, leaning into her mother's cool hand as she felt Celia's forehead and traced her cheek. Even her mother's forehead kiss erased the worst of the pain.

"Much better."

"I'm so glad."

The privacy curtain shifted as Dr. Mason stepped into the room, her typical smile adding to Celia's sense of contentment. If she could just lie here quietly and have these people around her all the time, she'd be healed in no time.

"How's my star patient?"

Celia flashed a weak smile. "I bet you say that to all your patients."

"Definitely. I only take on the best, you know." Janice Mason sat down on the bed, a very un-doctor-like move.

Even foggy, Celia knew this couldn't be good news. Her mother must have sensed that, too. She moved to stand beside Celia's head, the hand holding Celia's tightening.

"Surgery went well," the doctor started without preamble. "There were several tumors, and we took multiple samples for biopsy, as planned. We did proceed with a full hysterectomy."

Celia winced and Janice covered her hand with her own. "We felt it was necessary."

"I know," Celia said quietly.

"With all that we did, you'll be pretty sore."

"Already am."

"I bet."

Funny. Celia had been preparing for this over the past week, but now that it had happened, well, she felt...sorrow for the loss. They really had done it. Everything that made her female was gone. At least, that's how it felt. Celia wanted to curl up and cry.

That would be giving in. And Celia hadn't given in for a long time. Well, until lately, that is. So she made the only decision she could. She chose to face the situation like it was one of her headstrong clients. Direct and to the point.

"Results?"

"The frozen section done during surgery confirmed

cancer. We won't know much more than that until the pathology comes back for sure. We should have some preliminary reports by tomorrow afternoon."

"No hidden truths, right?"

Janice Mason looked at the I.V. keeping Celia hydrated and relatively pain free, then back at Celia. "Neither of the masses on your ovaries were benign, Celia. That much was apparent. And we found additional growths in the abdominal cavity. Anything more is pure speculation at this point. It's too early. But I would expect that, at the very least, you will be undergoing a fairly aggressive chemotherapy regimen."

All the surgical pain faded as Celia felt the brush of darkness overtake her. Tears welled in her eyes and she struggled to keep them from cascading over.

"Thank you," she said. "I appreciate the honesty."

Dr. Mason patted her arm. "We can deal with all the rest later. For now, get some sleep. As much as the nurses will allow, at any rate. I'll be in tomorrow afternoon and we'll talk more."

She patted both Celia's and Patricia's hands and left the room. Her departure left a silence that neither Celia nor her mother could break. Hospital noises faded until the lack of sound was its own profound echo...reminding Celia this was only the beginning. One battle. And there was still a lot of war to wage.

Celia would have liked to have curled up into a ball but since movement still sent pain, like shards of glass, piercing her abdomen, she kept her body still.

Her mind was a different matter. She couldn't stop thinking. Wondering. *Why is this happening to me? What did I do to deserve this?*

A single tear escaped as she fought the urge to scream. Then she felt a brush at her brow. Soothing her.

Lulling her back to sleep.

And somehow, Celia let it go, relaxed, and drifted off.

Nothing, Seth thought. You did nothing except draw some cosmic number. He continued to soothe Celia's forehead as her mother, face etched with deep lines of worry, lugged a chair over to the bed and reached for her daughter's hand again, this time holding it as though it were fine china.

Together, they kept watch through the night over the woman they both loved so much.

5

A NEW LEVEL OF UNDERSTANDING

By the time Dr. Mason dropped by late the next afternoon, Celia was starting to feel human again. Sore, but human. Her nausea had abated and she had even kept down a small bit of rather bland hospital food.

Short walks taken that morning had been an exercise in willpower. Those would get easier. At least, that's what the hospital staff indicated. Feeling so uncomfortable and wiped out was new to Celia. Now that the anesthesia had mostly worn off, nurses taking vitals made sleep pretty much impossible. All in all, she felt better than yesterday, though. And that was a surprise.

"Hi, Dr. Mason," Celia said as the oncologist walked in. Her voice still hovered a couple notes below normal.

"Hello. How are you feeling today?"

"Like I just finished a triathlon. Without the euphoria."

Dr. Mason chuckled. "That will get better." She glanced around. "Where's your mother?"

"I sent her home to get some sleep. She spent the entire night here. She's coming back later with Nicci for a visit."

"Good."

Celia noticed a subtle change in Dr. Mason's face, almost as if she were switching personas, from friend to doctor.

The shadow of impending knowledge tugged at Celia, trying to pull her down, to force her to come face to face with her fate. This is it. The big reveal. The definitive diagnosis. No matter what had happened before, this would be where her life changed forever.

Her heart started an uphill race as a familiar itch began to wind its way across her chest and up her neck. Her hand was already there, scratching, the IV tube trailing behind.

A sensation stilled her, as if someone gave her shoulders a comforting squeeze, calming her. Celia had no idea what it was, but it helped to keep the darkness at bay. She closed her eyes for a brief moment, then resolve straightened her shoulders and she made eye contact with the oncologist.

"You have the results from pathology, don't you."

"Some. Initial pathology looks to confirm that you have a form of ovarian cancer called Epithelial Ovarian Carcinoma." She paused a moment. "It's one of the most common types."

Common. That sounds good. Celia's heart thumped at a more normal rate as she repeated the word. "Common. That's good, right? That means you've had a lot of time to find a cure?"

"It means we've been able to find more effective ways to treat it."

But no cure? So much for that normal heart rhythm. "What stage?" Celia fell back on her research once again. Stage One would have been optimal. Just growths on the ovaries. Highly curable. Stage Two was more likely. It meant that the growths had extended beyond the ovaries, to her tubes and uterus. She had refused to look at stage three and four.

"We won't know for sure until we know how far it has spread."

Translation: it's spread.

"It's likely, though, that you will be at stage three."

"Three?" Her voice hollowed out as she felt the word echo back to her. Stage three. Worse than hoped. Much worse. Celia tried hard to listen to Dr. Mason, but the words continued to bounce around her mind like a game of Pong.

Stage three. The words hit the right side of her brain and bounced back. Stage three.

"Yes. I'm afraid so. Beyond the masses on the ovaries, we found visible growths in the lining of the uterus and in the abdomen. We don't know yet if any carcinoma exists in the lymph nodes. Stage four, as you know would mean the cancer has spread to other organs of the body. We saw no indication of that, which is good news. Again, we won't have the final results for several days." Dr. Mason sat down on the bed beside her. "Because there are so few symptoms, it's very hard to catch these cancers in the early stages. In fact, only nineteen percent are caught in the first stage."

Celia felt the room start to spin. She gripped the bedrail, but it didn't help. She knew better than to ask the question, but couldn't stop herself. "And the ones that aren't caught that early? Like mine?"

"Those are more difficult to treat."

Celia closed her eyes. "What's the bottom line, doctor?" she whispered.

"Chemotherapy will probably start sooner than we

would like. I'm afraid you'll only have a couple weeks at most to recover from surgery."

Celia turned to the window and watched the remnants of yesterday's storm move tree limbs fast becoming devoid of leaves. "I tried to keep my mind centered on the positive," she said. "I know all about stage one. Even stage two. I—I chose not to look at the other possibilities. At least not in depth. What..." She scratched her neck. "What is the survival rate at stage three?"

Janice Mason patted Celia's hand. "I think that's more than you need to worry about right now. Let's wait until we have all the facts."

Translation: it's bad.

"In the meantime, you work on getting your strength back."

Celia forced herself to smile, but knew it fell flat. "I will."

As soon as Dr. Mason was out the door, the smile disappeared and Celia stared once again at the clock on the wall.

Why did hospitals always put clocks right in front of your bed? Even the television was offset. But no. They wanted you to see the clock. Day in, day out. Minute by minute.

Tick, tock. Tick. Tock.

She closed her eyes to block out the sound, imaginary or otherwise. It took some real concentration, but the tick-tock faded. Coolness touched her forehead, like fingers combing through her hair. A gentle voice whispered.

Show me.

The playground at St. Mark's Elementary School

was a cold, gray expanse of concrete surrounding a two-story brick building that housed eight grades. A playground set with two swings served as the solitary structure available at recess. That, and one old, barely inflated ball, currently being haphazardly bounced in a game of four-square. Imagination was the only other equipment available.

Young Celia's auburn hair was half-pulled out of its ponytail. She knew her mother wouldn't be happy when she got home from school. Her uniform had a rip in it from an earlier fall to the cement while flying after a wayward ball. And a scabbed-over knee wound broke open again, the blood staining her white knee-high stockings. But none of that mattered. She needed all her concentration for the game at hand.

"Red rover, red rover, send Mary right over!"

A little brown-haired girl broke ranks from Celia's team and ran as fast as she could to the other side. She picked a spot between the two boys on the end, trying to break their hand-hold. But she couldn't. So she shrugged her shoulders and, with a smile only a girl could understand, grabbed the hand of the cutest boy and started yelling at the team she'd just left.

"Ceelie, they're picking all the girls! That's not fair. They're supposed to take turns." The blonde, pig-tailed girl next to her pouted.

"Yeah, Jenny. I know."

"They know we can't break through."

"Yeah, but we'll show them. We'll win anyhow." Celia broke the hand-hold with her best friend to hug her. "I know we will."

"But how?"

"We're gonna hold tight and not let them break us. That's how."

"Shhh. It's our turn," Jenny said. "Who's Keith gonna pick? Maybe he'll pick Bernadette. She won't break through. She can't break through anything."

"Hey! That's not nice."

"Well, it's true."

"But it's not right." Celia's answer was muffled by their captain's call.

"Red rover, red rover, send Bernadette right over."

Bernadette was petite, even for a ten year old. Her uniform was patched in a few places and she wore saddle shoes scuffed almost beyond recognition. Her brown hair always seemed to obscure part of her face. She kept to herself and only joined games when Sister Catherine insisted. You don't argue with nuns. Celia knew Bernadette was always the last one picked.

"This is gonna be easy," Jenny whispered.

"Shhhh."

Bernadette's stilted run didn't give her much steam and Celia and Jenny were easily able to hold on. Keith shuffled everyone so Jen was on one side of him and Bernadette on the other. Celia took Bernadette's other hand.

Another girl went flying to the opposing team and then it was Keith's turn again.

"Red rover, red rover, send Nathan right over," he hollered.

Celia saw Bernadette turn pale, her eyes as wide as a cartoon character in shock.

"What's the matter?"

"He'll hurt me."

"No, he won't."

"Yes, he will. I know it."

"He's your brother," Celia insisted. "He won't hurt you."

Bernadette looked away, but not before Celia saw the tears. She frowned. Something wasn't right. Bernadette seemed afraid of her brother. Celia didn't have any brothers, but knew from Jenny that they could be a real pain. Not someone to be afraid of, though. What would make Bernadette feel like that?

A recent talk with her parents popped into her head. They wanted her to be mindful of strangers. Some people just weren't very nice, they told her. And just like that, Celia understood the bruises Bernadette always tried to hide. She scowled at the school bully preparing for his run, then looked back at Bernadette.

"Okay. This is what we're gonna do," Celia said. "We're going to lock arms and not let him through."

Bernadette turned to Celia, shaking her head. "We can't hold him."

"Yes, we can."

"I can't." The panic was back in Bernadette's widened eyes.

"Yes, Bernie, you can. And you will. You hold on to me like this—" Celia linked the two of them together with a solid hand to arm grasp. "And you don't look at him. You look at me. You got that?"

"Y-yes."

"Good. Now, when I say, you take two steps back. That'll make it harder for him to break through. 'Kay?"

"I don't know—"

"Just keep looking at me. It'll work."

Nathan started his run, gathering speed as he crossed the playground. Celia kept one eye on Nathan and one on her partner, willing her to be strong. Just as Nathan hit, Celia yelled.

"Now!"

They both stepped back. Nathan's momentum

slowed. He grabbed both their arms and dug his fingers in, trying to break the hold. But they didn't let go. He slowed even further and was unable to break through. Finally, he stopped.

"You'll pay for that," he shot at his sister. He glared at both of them before forcing them to let him between them. He let loose of Celia's arm, but held onto his sister's hand.

Celia watched Bernadette's wide smile get wiped away and tears filled her eyes. Looking at Bernadette's hand, she could see the white, crunched look of a hand being slowly crushed.

Celia felt the fire of anger souring her stomach. She pushed Nathan, forcing him off balance so he had to let go of Bernadette. Then she stared defiantly at him for a long moment, turned, and marched directly over to Sr. Catherine. Tapping her foot, she waited impatiently until she had permission to speak.

"I think Nathan hurts Bernadette," she said without preamble.

Sr. Catherine focused on Celia. "Why do you say that?"

"'Cuz he said he would hurt her and she told me he meant it. And she's always got bruises. And she gets to school way early so she doesn't have to walk with him."

Sr. Catherine worked the beads at her waist as she and Celia watched the two siblings interact on the playground. The pain in the girl's face was evident. So was Nathan's fierce look. "Oh, dear," she said. "Dear, dear, dear. It makes sense. Why didn't we see this before?"

"'Cuz she hides it."

Sr. Catherine patted Celia's shoulder. "My child,

you've done well this day. Thank you for not being afraid to tell me. That was very brave." She walked over to Bernadette and Nathan, separated them and pulled the girl aside. Celia watched them speak, right up until Bernadette buried her face in the nun's habit. She turned away and saw Nathan watching them, also.

"You're gonna get your payback," Celia mumbled.

Doing the right thing didn't always make you feel better right away, Celia figured out. She wanted to beat him up for being mean. But that would make her as bad as he was.

Almost.

Still fuming, she walked the outskirts of the playground. Intent on fueling her anger at Nathan, she was almost on top of the little blond boy before she saw him. He leaned up against the fence and watched her. She did a quick side-step to keep from running into him and fixed him with a gaze filled with leftover anger. She didn't know him. He wasn't from her class.

"Who are you?" she asked.

"Seth."

"Do you go to school here?"

"No."

"What are you doing here if you don't go to this school?" Celia waved at the building behind her.

"Just—checking things out."

"Well, okay, I guess." Her anger diminished. "It's a nice school." Celia started to move away.

"Hey," he said. "That was a good thing you did for that little girl."

Celia turned back. "What do you mean?"

"Just that she'll be okay now, thanks to you."

"Oh," she said, puzzled. She looked over to where Bernadette and Sr. Catherine were just about to disappear behind school doors. "That's good, then." Her anger slipped further away. She turned back, but the little boy had vanished. Puzzled, she took a long moment to look around. He was nowhere.

Just then the school bell rang and she hurried to catch up with her class. Turning back just before going through the school doors, she still couldn't see the boy.

Celia continued to stare out the window of her hospital room, but her mind was awash in the childhood memory she'd just relived. Funny. She hadn't thought of, or seen, Bernadette for years. They'd been good friends all through school, but Bernadette had lit out for Harvard after graduation and never returned to Seattle. Celia barely remembered the incident, but now, in retrospect, she realized that Bernadette had been severely abused by her own brother. The world was a sick, sick place sometimes.

A wistful smile touched Celia's lips. She'd made a difference that day. And she was glad the memory had returned to remind her. It felt good, even after all this time.

She'd made a difference then. She could make a difference now, too. For herself. It was time to stop wallowing in self-pity. Time to let this cancer know who the boss is. And who is going to win.

She reached for the call button just as her door opened. Her best friend Jen walked in with her pre-school kids in tow. Blonde and petite, Jen looked like a cheerleader, even after two children. She could light up a room just by walking in. And she lightened Celia's mood considerably.

"Jen, great timing. Could you get my robe? I want to go for a stroll around the floor. I'm going to need all the strength I can muster and now's as good a time to start as any."

6

THE DREADED CHEMOTHERAPY: HEY, THIS DOESN'T SEEM SO BAD

The phone's soft jingle woke Celia from a lovely dream. She'd been on an escorted tour around countryside filled with lush grass and spring bloom. A handsome escort with the most amazing brown eyes and white-blond hair had been beside her, reining the horses that pulled their carriage. She sighed as she fumbled for the phone, residual soreness from the surgery reminding her of the difference between dreams and reality.

With a glance at the Caller ID, she clicked talk. "Hi, Mom."

"It took you a long time to answer. Is everything all right?"

"Yes. I'm fine. I just took a little nap before Nicci gets home from an after-school play date."

"See. You're still tired. You should have stayed here longer," her mother said.

"Mom, it's been two weeks since surgery. I couldn't have made it through those first few days without you, but I needed to get back home. Admit it. It was getting hard for you, even with Jen's help, and Dan's, to get Nicci to and from school." Celia's ex might have his shortcomings, and didn't know what was going on beyond the word "surgery", but he'd been very solicitous and helpful these past couple weeks. Still, her mother grew very quiet at the mention of his name.

"Plus, Nicci needed some normal. She was getting way too quiet, too worried. She needed to be home."

"That girl carries the weight of the world on her shoulders," Patricia said.

"I know. Coming home and getting back to her daily routine seems to be working. She's over at her friend's watching some mind-numbing tv for—" Celia checked her watch—"another hour or so."

"Well, how about dinner? Are you all set?" her mother asked.

"You cooked enough food to supply a Navy ship heading out for a six month tour. Nicci and I are going to get fat if we eat everything you've stocked us with."

"There's nothing wrong with that. You need some weight on you."

Celia rolled her eyes. Did she eye Nicci with the same you-need-to-eat-more look that most mothers seemed to use?

"So," her mother changed tactics. "Are we set for tomorrow? I'll pick you up around nine?"

"Yes. That works great. Nicci will have left. She really wants to go with us, but I don't want her to miss any more school. I had to promise her a lot of details about my experience to get her to agree."

"That sounds just like our sweet Nicci. Now, you're sure you want me to drive?"

Celia grinned. Her mother had lived in Seattle all her life and yet managed to avoid ever driving the downtown corridor. "You'll do just fine. Remember, I'll be giving directions. And I know Seattle like the freckles on Nicci's cheeks. There's zero chance of getting lost."

"All right, then. I'll see you in the morning."

"Hey, Mom?"

"Yes?"

"Do I thank you enough for all the help you give me?"

"Yes. You do. But you don't need to. You're my daughter. Of course, I'm going to help."

As Celia hung up the phone and lay back, she closed her eyes and wished for a few more minutes of slumber. She wanted to see those eyes again. She'd been comfortable with the man from her dreams, almost as if she knew him. The memory of his face already faded, slowly being relegated to her subconscious. Maybe he would wait there for another day's dreaming. One could always hope.

She stretched, careful not to aggravate her still tender stomach, rolled over, and pushed herself up. Time to find her energy and make things look good for her daughter. Celia's brows knit together. Her daughter had been acting way too somber lately. Watching her recover from surgery hadn't helped. It was pretty obvious that Nicci was worried—and whom she was worried about. So tonight, it was time for a night off. She reached for the phone. Since she wasn't allowed to drive yet, she'd see if Dan might drop off a movie for them. And she'd make Nicci's favorite meal—macaroni and cheese with polish sausage. And Kool-aid, of course.

Long after Celia left the bedroom, Seth stayed, his

memories filled with the acute awareness of having her seated next to him.

"I, too, enjoyed the ride, milady."

Celia opened some non-descript magazine from the table, but scanned the waiting room instead of reading it. Warm colors and pleasant, relaxing photographs adorned the walls of the outpatient oncology suite, all designed to make you feel at ease.

Except it's hard to relax when you're about to fill your body with caustic chemicals. The hint of disinfectant ruined the soothing effect, anyhow. She tossed the magazine down. Maybe pacing would help, adding her footfalls to a carpet that had probably cushioned many before her. Before she could stand, an older woman in scrubs opened the door to the inner sanctum.

"Celia?" she called.

Here comes my new reality. She pushed herself out of the chair, shuffling feet that felt heavy, as if earth's gravity had just spiked higher.

She and her mother were ushered into a room designed to put people further at ease. An LCD television screen with DVD, a CD player for music, even a mini-fridge with juices. She knew from the literature that she could order lunches with a simple phone call while she was held captive by the chemotherapy. Celia glanced at the I.V. pole.

"Go ahead and have a seat." The nurse indicated a padded recliner. Celia's eyes widened in pleasure as she sank back. The chair was quite comfortable.

"My name's Mary and I'll be your primary caregiver today. There will be others in and out as needed, also. Oh, here's one of them now. She'll get your vitals while we talk."

"All right." Celia clutched the arm of the recliner as the aide prepared to take her vitals, certain that her blood pressure would be abnormal to say the least. She could hear the blood rushing through her ears as if she had a seashell held up to one.

"Did your chemotherapy get explained to you in full?"

"Yes, but I've got some questions."

The aide placed a thermometer in her mouth and Celia held up her hands.

Mary laughed. "It's okay. We can wait."

When she could talk again, Celia fired off her first question. "I was told that I'd be receiving a platinum based therapy—Carboplatin, right? In conjunction with Taxol?"

Mary consulted the chart. "Yes. You'll receive those both by I.V. and intraperitoneal injection through the port catheter. You had that implanted in your chest wall during your staging surgery."

"Yes, that was loads of fun." Celia scrunched up her nose. "Will I be getting the recommended dosage through both methods? Or half the dosage through I.V. and half through the port cath?"

The aide was done taking her pulse and wrapped a blood pressure cuff around Celia's arm. Celia shifted in order to see, but it did no good. The aide still blocked her view. Tempted to be rude and nudge her aside, Celia chose the high road. She tapped her fingers until the aide was done.

"Blood pressure is up a bit," the girl indicated.

Mary checked. "Not enough to be an issue. She suggested the aide finish taking vitals later and turned back to Celia. "I saw that you're a pharmaceutical rep, so I figured you'd have more questions than most. The reason we do chemotherapy both ways is so we can bombard the cancer cells. You will get more medication this way. Unfortunately, that sometimes increases the side effects. But it's been determined through multiple studies that this is the most effective way to treat your diagnosis."

"What about other medications? For nausea and other symptoms."

"You most likely won't need or receive any other medications here. At least not yet. You'll have a home regimen for nausea and I recommend you follow it whether you feel ill or not. Did you fill your prescriptions?"

"Yes."

"Are you aware of the possible side effects from the chemotherapy drugs? The most prevalent ones are nausea, diarrhea, fatigue, appetite changes, and hair loss."

Celia's hand tangled in her hair. "I'm aware of them," she acknowledged, feeling like a man being led to the guillotine. "Do you see a lot of women lose their hair."

"Some. Men, too," Mary said. "I'd be prepared for it. Have you thought about options? Hats? Or wigs?"

Celia waved her hand, still not ready to go there. "I decided to deal with it when I have to."

"I can understand that. It can be nice to be prepared, though. Just in case. Has anyone mentioned that we have on-site counseling available if you should feel the need?"

"Dr. Mason mentioned it. I...don't feel like I need that. At least, not right now."

"That's fine. If you do, just let us know and we'll

match you up with someone."

Celia knew they were about talked out. There was nothing else to delay the process. She glanced at her mother, who was as white as the chalk against a blackboard. "Are you okay, Mom?" she asked.

"Yes, honey. Just worried."

"You don't have to stay here for the whole time, you know?"

"I want to be here." She held up a bag. "I've got my crocheting." Her attempt at a smile looked more like the zig-zagged line on an EKG tracing, but Celia fed it into her soul for encouragement.

"Okay, we've got a few more questions to ask before we proceed." Mary said.

This was turning into another pre-op session. And Celia was starting to chafe, running her hands back and forth along the arms of the recliner. She was tired of answering questions. Tired of reviewing her medical history, which had been pretty much non-existent until a month ago. Tired. Period.

Mary set her pen down. "That's about all we need to get started."

"About time," Celia mumbled.

"I'll take a quick look at the port site, we'll get your I.V. started, and get your chemotherapy meds running. You will need to stay still for the first couple of hours until we gauge your body's reaction to the medications. After that, you can get up and move around if you want. Do you need to use the facilities beforehand?"

"Yes."

When she returned, Mary had everything laid out for the I.V. Celia couldn't see the needle, but noted the length of the package it was in.

"I hate needles," she muttered.

"You're not alone. Try to get comfortable and I'll help you through it," Mary said.

Celia settled into the recliner with a slight shiver.

"Are you cold?"

"No. At least, I don't think so."

The blinds on the window were drawn, but provided the only focal point that kept needles out of Celia's peripheral vision. Celia tried to draw a deep breath, but couldn't. Drawing quick, shallow breaths, she counted slats in the blinds.

One, two, three...

"Try to breathe naturally," Mary said as she tapped lightly across Celia's hand in search of a vein.

Four, five, six...

"You're going to feel a little pinch."

Celia started to count out loud. "Seven, eight, nine, ten...ouch!"

"I know. But it's already over."

Celia chanced a look as she felt tape being applied. All done? "Good," she tried to joke. "Does that mean I can go home?"

"Not quite yet," Mary smiled as she picked up her supplies. "I'll be back with your meds in a moment."

Dr. Mason popped in on Mary's exiting heels.

"Hi, Celia. I thought I'd stop by on my way to the office and see how it's going for you." Today, her T-shirt was a splash of rainbow colors with a large peace sign across the front.

"Fine, I guess."

She glanced at the chart then at the I.V. pole. "They're ready to start?"

"Just waiting for the chemicals."

Dr. Mason sat next to Celia's recliner. "I know it's hard, but try not to think about the down side of this.

Remember that these *medicines* will be attacking the cancer. They are fighting *for* you."

Celia ran her free hand through her hair. "It's hard. I can't stop thinking about the side effects and wondering how many good cells they'll be killing at the same time. Research says I have a pretty good shot at losing my hair. Not to mention my ability to eat for a while."

"Let's take it one day at a time. You feel good now. And, believe it or not, you'll feel good when you go home today."

Celia knew the skepticism was transparent on her face but she held her tongue.

Janice Mason chuckled and stood. "Try to relax. Today really will be a breeze."

Mary returned, arms laden with I.V. bags and accoutrement.

"I'll stop in later," Dr. Mason said.

"Bye, Doctor."

Seth watched as Celia glared at the intravenous bags the nurse placed on the pole. Lips that had disappeared into a thin, almost white line gave evidence of her anger. Good. Anger would help her fight.

As the bags were connected to her port catheter and to the I.V. in her hand, he saw the trembling before anyone else did. First, her hands. Then it cascaded up her arms. Her legs started to shake, too. And finally, the thin lines of her lips gave way to tremulous motion.

"Are you cold?" the nurse asked, reaching into an in-room warmer for a heated blanket and covering Celia up to the chin.

"N-no."

Her mother, seated beside her, clasped Celia's hand in hers.

Seth craved the ability to do that. To provide tactile relief for her distress. He thumped his hands together in his own show of anger. This was too much, too hard to watch. How could he be expected to witness this and not help? What hell had he been thrust into? And what had he done to deserve this punishment? He hung his head as he saw the unshed sheen of tears in Celia's eyes. If it was hard for him to watch, how much harder was it for her to live? He knew she had not earned this penance.

As the nurse left, he leaned in and embraced her face within his hands.

Celia shifted his way, almost as if moving into his embrace. He didn't know how long he stayed there, holding that inanimate touch until her trembling ceased. Her eyes closed and her body relaxed.

She slept.

With the intense relief of a man who'd been tossed a life preserver, he removed himself to the corner of the room and kept watch along with her mother, whose crochet needle wove silent strands. Occasionally, the needle stopped as a hand reached up to wipe a damp cheek.

Walking out of the building, Celia and her mother turned in unison to look back at the façade. Her first chemotherapy appointment was done.

"What do we do now?" Patricia asked her daughter.

"Um, I don't know."

"Well, how are you feeling?"

Celia's brow creased. "Actually? I feel fine." She laughed, a short hoot, like a prisoner given a temporary reprieve from torture. She knew more would be forthcoming. For now, though, it was a moment to enjoy. "Seems kind of anti-climactic, doesn't it?"

"I'm just glad you feel well. Would you like to get some dinner?"

Celia threw an arm around her mother's shoulders and drew them toward the street. "Well, since Nicci will be at her Dad's until after dinner, why don't we do some shopping first and then get a bite to eat?"

"That sounds lovely. You know this area. Where would you suggest?"

The rain had stopped, so they wandered the shops of downtown Seattle. In one boutique, Celia found a row of hats and began trying them on. "After all, there's a very good chance I'll lose my hair," she said with an attempt at a smile.

She reached for the red and purple one, but Patricia stopped her. "Sorry, dear," she said placing the hat back on the rack. "You'll have to wait a few more years before you can wear that one."

"Well, then, how about this one." She grabbed a brimmed straw hat with a muted yellow ribbon around it. "For the summer."

She perched it on her head and searched for a mirror. It looked good—at the moment. How would it look in a month? Celia pulled her hair tight and shoved it up underneath the hat. Covering what little hair still showed, she imagined herself without it. Her eyes seemed larger. She leaned in and wiped at her cheek, frowning.

Her freckles seemed larger, too.

She had great cheekbones. They seemed more pronounced now, though. Of course, if she lost much weight due to chemo, that could be a disadvantage. She would look way too hollowed out.

Her color seemed fine. She'd been gifted with just

enough to look lightly tanned. As she ran her hand over her face, she wondered if she would lose that color, become ashen like most sick people do.

She hoped not.

Yanking the hat off, she tossed it back on the rack and turned to leave. This was no longer fun.

Her mother broke the silence as they moved on. "Honey, you can always get a wig."

Celia snorted in disgust. "Those things look more fake than anything. Wearing a wig is like putting a neon sign on your forehead. Look at me, it says. I've got cancer."

She set a pretty strong pace and it took a bit for Celia to re-focus and see her mother lagging behind. Filled with remorse, she ran back the few steps.

"Mom, I'm so sorry."

"That's okay, dear."

"No, it's not. I—I got so wrapped up in my own issues I forgot about your needs." She hugged her mother close and whispered in her ear. "That's your job from now on, Mom."

"What?"

"You get to remind me when I'm acting too selfish. Keep me grounded in the fact that there is life to be lived and people to notice."

"Oh, honey—"

"I'm serious, Mom. One of the things I like about myself is that I take others needs very seriously. I don't want to lose that just because I've got some illness."

She stopped in the middle of the sidewalk. Strangers were starting to step to the side to pass them but Celia remained still. "This is serious, Mom. Promise me."

"All right. All right," Patricia said, glancing from side to side. "I promise I'll tell you when you are getting *too* selfish."

"Good." Celia nodded and linked arms with her mother as they walked on.

"I will, however," Patricia said, "also remind you when you need to be *more* selfish. Deal?"

Celia grinned. "Deal."

In the next store, Celia again browsed hats, then went in search of her mother, who stood in front of the mirror holding a feminine and romantic handkerchief-hemmed dress against her body. A dress unlike any Celia had seen her wear before.

Curious, she watched her mother for a few moments. She moved from side to side, the soft hem swirling around her calves. And...was that humming Celia heard? Her mother never hummed. There was clearly a mystery here that needed solving.

Patricia looked up and caught Celia's obvious interest. When she dropped the arm holding the dress at the same time as her other hand rushed to cup her cheek, Celia's mouth dropped open.

Was her mother actually blushing? "Mom?"

Patricia Milbourne, always so calm and collected, flustered her way through hooking the dress on the closest rack possible, as if touching it any longer would burn her.

"Mom, what is up?"

"Nothing, honey."

"Bull." Celia's mother may have held her silence sometimes, like when Celia had chosen to accept Danny's marriage proposal. But she never out-and-out lied. "Something's going on. You're acting like a giddy—"

Celia froze. Could it be? Her mother had never shown a bit of interest in any man since her father's passing. Heck, she'd never looked askance once they'd met back in high school, if her father's stories were at all accurate. Was she—interested in someone?

"Are you...have you..." She didn't even know what to ask. And her mother's blush had deepened. "You *are.*"

Her mother stood mute, toying with the strap of her purse.

"You're seeing someone!"

Patricia opened her mouth then closed it. Looked around like any exit would do at the moment, then raised her arms in supplication. "No. I'm not."

"That's—"

"But maybe I'd like to. There is someone..."

Oh. My. God. Celia couldn't believe her ears. So many things whirled around in her head it was impossible to sort them out. One thing, one emotion, edged the others out. Happiness. For her mother, who stood fingering a decidedly un-Mom-like dress. How she personally felt about it, she'd sort out later. For now, though, astonishment that her mother was interested in someone, and happiness that her mother had finally embraced life after five years of being a widow, overshadowed everything.

Celia closed the distance between them and hugged her mother. Tightly. "I'm happy for you, Mom."

"There's nothing going on. Really. He's just a friend. A part of our bridge group."

"Friends have never made you blush before," Celia said. "And if he's someone who interests you, I think you should go for it. Ask him out."

"Oh, no. I couldn't."

Celia grabbed her mother gently by the shoulders. "Yes, Mom, you can. Don't waste another minute." She buried the shadow around her, just for a moment. "Ask him out. Find out if you really *do* like him."

"I don't know. I'll...I'll think about it."

"Good. But don't think too much. Just ask him out. Coffee, Mom. See if he wants to have some coffee."

"But we have coffee when we play bridge."

Really? What was it going to take to convince her mother to go for it? Celia stood there staring, waiting, until finally, her mother acquiesced.

"Maybe I could ask him for coffee."

"Thank you," Celia said. "How long have you felt this way?"

Patricia shrugged. "A while, I guess."

"And you didn't tell me?"

"I didn't want to distract you."

"With this kind of stuff, Mom? You can distract me anytime you want."

Linking arms, they searched a few more stores for a deal they couldn't live without, but came away empty-handed, except for the dress Celia had insisted her mother go back and buy. After dinner, they worked their way to the car. Celia stopped before unlocking it and searched the Seattle skyline, taking the moment to imprint her mind with this memory. So she could draw it out and relive it when she needed the distraction.

Today is a good day.

Nicci, of course, was a bundle of questions after they picked her up. Celia tried to explain it as best she could, but couldn't allay her daughter's certainty that she was hiding some deep physical misery.

"Really, honey. I feel fine."

"But you said that the drugs would make you sick." Nicci pulled her mother's face closer. "Are you trying to look good for my sake?"

"No," Celia laughed.

"'Cuz you don't have to fake it, Mom. I'm old enough. I'll take care of you."

Celia hugged her daughter tightly, a love-infused smile filling her face. "I know you will, Babydoll. And I'm counting on it."

Celia declined her mother's offer to spend the night, preferring to concentrate on Nicci while nausea was not an issue. So Patricia dropped them both off for a quiet night together.

As Celia took the popcorn and Kool-Aid to the couch, Nicci picked the movie.

"*Girl Meets World*?" Celia groaned.

Nicci's eyes sparkled. "You bet!"

"Haven't you had enough of that show yet?"

"Mom! I'll *never* get tired of *Girl Meets World*."

Celia ruffled her daughter's hair. "I know." Hand to forehead, she affected her best Scarlett O'Hara expression. "If we must, we must." Falling back on the couch, she dragged Nicci with her and the movie was delayed for several minutes by a gentle tickle-fest.

Later, curled up in blankets with Nicci lost in the movie, Celia let her thoughts wander. For a day she'd dreaded when it began, it had turned out pretty darn well. How strange was it that she'd been filled with all these caustic, cancer-killing chemicals, yet she felt fine? She couldn't quite wrap her mind around it. She was quite certain it would change. It had to.

So far, she had managed to keep her condition from everyone but her mother and daughter and best friend. That wouldn't hold for much longer, though. She needed to let her boss know when she would return to work. They would need a plan in place for those days when she didn't have the strength to see clients.

She'd need to talk to Tana and the rest of her team after that. They had a right to know she wouldn't be able to give one hundred percent for a while.

And she needed to tell Daniel. Asking Nicci to keep a secret from her father wasn't fair. Daniel had a right to know and... Celia took a deep breath. There were decisions to make. Just in case.

She hugged Nicci tighter and forced her thoughts to the far reaches of her mind. It was time to concentrate on her daughter.

After the movie, she tucked Nicci into bed and kissed her goodnight. As she started to close the door, her daughter spoke up.

"Mom?"

She paused. "What's up, Babydoll?"

"Could you leave the door open?"

Celia frowned. Nicci always slept with the door closed. "Sure." Heading back downstairs, she couldn't help but wonder if this was another casualty of her diagnosis.

The next day was Saturday and Celia was happily surprised that she still felt well. A bit off in the energy department, but she had planned for a slow day. She and Nicci walked up to buy groceries first. The freezer was stocked, but the cupboards were bare, and if Nicci had to have toaster waffles instead of her favorite cereal one more time, the girl would probably revolt.

After the store, Nicci played at a nearby friend's home while Celia took a short nap. She woke up refreshed and alert. And still very surprised.

She needed to clean. The sun drew her, though. After picking up Nicci, they walked to the park to absorb some Vitamin D.

That evening, Celia sat with her planner and tried to map out the next few days. She couldn't plan too much, but a few phone calls to clients would help. No contact meant no sales. She could use some commissions to shore up her sagging paycheck. Her base pay wasn't quite enough to keep up with the bills. Celia counted on her commissions to make ends meet.

She tapped the pencil on her date book. She would call her boss on Monday. Thankfully, the trade show she'd missed had been the last one of the season. Normally, her life for the next few months would be filled checking in with current clients and cold-calling others. If she worked on that each day she felt well, she should be able to keep up with her minimums.

She hoped. Health was her top priority, but the mortgage was a very close second. They had only been here a few short months. Celia stared at the taupe walls she and Nicci had painted all by themselves. Most people would never hand a nine-year-old a paint brush, but that day was forever etched in Celia's mind. Nicci took low and she took high. They met in the middle with almost as much paint on them as on the walls, giggling the whole time as they swatted each other with their brushes. Later, after Nicci was safely tucked in bed, Celia had smoothed the rough spots and cleaned up.

No matter what, she wanted to hold onto this house. For Nicci. Celia shook her head. Who was she kidding? She wanted it for herself just as much.

She pushed up from the dining room table and felt more tired than she had all day. After checking the doors, she changed for bed and climbed in without her usual nighttime rituals.

Maybe, she thought, she would see her handsome

escort again for another ride in the park.

7

THE DREADED CHEMOTHERAPY: REALITY RE-DUX

Three days after chemotherapy...

Celia had only a moment's notice as the nausea crossed from unpleasant sensation to miserable reality. The putrid scent led the way and gut-wrenching cramps followed. Clutching her stomach in an attempt to ward off the pain, she barely reached the toilet, gagging the entire way. At least she wouldn't be cleaning the bathroom floor. This time.

The convulsions continued and took every shred of energy she had. Finally, her body relented and her throat began to ease. Vigilant for the next vile round, Celia sagged to the floor beside the bowl. Exhausted, she could feel her body shaking with the effort it took just to stay upright. Unable to stop the tears, Celia let them flow. Just this once. Hell, she couldn't stop them if she wanted to anyhow. How was she—or anyone else, for that matter—supposed to tolerate this? The disease was bad. She knew that. This was...well, you just couldn't prepare for this kind of sick.

Celia shuddered as she wiped the remnants from her stomach off her mouth. She rolled her tongue across her lips in disgust at the sour taste. Right at this moment, the treatment seemed much worse than the disease.

She rested her head on folded arms, desperate to grasp a moment's peace. *Please, please, please. Let me forget it all. Just for a little while? That's not too much to ask, is it?*

A coolness touched her forehead like an invisible hand bathing her with a cold cloth. It felt like ice cream on a scorching hot day. She leaned into it, desperate for the respite it offered.

Show me.

The words were so faint, she barely heard them. Or maybe she just thought them? Celia frowned as she studied the bathroom. No one else was there.

Show me, she heard again. Then everything went gray...

The antique white furniture sent a wave of nostalgia through Celia like she'd just come across a favorite old movie playing on television. She'd argued until she was blue in the face about that furniture being too babyish for a young woman of her age. Her parents had refused to understand.

The only piece that teenage Celia had loved was the dressing table in a rich dark cherry that went with nothing, but was the focus of her time in this room. Looking back now, though, the twin bed, nightstand and dresser were salve for her soul. She missed them.

The posters surrounding the mirror told her this was during her Tom Cruise phase in the late 1980's. She had been over the top in love with him. The tinny music coming from the AM/FM/Tape player made her even

more homesick. *Hold On To The Nights*, by Richard
Marx. Teenage Celia hummed along with the music as
she sat in front of the mirror and applied what little
makeup her mother would let her wear. Mascara and a
lightly colored lip gloss.

That dispute had been a real struggle of wills
between her parents' old fashioned views and her
modern day reality. Celia shook her head at the
memory. Her perspective now was quite different from
what Celia the teenager thought. Anxious to fit in, to
have what her peers had, she had argued for days about
make-up, to no avail. And had been devastated by her
parents' steadfast refusal. Now, it seemed so petty.
So...unimportant.

The girl began to brush her unruly locks into an
obedient hairstyle. Celia knew it would never happen
and watched as she eventually gave up, pulling it into a
ponytail. She opened the middle drawer and reached for
a small spritzer of Binaca. She slipped it into the pocket
of her acid-wash jeans, but her hand stayed just for a
moment as she prayed she would finally get the chance
to use it.

Celia smiled as she remembered what her teenage
self was thinking about.

The doorbell chimed and the stool went flying as
young Celia rushed to get downstairs before her parents
could interrogate her friends. Grabbing denim jacket
and purse, she tossed a quick wave and a "g'bye" over
her shoulder and launched herself out the door.

Her two best friends in the whole wide world, Jen
and Bernie, waited for her. They screamed in unison
and jumped up and down as they hugged each other.

Tonight was date night!

Well, sort of. That's what they had decided to call it,

at any rate.

Tonight they were going to the movies as a group. With boys! And one boy in particular. Young Celia clutched a hand to her chest as her heart thumped wildly. In her class, he was the boy all the girls wanted.

Yesterday he'd actually asked if *she* was going to the movies tonight. Her! Celia Louise Milbourne!

"Thinking about Danny again?" Jen said with an exaggerated roll of her eyes. Bernie, behind her, grinned widely.

"He's just so—" Celia sighed. "—so wonderful."

Both girls sighed with her. "Yeah. He's wonderful, all right. You are *so* lucky," Bernie said.

Celia patted the pocket with the breath spray tucked inside. Maybe tonight would finally be the night.

After being dropped off at the mall by Jen's mother, the girls walked to the bustling food court, bought sodas, and positioned themselves so they could see the entrance to the multiplex. There was no way they wanted to be the first ones there.

Once most of their group arrived, they tossed their pops in the trash and casually joined them. Celia's hopes plummeted as she watched two girls from her class cling to Danny. Daggers of ice froze her heart mid-beat when he laughed at some little nothing they said.

At that moment he looked her way—and winked! Any daggers disappeared and her heart missed beats for an entirely different reason.

Danny, a golden-haired transfer from California and the cutest boy in school, had only been here a little while. He didn't talk much and that air of mystery made all the girls want him.

He'd winked at her! Maybe he would sit beside her.

Maybe even put his arm around her. Oooh! That would be heaven!

Jen and Bernie were busy talking to the other boys who'd come in at the same time as Danny. They managed to remain by the boys' sides as everyone filtered into the theater. Even better, the boys followed her friends into the same row and sat down next to them. Celia's own hope dwindled as a glance over her shoulder verified the two girls were still cemented to Danny's arms.

"Go tell them to beat it," Jen hissed.

"No!"

"Then tell them their mom is outside."

"Shhh. They'll hear you."

"Well, you've got to do something."

"No," Celia said, twirling the thin jelly bracelets on her wrist. "It has to be his idea. I'm not going to chase after him like some hussy." Hussy. What a great word. She'd found it in one of her mother's old boxed-up books. Those girls *were* hussies, the way they were hanging all over him!

Celia checked for seats. Jen and Bernie had somehow managed to leave two seats open. One for her...

Danny entered with the other girls, glanced at the seat next to Celia, and went right past it.

Celia's stomach constricted as if she had tightened her belt too far. He wasn't going to sit here. In fact, he'd probably only been acting friendly when he asked about the movies. It was so obvious now that he didn't feel for her what she felt for him. At first, Celia kept her eyes frozen on the popcorn commercial currently playing. Then, when Danny moved into view again, she stared at the wall, at Jen, anywhere but at him.

It was an impossible feat and her face flamed as he ushered the girls into seats. He looked back at her and she focused again on her bracelets, twirling them like crazy, so he wouldn't see her mortification.

She had misread everything! He didn't like her. Didn't even think she was worth more than a second glance.

She just wanted to shrivel up and die.

"Mind if I sit here?"

Celia scrambled to catch her purse as the voice shocked her right to heaven's gate.

"N-no."

"Thanks." Danny settled in and grinned. "I was hoping we'd sit together."

"But what about..." Celia crooked her head toward the two girls.

"Oh, they're all right," he whispered. "They talk too much, though, and I'd never hear a bit of the movie." He smiled.

Celia felt her body melt into a pool at his feet.

Say something. Anything. Just sound smart.

"Oh."

That's it? Oh? That's all you could come up with. Way lame. A struggling smile was the best she could do for cover.

He nudged her arm. "You should do that more often."

"What?"

"Smile. You're pretty."

Her face turned as red as a Hot Tamale candy and she turned away with a mumbled thank you to try to hide it. The dimming lights saved her.

She didn't see the previews.

And couldn't remember much of the movie, except

the weird name. *Beetlejuice.*

She clutched her hands together, then unclenched them when she realized her palms were damp with sweat. She tried to casually wipe them on her jeans, praying the dark theater hid the action.

Celia almost yelped when Danny reached for her hand. She felt like she was going to explode. In fact, sitting still was the hardest thing she'd ever done. What she really wanted to do was run around the theater and proclaim to the world that Danny Wallman was holding her hand.

After the movie the group wandered the mall. A couple other friends joined them, including a tow-headed teenage boy Celia barely saw. She only had eyes for Danny, who had captured her hand again. In broad daylight! And in front of their friends. That had to say something! The two girls who had walked in with Danny scowled at her. Celia grinned like she'd just gotten her braces off. The world was absolutely, positively perfect at this moment. She prayed that it would never, ever change.

Danny's hand felt like a soft, warm glove. The heat wove its way up her arm and throughout her body as he interlaced their fingers.

Celia sighed. It was just like in the movies. Only better.

Focused on their hands, she didn't notice them lag behind the group. She didn't even question Danny as he drew her into an alcove.

Before she could react, he gave her a hasty, forever-immortalized-in-her-heart kiss, then pulled her back to the group. A group she didn't see. A mall that no longer held any interest.

Celia's hand covered her lips. They felt all tingly,

like after eating Pop Rocks. Her first ever kiss by a boy! She remembered the breath spray in her pocket. She'd never gotten a chance to use it. Glancing sidelong at Danny's grinning face, she knew it hadn't mattered.

Because she knew that finally, after all the waiting and wondering, she was really, truly, hopelessly in love.

Images from that day continued to fill Celia's mind as a knock on the bathroom door roused her.

"Mom? Are you okay?"

She focused on her surroundings, surprised she wasn't still at the mall. She was in her own bathroom. And she wasn't a teenager anymore. She was an adult. With cancer. And a child knocking at the door.

It had seemed so real. A vivid, happy memory from her past and an answer to her plea to forget it all. Just for a little while. Her lips quirked up at the corners despite a stomach that still complained. That day, with Danny? It *had* been love. She had the daughter to prove it.

"Mo-o-m!" The door handle rattled as Nicci opened it.

Pasting a tired smile on her face just in time to alleviate Nicci's concern, Celia settled her daughter onto her lap on the floor.

"I'm fine, Babydoll. Just a little sick is all."

"You were more than a little sick, Mom."

"Yes. I was. But I'm better now," she ruffled her daughter's hair, "because you're here. Did you have a good day at school?"

"Yes, except Dad was late to pick me up."

Well, she had loved Danny at one time, Celia thought with consternation. "I know your dad isn't always on time. But he means well and he does spend a lot of time with you."

"I know, Mom. But does he *have* to act like I'm his little baby all the time? All those squishy hugs in front of my friends! It's embarrassing."

Celia laughed. Now that was the Danny who was hard to resist. "I'll talk to him."

"Thank you."

"Don't expect much. He's a tough man to change."

In a moment of rare adult insight, Nicci rolled her eyes in a "don't I know it" maneuver. Getting up, Nicci turned before leaving. "Hey, Mom?"

Celia pushed herself up from the floor, groaning at stiffened muscles. "Yeah?"

"Do you think maybe it's time to tell him about...you know? How sick you are?"

Celia saw the worry in her daughter's face and her throat constricted with regret. Nicci was being forced to grow up way too fast because of her mother's disease. Another item to add to the unfair list, which had gotten pretty long lately. She sat on the side of the tub and pulled Nicci down beside her, wrapping an arm around her daughter's shoulders.

"This is pretty tough on you, isn't it?"

"It's tougher on you." Nicci straightened. "I can handle it."

"Oh, Babydoll, I know you can. I just hate that you have to." Celia wanted more than anything to give her daughter the happy, carefree childhood she'd been privileged to have herself. The fact that Nicci now sought out her mother before doing anything else when she got home from school was proof that carefree had gone out the window. And Celia had no idea how to fix that. She hadn't even told Nicci how sick she was. She knew, though. It showed in how she cleared the table without being asked. How she made her bed in the mornings. Heck, she'd even started getting up to her alarm, instead of Celia waking her the requisite three times before she rolled out of bed. Celia wanted more than anything to keep things normal for Nicci. She glanced around at the bathroom they were currently sitting in and almost laughed. There was no normal anymore.

"Mom?"

"Hmmm?"

"How bad, I mean... How sick..." Nicci's voice trailed off, like she both wanted to know and didn't.

Celia knew that feeling well. She hugged Nicci tight for a moment. Having never lied to her daughter, she wouldn't start now. But there were depths to the truth and she wasn't above masking the worst of it, at least for a while. "It's pretty serious. They couldn't get quite everything with the surgery. That's why I'm having this chemotherapy. To get the rest of the bad cells."

"It's cancer, right?" Nicci's words came out in a whispered rush, as if saying it jinxed them for all eternity.

"It is a form of cancer, yes."

"I read a book from our library. It talked about how medicine like you take attacks the bad stuff."

When had her nine-year-old daughter become so grown up? "It does."

"But it also attacks some of the good stuff. That's what makes you so sick."

"Uh huh," Celia said.

"But, Mom? This sick, like you feel now? It's going to go away. That's what I read. And the cancer will go away with it. I know it will. Until it does, I'll take care of you, okay? Like you took care of me when I was sick. That's my job."

Celia nodded, unable to form a coherent response for her daughter. Tears filled her eyes. She should be strong for Nicci. She needed to be strong. Instead, the child she loved more than life itself had just offered her own strength to shore Celia up. It shouldn't be her daughter's job. She should be out planning sleepovers and homework parties.

She needed to tell Nicci she didn't have to be strong for her. But as she stared into the dark, serious eyes of her daughter, she knew that Nicci didn't want to hear that. She needed to help, wanted to more than anything.

"I know you will. I wish you didn't have to, but I appreciate you more than I can say. I love you so much, Babydoll."

"Love you, too. But..."

"What?"

"Well, if you could tell Dad..."

The thought of having to tell her ex-husband the depth of her illness sat like sour milk in an already fragile stomach. Still, this was one thing she could give Nicci. An outlet. Someone to talk to, or to give her that sense of normal she'd need in the coming weeks and months. Yes, it was time. "All right. We're done with secrets. I'll call your father tonight."

Dan was at the house within half an hour of Celia's call. Nice and prompt. She'd hoped that he would be late. He usually was. The man may have his faults, some of which had become intolerable to her, hence the divorce. But in his own way, he still loved her. And she still held a lot of affection for him. This wasn't going to be easy.

He came in without knocking, as usual. And dripping wet. October had melted into November with a rainy vengeance. "Ceelie? Where are you?"

"I'm in the living room, Dan. Come on in."

Seth sat on the arm of the couch, next to Celia, in an attempt to bolster her courage. He doubted it would work, and it was possible he sat here for his own sense of need. Either way, he would be with her.

She was enveloped in a large comforter in muted blues and grays which contrasted with the tans and greens of the room. The warmth of the blanket stopped her shivers as she hugged it to her chin.

Dan's eyes looked like a startled cat when he entered. They never left her face as he sat down on the coffee table in front of her.

"What's up, Ceelie? You sounded pretty serious on the phone." He leaned in to brush a strand of hair out of her eyes.

Seth forced his fists to relax, one finger at a time.

"I thought surgery took care of everything," Dan said. "Have you got the flu?"

"No, Dan. It's not the flu."

Seth's gut went taut as he heard the quaver in her voice. He wanted so badly to help her.

"What then, if not the flu?"

"I'm sick, Dan. I—I have cancer."

To Dan's credit, he didn't flinch and remained in close proximity to Celia. His skin tone, however, turned decidedly ashen. "Ca—". He stopped, gulped air, and tried again. "Cancer?"

"Ovarian cancer, to be precise."

Dan's face crumpled. "That's bad, isn't it?"

"It's not good," she said.

Seth watched her tense. Her lips became thin lines as they usually did when she was stressed. And she was starting to scratch. He rested a hand lightly at the base of her neck in the hopes that it would help. Whether it was his unfelt touch or her own ability, the muscles underneath his hand eased.

"I mean...you know what I mean," Dan said. "You hear about it in the news. It's one of the worst kinds of cancer, right? Like the diabetic cancer?"

"You mean pancreatic cancer?"

"Yeah, like that."

"Well, I'm trying not to think that way, but yes, it does not have the best cure ratio."

"Do you know how—"

She tensed and didn't respond. Seth felt her fear. It mushroomed out of her, hemmed her in like a deep fog. And, for a moment, the panic immobilized her tongue. It was too early for the question. Dan wouldn't dare ask her how long, would he?

"—how long you've had it? I mean, how far along is it?"

Expelling a deeply held breath, she answered with barely any waver in her soft voice. "There are four stages to this cancer," she explained. "Stage one and two are fairly recoverable. I have stage three."

Dan's posture gave way and he slumped to the floor in front of Celia.

Petty satisfaction pulled at Seth's lips.

Celia straightened and continued as if anxious to get it all out there and not have to say any more. "Stage three means that the cancer was in more than just my ovaries. It has spread to my uterus, lymph nodes and abdominal cavity."

"Is it meta—, meta—"

"Metastatic? It hasn't shown up in any other organs, if that's what you mean. That would be stage four."

Dan seemed close to losing it completely. Head in hands, he started rocking back and forth, the word "cancer" whispered with each exhale.

Come on, man. Pull it together. Celia needs you. Seth wanted to thump the man for being so weak. Just when Seth thought he'd try to give Dan a good pounding, Celia's ex-husband sat back up. His face was still white, but there was a resolve showing that hadn't been there before.

About time.

"What can I do to help?"

Celia breathed deeply. "I've got my treatments under control." She swallowed as if another gagging spasm was about to come on. "At least, I'm covered for transportation. I could use your help with Nicci."

"Sure. Whatever you need. I can pick her up from school or take her more weekends. Anything," he said in a rush.

"It's more than that, Dan. She's acting all grown up around me. She won't cry. She won't talk to me about how this is affecting her. She's trying to be strong for my sake." She sighed.

Dan did, too. "That's our Nicci."

"It sure is. But she needs to be able to let go. Get it off her chest. That's what I need from you more than anything. Get her talking. Give her a shoulder she feels safe crying on. And give her life beyond sickness to focus on, at least in bits and pieces."

"God, you're right. This has got to be incredibly hard on her."

"I think it is. She's a strong girl. After all, she's our daughter. But she needs a break from," Celia held her arms out, "all this. She needs a break from me."

"I'll talk to her, try to help her deal." He paused.

"I'm so sorry, Ceelie."

"Yeah," she nodded. "Me, too." She gulped some air and Seth knew she'd run out of time. Celia tossed the comforter aside. "—Back in a bit," she said, a hand over her mouth as she rushed out of the room.

It was more like half an hour before she returned to the living room. Nicci was home from her friend's house and playing video games with her Dad. Her face was more animated than Celia had seen it in some time. It made telling Dan worth it. She'd have to look at his puppy dog eyes every time he caught sight of her, but Nicci would have someone to talk to. And that was what was important.

Five weeks later, after her third dose of chemotherapy, Celia felt her stomach sending up little waves of displeasure as she stood in front of the mirror. It wasn't the chemo, though. She had another two days before that would kick in. Funny how easily it all fit into a schedule.

Chemo on Friday.

Feel fine on Saturday.

Tired on Sunday.

Heaving until your stomach had yanked itself inside out and lodged in your throat on Monday. Dead tired and able to do nothing but sleep on Tuesday. Then you spent the next two weeks slowly regaining your strength, only to go through the entire process again.

No, it wasn't nausea that made her sick at this moment. It was her reflection. She stared at what was left of her hair with disgust. She was afraid to brush it these days, so much came out.

Nicci walked into the bathroom with one of her own scarves. "Here, Mom. Try this," she said with a touch too much brightness.

"Ooh, it's blue. My favorite color."

"I know." Nicci beamed.

Celia set the triangle at the edge of her forehead and pulled the ends together to tie in the back. Tucking a few strands in that stuck out in unlikely places, she turned to the mirror. That was what gave you away as a cancer patient. You couldn't let a few bangs peek out, a few wisps go astray. Nothing showed because eventually nothing was there to show.

She moved her head from side to side, trying to get a glimpse at the back, which still seemed full. Not bad. For now, it would do. And much better than staring at her ragged hair all the time.

She turned to Nicci with a smile. "Well, how do I look?"

"Smashing, Mum. Just smashing!" Nicci's overstated British accent had them both laughing.

"Good, then let's go out and see the world."

An hour later, she was ensconced in a chair and flanked by Nicci and Jen, who were having much more fun than she thought they should.

"Try this one on, Mom!" Nicci said. She held out a flaming red, tightly curled wig.

"I don't think—"

"Ah, come on, Mom," Jen mimicked. "Let's see what it looks like."

Celia glared at her best friend as she contemplated changing her status from bestie to not-so-greatie. She reached for the wig and tugged it on. As she flipped her head up, the curly bangs were so long they covered her eyes. She blew at them, but they wouldn't budge. Quite certain she looked like an orange, permed sheep dog, she parted the bangs with both hands. Nicci and Jen were holding on to each other so they wouldn't fall. They were that weak from laughter.

It wasn't funny. Not one bit. Still, as Celia watched the joy in her daughter's face, her anger faded. Her daughter was happy. Happier than she'd been since, well, since this whole mess had started. And Celia's pain disappeared as she caught Jen's eye. She tossed her a quick nod of gratitude.

"I don't think this is the right color for me," Celia said, sending the two into another outburst of laughter. Several minutes later, they wiped their eyes and began searching anew.

It was time to rein them in, Celia decided. "Hey, could we try for something close to the color my hair actually was?"

For the next half an hour, Celia tried on wig after wig. None of them looked right. None of them looked...like her hair.

"Maybe," Jen said, "we're going about this the wrong way." She started searching again. After a bit, Celia heard an "aha!" come from the back room. Jen reappeared, hands behind her back.

"Celia," she said. "Do you trust me?"

"Today? I'm not so sure."

"Ah, come on," Jen grinned. "It hasn't been that bad, has it?"

"No," Celia said with a note of wariness.

"Good. Then close your eyes. I don't want you to see this wig before we've got it in place."

Opening her mouth to protest, Celia stopped and snapped it shut. Obediently, she closed her eyes. It felt strange as they settled the wig on her head and she felt them brushing it out. It felt...lighter than the other ones.

"Okay, you can open your eyes now," Jen said.

When she did, the person in the mirror amazed her. The wig was lighter than her auburn hair had been, but not by much. Instead of finding something long and wavy, like hers, this one had trendy bangs and fell in layers to a little below her shoulders.

It looked good.

She turned her head from side to side and watched it move with her.

She looked good. Better than she thought possible. She moved closer to the mirror. The layers made it hard to tell it was a wig. And they framed her face, emphasizing her blue-green eyes.

She twisted around to Jen and Nicci and found them standing perfectly still, fingers and arms crossed in front of them.

"I like it."

"Yippee!" they both shrieked.

Leaving the shop a short while later, Celia tried to act normal but couldn't help a few quick head-turns to feel the wig swirl and settle. It wasn't quite a natural feel. Still, it reminded her of how her own hair had felt when it had been full. It was nice. More than nice, actually. She flicked her hair again, deciding it was uplifting in a most satisfying way.

"Celia?"

The deep voice came from further up the street and Celia watched the man draw near. Recognition smacked her in the face. *Not him.* She whirled around, looking for somewhere to hide, some plant to crawl under. There was nothing. No escape.

She faced the tall man, noting his impeccably cut suit, his perfect nails, his groomed dark hair. Dr.

Michael Worthington. Plastic surgeon extraordinaire. And the man that made the hearts of most women thumpety-thump much faster whenever he was near.

He was a client. One who had asked her out when she was Mrs. Daniel Wallman. He'd assumed she was unmarried because she carried the same last name as her well-known physician father. She had chosen to use that name recognition for her job, so everyone knew her as Celia Milbourne. She'd officially taken the name back after the divorce.

Dr. Worthington had asked her out again once she and Danny had separated. She'd been tempted. Who wouldn't be? But there was something just a tad bit tainted about the man. He looked too perfect, if there was such a thing. She'd gladly fallen back on the old it's-not-good-business-to-date-clients   line   and gracefully handed off his case to another rep.

Still, to run into him here. Now. She wasn't ready to let the professional side of her life know about her illness. Her hand brushed along her head, feeling the wig to make sure it was in place. Maybe he wouldn't notice.

He stopped a few feet from her, arm reaching for her hand, and his perfect smile faltered, just for a millisecond.

He knew.

He recovered so fast no one else noticed. Except Celia. She saw the perfect hand drop to his side. The perfect sparkle in his eyes diminish as the physician in him took control. And the perfect smile settled firmly back in place.

She saw herself reflected in his face. The high color was gone, replaced by her new pale, semi-ghostly look. The obvious absence of hair was like branding the word across her forehead.

Cancer.

"Celia? Are you all right?" he asked.

She opened her mouth to speak, but nothing came out. No words. Not even a squeak.

Jen stepped in and rescued her. "She's just a little tired, is all. Hi, I'm Jen."

"Michael Worthington."

Celia leaned toward Jen. "Client," she whispered.

"Oh, you're one of Celia's clients."

"Yes. Or, I was."

Celia watched him medically appraise her condition. "How are you feeling?" he asked her.

"Fine." Celia plastered a happy face on. "Just fine."

"Well, that's good to hear, then," he said.

Jen looked at her watch. "I'm sorry to have to cut this reunion short, but we need to be going."

"Certainly." He reached for Celia's hand then. "Call me if you need anything, all right?"

"Um, sure."

Now his other hand settled gently on the back of her shoulder. "Seriously. If there's anything I can do to help, call." He let go of her then and reached into his pocket, pulling out a business card. "My private line is listed on the bottom."

Wow. Unsure if this was another come on or a bona fide offer, Celia thanked him and hurried on toward the car, fighting the urge to turn around. She didn't need to. She knew he was rooted in his spot. Staring at her back. At the back of a woman he had wanted to date at one time. And now when he looked at her, he saw only a medical condition. At least, that's how it felt to her.

She slumped down in her seat. Damn. Would he keep this to himself? Probably. She wasn't ready to tell her clients she was ill. It would have to be soon, though. She knew that now.

At home, ensconced on her own couch with her comforter around her, Celia watched Jen putter at dinner preparations in the kitchen. Nicci happily assisted, if the banter between them was any indication. Celia didn't feel up for a party, but Jen's husband, Keith, would be here in an hour or so with their kids. What had started out as dinner for three had morphed into some sort of celebration. Even her mother was coming over.

The trip to the wig shop had drained the last of Celia's energy, though. With Nicci occupied, she closed her eyes, giving in to her exhaustion.

"Mom?"

Celia struggled to come out from under the shroud surrounding her brain. "Mmm?"

"Everyone's here and dinner's ready. It's time to eat?"

Celia opened her eyes to find her daughter's face less than a foot from her own. She held up a hand so Nicci would back up a bit. "I don't know, honey. I'm tired. I think maybe you should all eat and I'll just lay here and doze." She tried to roll over but the couch wasn't wide enough, so she settled back down into the pillow as Nicci headed for the kitchen.

"She doesn't want to eat," Nicci told Jen. "She says she wants to sleep."

"Well, we'll just have to do something about that."

Before long, slumber became impossible as chairs ended up all around her. Celia tried. She kept her eyes closed and willed herself to sleep. But the lively conversation drew her in and finally, she gave up.

Propping herself in more of a sitting position, she

eyed the group. "With all this noise, who can sleep?"

"That's the idea," Jen said with an innocent smile on her face.

"Yeah," Celia said. "I got that. Okay, someone. Get me a plate of this food you're all saying is so good."

Nicci, Jen and Celia's mother all jumped up and rushed to the kitchen.

"A *small* plate," Celia said.

The next couple of hours were spent eating Jen's homemade spaghetti and listening to Keith's bad jokes. Nicci occupied Jen's rambunctious sons with crayons and coloring books while the adults discussed politics, finances, the weather, and a myriad of other topics.

Celia listened. And watched. And occasionally spoke. Even tired, she was happy she'd joined the party. For a few hours, nothing bad intruded. No plastic surgeons, no nausea, no cancer. This—family and friends gathering—this was what life was all about. And she was surrounded by the best of both.

A short while later, Celia watched as Nicci let the last of their guests out and locked the door. Her daughter shut off the lights, came and kissed her goodnight and went upstairs to bed as if their roles were reversed. A shadow touched Celia's mind, another worry about what this was doing to her daughter. She pushed it away. The night had been too good to end on that note.

Celia drifted off to sleep on the couch with the evening's memories playing back in her mind.

The next day her doorbell rang precisely at noon. She gave one last little tug of the wig as she headed downstairs. She'd invited her boss, Tom, and her assistant, Tana, over for lunch. Assistant was no longer the right title, though. Tana had slid into the role of team leader over the past six weeks and, from what Tom said, she was doing a stellar job at it. A twinge of jealousy pinched the back of Celia's neck and she rubbed it away. Not because Tana was doing so well. Because Celia missed working. She missed talking to her clients, a lot of whom had called her father a friend. She missed...normal.

She'd spoken to each of them regularly. Today she would see them for the first time since she'd started chemotherapy. Or rather, they would see her. Both were more than people she worked with. Still, Celia shook her head at the nerves fluttering around in her stomach, as if she were going to a job interview rather than meeting with people she already knew. And counted as friends.

Checking the wig one last time, she opened the door to greet them. She never got the chance as Tana threw her arms around Celia.

"It is *so* good to see you!" She pulled back abruptly. "Oh, I'm sorry. Am I hurting you?"

Celia shook her head.

"No? Great! It's just *so* good to see you! And wow—" Tana looked Celia over from head to toe, "—that wig rocks! It's absolutely perfect on you. In fact, I think when your hair grows back in, you should keep it in this style."

Tana's enthusiasm was infectious and Celia laughed, throwing her hands up in the air. "Tana, you are crazy!"

"That's me," Tana said as she stepped through the door.

"I was beginning to think she'd forgotten me. Her own boss, left standing outside in the freezing rain," Tom grumbled with a grin of his own. He gave Celia a one-handed hug. The other held take-out Chinese. Their lunch.

"You were high and dry on that porch, Tom, and you know it." Tana flopped down on the couch. "It's just been *so* long since I've seen Celia. You look much better than I expected."

"Thanks. I think," Celia said. "And thanks, Tom, for picking up lunch. My energy—"

"No worries," he cut her off. "I, however, am starving. Where are the plates?"

Two hours later, after a hearty lunch that Celia could only pick at, they had ironed out the schedule for the next few weeks and caught up on all the company gossip. Tana kept the conversation lively and Celia was more than content to listen. As Tana went on about one more thing, Celia drifted off and started as she woke up, her head whipping forward.

"Time for us to go. We've overstayed our welcome," Tom said.

"Never," Celia answered. "I feel like an old lady sometimes, the way nap time comes around and my eyes just close all on their own."

"Don't you worry. We can see ourselves out." Tana placed the comforter over Celia's lap and kissed her cheek. "I know I've already said it, but it's so good to see you looking so well."

Celia grasped Tana's hand. "You're good for my soul, Tana. Thank you for coming over."

"We wouldn't have missed it for anything." Tom patted her arm.

"You're right about that. In fact I—"

"Come on, Tana. Time to let the nice lady sleep." He was laughing as he nudged her out the door.

Celia snuggled deeper into the couch. The wig shifted so she pulled it off. Holding it in front of her, she realized how silly she'd been about not wanting one. This afternoon had seemed completely normal.

Maybe the wig was her good omen. Maybe things would turn around. Maybe, just maybe, she would see normal again.

8

TURNING THE TIDE

"Hi, Mary," Celia smiled as she cozied up to the now familiar recliner. She'd been coming here every three weeks for three sessions now. Over two months of chemotherapy and its side effects. Months of trying not to let the world in on her dark little secret. Long, harsh, gray, winter months of praying each night it would all go away. And waking up each morning to find it hadn't.

"Hello," Mary said. "How are you today?"

"I think, so far, that today is a good day. I managed to straighten the house before I left to come here."

Mary chuckled. "That *is* a good start. Does that mean you're feeling better?"

"I wouldn't go that far." Celia watched Mary writing chart notes and anxiety began to settle over her like an icy blanket. When she spoke, her words were a whisper. "I, um-m, I'm getting a little scared."

Mary set her pen down and swiveled around in her chair to focus on Celia. "In what way?"

"Well, the drugs seem to be having a cumulative effect on my energy level. And I've still got five sessions left." She rubbed her arms. "Is my body going to be able to handle it all?"

"We do a lot of labs to help determine that." Mary glanced at the chart. "Your white blood count has been flirting with levels low enough to warrant a delay in your chemotherapy. Dr. Mason noted that it was okay to proceed with this session, though. Do you want to cancel today and talk to her about it?"

"I don't think so. I'd rather get it over with, if my body can handle it. If Dr. Mason thinks it's okay..."

"Is your reaction to the medications lasting more than a few days?"

"No. Except for the lethargy."

"You will rebound, but probably not until you've completed your chemotherapy." Mary patted Celia's hand. "I wish I could give you better news."

"I know," Celia sighed.

"Ready to get started?"

"Might as well get it over with."

She had talked her mother into staying home during these treatments after the first one. Six hours was a long time to sit in a chair and, to be honest, they'd run out of things to talk about. Celia's time chained to the I.V. pole was better spent helping Tana by calling clients and organizing work schedules. She'd pretty much become Tana's assistant. She didn't mind. And Tom had continued to give her a salary because of it.

Celia frowned. It didn't quite meet her bills, though. Her savings account was getting dangerously low and she would soon be tapping her one remaining source, a small trust fund from her father's estate.

She looked at the pile of work on her lap. Work she wasn't in the mood to do. So she popped *Pretty Woman* into the DVD player, fully intending to spend a couple hours lost with Julia Roberts and Richard Gere.

About the time the Vivian Ward character went shopping for clothes on Rodeo Drive, Celia was interrupted by a knock at her door. She paused the movie.

"Ms. Milbourne?" the slender woman asked as she entered. Her face was framed by a mass of blonde-brown curls that stylists spent their lives trying to recreate.

"Celia. I'm not much on formalities."

"Me, either." The woman held out her hand. "I'm Laura. Laura Holmes."

"Ah, the resident listener. I've heard about you."

Laura held up her hands and laughed. "None of it good, I'm sure."

"Quite the opposite, actually."

"In that case, my true reputation precedes me. Mind if I have a seat?" Her voice had a lilting sing-song quality that could make an angry grizzly go mellow.

"Sure. Time to check and see how I'm holding up, is that it?"

"To some extent. Also to see if you have any needs that aren't being met."

Celia frowned. "I'm curious. What made Mary contact you?" She was quiet a moment, then snapped her fingers. "I used the word 'scared' this morning."

"I happened to be in the building already and yes, Mary pulled me aside and mentioned that you were having some issues."

Celia nodded and indicated the recliner, her eyes sparkling with fun. "I'm already on the couch, so to speak."

Laura chuckled. "I'm not a psychoanalyst."

"You sure?"

"Trust me. I'm sure. It's one thing to help someone

with their grief and anger. It's quite another to have them confessing their sins to you." She shuddered. "Way too much information."

"Oooh, now this sounds interesting. Care to dish up something spicy to help me while away the hours?"

"Sorry. Confidentiality laws," Laura answered with a mock-stern voice.

Celia calmed her delight with an effort. "So...what do we do now?"

"Let's start with some basics and see where things go. You've been in chemotherapy for what, a little more than two months now, right?"

"Mmm-mmh."

"What side effects have you been dealing with?"

"You mean—" she waved a hand at the scarf on her head. "—besides the hair loss?"

"That is the toughest one to handle, isn't it?"

"Is that vain of me?"

"Not at all. And you are not alone. It's easier to focus on that than the other complications. And you see it every time you look in the mirror. The constant reminder becomes the poster-child for your illness."

"You sound like you know."

Laura nodded. "I'm a survivor. Ovarian. I just crossed the five year mark, so I'm considered to be cured."

A gut-wrenching resentment boiled up and Celia struggled for a long moment to stifle it. "Stage one?" Celia asked, trying unsuccessfully to keep the bitterness out of her voice.

"Stage one," Laura confirmed. "I got lucky."

"And I didn't."

Laura cocked her head. "You have a tougher road to travel than I did."

"Yes," Celia said. The resentment was still there under the surface, barely held in check. It wasn't Laura's fault she'd gotten a better deal. *Luck of the draw.*

"So, what other side effects have you been dealing with?"

Celia looked out the window at the gray drizzly day, tapping her hand on the arm rest as she contemplated the overabundance of complications she'd dealt with. "Nausea, diarrhea, loss of appetite. Speaking of which, they tell you that's a side effect but they don't manage to get through to you just how lousy food is going to taste."

"It was weeks before I could sit down to a meal and not be disgusted," Laura agreed.

"I miss milkshakes. Who could ever imagine that milkshakes would taste bad? That was my comfort food. Fresh banana or chocolate—or even better, both!"

"Don't tell anyone, but mine was Twinkies."

"Ooh. That's bad."

"Yes, and I haven't been able to eat one since."

Celia stopped tapping. "You mean—"

"Hang on. I'm not saying you won't get your taste for milkshakes back. I haven't eaten Twinkies because I finally read what they were made of. It was more of an I-don't-want-that-in-my-stomach kind of thing."

"I know what you mean. Not that it matters much. I have to be careful what I eat or drink these days anyhow."

"White blood count been low?"

"Yes. So comfort food doesn't comfort anymore, and I have to steer clear of the raw stuff until my labs are better. That doesn't leave me with many options." Celia grimaced in displeasure. "You know, I've tried to do some research about whether or not food could have contributed to my cancer. There isn't much out there on the subject, though."

"I don't think there is much to substantiate food as a cause, but ovarian cancer does show up in higher numbers with high fat, low fiber diets. There are a lot of factors that can lead to this diagnosis, though. Age, family history, whether or not you've had children—those are the most prevalent factors in determining the risk for ovarian cancer."

"Yet I don't fit any of those molds." Celia's voice echoed the words as she felt her face warm and the familiar itch working its way up to her neck. "I gave birth to a daughter. There's no known family history of ovarian cancer. And I'm only thirty five years old. It pretty much sucks."

"I agree. It does."

Silence filled the aching holes of despair that Celia worked so hard to suppress. Dwelling on the negatives did nothing to help her situation. "So—" she said, "—we've discussed the cancer and my symptoms. What do we do now?"

"How about we watch Vivian and Edward fall in love." Laura indicated the television.

"Sounds good to me." Celia tapped the play button.

When the movie ended, Laura reached for the ejected DVD and handed it to Celia. "I should probably get going."

"This is the kind of job I could handle," Celia said. "You get to sit around, chat, and watch movies. Nice."

Laura smiled. "Actually, I'm a volunteer."

Celia's eyes widened.

"Oh, I'm a social worker by degree and work in home health and hospice. But my work with cancer patients is unpaid. That way, I get to do this." She handed Celia a business card. "This is my work information. On the back you will find my home and cell numbers. So you call me at any time, okay?"

Celia's eyebrows shot up. She was floored by Laura's offer. "You know—" she said, "—I have the best support system in the world. I've got a Mom who will take me anywhere, anytime. She hardly ever lets me cook. She watches my daughter for me. I've even got an ex-husband who is more than willing to help. And a daughter who has become my little nurse on the bad days. Friends are willing to help, too. But I can't...burden them beyond what they already have to endure. I won't."

"How about what you endure?" Laura asked. "You must feel anger. Pain. Fear?"

Celia's head came up. "I try not to give in to it."

"A fighting spirit definitely helps. However, you will have weak moments."

"Don't I know it."

"That's what I'm here for. Although, I hope you'll share the good news moments with me, too."

"I don't know. You're taking on an awful lot here..."

"I only take on two volunteer clients at a time so I can offer a twenty-four seven shoulder. And I hope we'll become friends." She rested a hand on Celia's arm. "I know what you're going through. I've been there. So if you wake up afraid at five in the morning, call me. If you're planted beside the toilet bowl at one a.m. cursing the gods for what they've done to you, call me. And, if you want to celebrate the good news with someone who knows just how good it feels to get that news, call me."

Celia ran her hand slowly over the business card,

speechless. Tears welled in her eyes. This gift, from a relative stranger, touched her heart in ways nothing had since that fateful day when she'd been told she had cancer.

She looked up at Laura, giving the card a little wave. "Thank you. This is one of those good news moments."

"And I'll be praying with you that there are many, many more."

After Laura left, Celia lay staring at the hated I.V., watching the drip, drip, drip of medicine. Dread soured her stomach at the bout of chemotherapy reactions soon to come.

Damn it. She scratched her neck. *I'm not going through all of this for nothing.* She placed a hand on her abdomen. "I'm still fighting you, cancer. And I plan to win." She picked up her cell phone. Time to make some plans.

The next day was Saturday. Celia took one last look in the mirror and headed across the hall to rouse her daughter.

"Up and at 'em, Babydoll. We've got somewhere to be and I need you to get up."

"Where?" the mumbled question floated up from under the covers.

"It's a surprise. So get your behind moving, okay?"

Nicci's head appeared. "A surprise? What kind of surprise?"

"I'm not telling. I've got Sunday breakfast ready downstairs, though, so hurry."

"Hey, it's Saturday."

"So?"

"So—it's S-a-t-u-r-d-a-y!"

"Well, this week we're having Sunday breakfast a

day early."

"Cool!" Nicci vaulted off the bed and started looking for clothes.

While Nicci ate, Celia called her mother. "Hey, Mom."

"Celia! How nice. How are you feeling this morning?" This had become her mother's normal opening question.

"Better than usual."

"That's excellent news, honey."

"Do you have any plans today?"

"Nothing I can't change. Why?"

"I don't want to bother you if you're spending the day with Mack." Celia had watched with happy interest as the slow-moving romance blossomed. It meant everything to her that her mother had a companion. And she'd done it herself. Taken the initiative and asked him out for coffee shortly after Celia's first chemo. Neither had looked back since and it was supremely satisfying to be even a small part of their friendship. Mack was a kind and generous man with a quirky sense of humor everyone loved.

"Mack had to help his son with something, so I won't see him until tomorrow." The hint of regret touched Patricia's voice. "Where are we going?"

"It's a surprise. Nicci and I would like to pick you up in a little while if you're willing to spend the day with us."

"Always. I'll be ready."

Two hours later, they drove into a parking lot that was more like a front yard cemented over. The small, sage-colored building had probably been a home at one time, but now housed a day spa called *Breathe*.

"I pass this place a couple of times a week and have

always wanted to stop in and see what it's like."

"Have you set up a tour?" her mother asked.

"No. I've set up appointments." She tapped Nicci on the shoulder. "For all of us."

Nicci squealed with delight.

"You don't need—"

"Yes. I do. My illness has had the upper hand for too long. I'm done letting it live my life. And yours." She hugged Nicci. "And my daughter's. So today we get to have fun. This is my treat." Celia sent a nod of thanks up to the heavens for the money her Dad had left her. She'd be tapping into it for this little venture. But it was going to be worth every penny.

Half an hour later, they lounged in their spa robes in comfortable, padded chairs, sipping custom lattes, with cocoa for Nicci.

"Celia?" the attendant asked. "Ready for the stylist?"

"You bet," Celia said. "Mom? Nicci? It's time for me to take control and I'd like you both to be there."

Celia sat in the chair and let the stylist remove her scarf. She fought the urge to let her breath out in a big whoosh. It was the same every time she saw herself. The warmth-that-did-not-warm spread through her body as she braced for what she would see.

The woman in the mirror looked quite different from two months earlier. Her cheeks were hollowed. And yes, those slightly prominent cheek bones had become the beacons she'd expected, announcing to the world that she had lost too much weight. Her skin had gone pale, but not ashen. That was a blessing.

Her hair, though, was one of the most infuriating parts of this whole process. Celia reached up to touch one of the wisps that remained. Only thin little sections were left. Her glorious auburn hair had succumbed to the cancer-fighting agents.

She eased her hand away.

"Ready?" the stylist asked.

"What are you doing, Mom?"

"I'm going to get my head shaved."

With the innocence of a child, Nicci's shocked look switched instantly to curiosity. "Can I watch?"

"You bet!" She turned to the stylist. "Go for it."

Removing what remained of her hair didn't take long. Celia stared at the image reflected back at her in the mirror. Her eyes seemed so large. Like light-colored snowman coal in an oval, white face and hair-free head. She moved as if in slow motion, running a hand over the smooth surface. It had a bit of a shine from the moisturizer.

Strange. There had been so little hair left. And yet, this was hugely different. Without that thin layer, her head seemed so—big.

She felt the stillness around her and turned. They all waited. Her mother and daughter. Even the stylist seemed to be holding her breath.

Looking back at the apparition in the mirror, a grin spread across Celia's face. She took one last look and then laughed. Long and heartily. Until her mother and Nicci were laughing with her. In fact, before long they all had tears in their eyes from the laughter spilling over.

Wiping eyes still filled with pleasure, Celia hugged her family tightly.

"Can I get my hair shaved, too, Mom?"

Everyone froze as their faces traded smiles for wide-eyed looks of disbelief.

"You don't really mean that, right?" Celia asked.

"Sure. You look totally cool. And I think it would

make us look like twins."

Celia sat down, pulling Nicci with her. "Babydoll, that's the nicest compliment I've ever gotten." She hesitated for only a moment before touching her daughter's long auburn hair. Running her hands through the waves, a lump of nostalgia stuck in her throat. She shook it off. "But I think not. I love your hair and I'm not ready to see it gone. Besides," Celia continued, the twinkle back in her eyes, "one big bald head in the house is quite enough."

She tickled Nicci who squealed and gave up.

"Okay, 'kay!" she giggled.

"Okay then, musketeers, on with the day. Next up, massages for everyone."

Seth couldn't stop staring. Unable to move, his eyes saw nothing else. No one else. Only Celia. She looked...luminous. A flash of memory—women who wore their hair in massive concoctions of curls—came to mind. He didn't like it. Today's freedom to let your hair loose seemed much more his style.

Still, this absence of hair. It made every beautiful curve stand out. The shadow of her eyebrow line arched just right over eyes that dared you to look away. Her cheekbones showed more now, but were still a long way from making her look austere. At the moment, her cheeks were filled with the color of high emotion and a wistful smile turned up the corner of very kissable lips.

Celia Milbourne was more beautiful bald than any other woman he'd ever met...or seen, for that matter. He was certain of it.

Celia moved through her house as if dragging a two

hundred pound weight. The blankets and popcorn bowl lay where she and Nicci had watched a movie. Celia had fallen asleep a quarter of the way through.

She flipped the lock on the front door and headed to the back of the house. What little counter space she had was covered with dirty dishes. Plates made it to the dishwasher. But the silverware slid out of her hands before she could make it to the sink, clattering against the vinyl floor. Reaching down, Celia felt like the whole world had turned on its axis. Everything was spinning.

She sat on the floor and waited for the spell to pass, then picked up the forks and spoons, tossing them into the sink. Giving up on any more clean-up, she climbed her stairs like a zombie and found the energy to get ready for bed. Barely.

Pulling the covers back, she noticed a card on her pillow. The front seemed to be a caricature of her—bald head and all. Inside it said:

Thanks. I had fun today. Love you, Nicci.

She ran her hand over the letters as joy temporarily beat out her exhaustion. It had been a fun day. Drawing the quilt up around her neck, Celia switched off the light and fell asleep almost instantly, card clutched to her chest and a quiet smile still on her face.

Nothing had changed in Dr. Ted's office. Diplomas still dotted the walls. His desk was the same dark cherry covered in an organized mess of files. Celia rubbed the familiar arm of the stuffed chair she sat in. She looked toward the picture of his daughters and laughed. Even his stethoscope remained in place.

No, nothing had changed. The menace she'd felt at her last visit here had dissipated, but the atmosphere had not quite returned to the comfort of old. Still, it felt good to be here now.

The door opened and Dr. Ted grinned widely when he saw her. "This is a welcome surprise."

She stood just in time to be enveloped in one of his customary bear hugs. Hugs that were better than her favorite chamomile tea. "It's good to see you, Dr. Ted," she said with a laugh.

He set her away from him and gave her the physician's once over. Worry creased his brow, but his smile was quickly back in place. "You look good."

"I look like hell."

"You *look* like you've been undergoing a difficult chemotherapy regimen," he countered.

"I can't argue with that," Celia said. She sat, but not in defeat. She held up her chin as if trying to emulate the Queen of England as she spoke. "Except that, as of last week, I'm done. Five months of grueling chemo finished."

Dr. Ted settled a hip on the edge of his desk. "I know. We've all been counting the days. I'm very relieved for you."

"The thing is, in my mind I know the chemotherapy is over. My heart and my body have yet to get the message."

"You have to give yourself some time to recover from the effects of the medication."

"I know that, too. And maybe it's too soon to see any changes." Celia shook her head. This was a stupid idea. He couldn't give her guarantees any more than Mary or Dr. Mason could.

Dr. Ted cradled her hand between his own. "What's up, honey? What's on your mind?"

"I just—" Her voice cracked and she took a big gulp

of air before continuing. "I'm still so tired. I couldn't even drive myself here today. Mom had to drop me off. I'd...just like to know when I'll get my life back."

"Soon."

Celia pictured the pile of laundry in her mud room, the groceries that Jen was picking up for her right at this moment. And the bills that were more and more of a struggle to pay.

"Soon sucks!"

Dr. Ted let go of her hand and stood. "Sometimes, it does." He knit his brows. "Do you know what your white count has been doing?"

Celia pulled pages out of her purse and handed them over.

Reaching for his glasses, Dr. Ted perched them on his nose and glanced at the sheets. "This is encouraging, Celia. Your white blood count is coming up."

"Not very fast, though."

"No, but the important thing is that your body has indeed started to rebound. I think you'll soon see daily improvements."

With a deep sigh, Celia stood up. "I don't much like this forced inactivity, but I guess I can give it a while longer."

"Good. And if you get frustrated, you come on by. We'll get some Chinese take-out and I'll let you beat me at a game of chess."

Celia chuckled. Their skills were pretty much dead even, as was their win/loss ratio. Dr. Ted was way too competitive to throw a game. "I'll win without your help, thank you very much."

Seth watched Celia wait for her ride, seated on the

cement planter outside the medical office. He remembered that day, almost eight months ago, when she'd come flying out these same doors, panic written all across her face. Today, while not exactly calm, she wasn't frantic. She turned her face up to the spring sun with a wistful smile, as if a good memory had just come to mind.

He saw everything in vivid color. How the sun picked up the highlights in her wig and made them look like streaks of red-gold. How her blue-green eyes squinted in the bright light, yet she didn't dig for her sunglasses. How she was content just to sit there and breathe.

Today, Celia Milbourne was enjoying the moment. Tomorrow, she would feel a little bit better. And day by day, her strength would return. Her activity level would increase. Her life would resume what, for her, was normal.

He was so happy for her. For the respite she could now enjoy. Still, the ache in his heart spread like a mushroom cloud. There was nothing he needed to be here for now. She didn't need his help.

He should go.

He just didn't know if he could.

9

LIFE RETURNS TO NORMAL

Celia loved sunshine, even more so since chemotherapy. Nowadays, warmth had taken on a whole new meaning. She closed her eyes and turned her face to the sun as the heat washed over her. She listened to her body. No flush crawled up her neck. No clammy sweat erupted. This didn't feel like a hot flash. It felt more like freedom.

She was free from drugs. Free from the aftermath. Free from thinking about cancer every single waking moment of her life.

The neighborhood store had once again become a place she could reach on foot. Arms outstretched, Celia twirled in a circle and followed up with a couple of skip-steps. That was all it took to deplete her still-diminished energy level and she braced herself against a fence, panting like a dog in sweltering heat.

"Are you okay, miss?"

The deep, mellow voice didn't sound young. Then again, it didn't sound old either. In fact, as Celia straightened to see the man who stood at her side, she thought it sounded just right.

"Um, I think so."

Taller than her by several inches, his groomed dark hair said business. His t-shirt, shorts, and high-end running shoes said he kept in shape. And his green eyes definitely said Irish.

He smiled then and Celia's stomach sloshed to jelly.

"Are you sure you're all right?" he asked.

"Yes. Just—winded."

"Chemotherapy?"

Celia's good mood underwent an instantaneous transformation, just like her face, which went from warm exertion flush to red-hot, how-could-he-know crimson. Old fears cut straight to Celia's gut, agitating acids into a nausea she forcibly suppressed. Both hands reached up automatically to make sure her scarf was securely in place. It was.

She glared at the man. How did he know? He said the word so casually, like he was inquiring about the weather.

Unprepared to answer his question, Celia mumbled a thank you, tugged the scarf lower on her forehead, and moved off.

Cute guy apparently didn't deter easily. He fell into step beside her. Celia kept her head pointed forward, but had to fight the urge to glance his way.

"My name's Brad."

"Great."

"And your name is—"

She whipped around. "What are you doing?"

"Striking up a conversation?"

"No. You're playing nice with the sick lady. Well, I'm fine. So just go on your way and leave me to take care of myself. I can handle it."

His grin widened, if that was even possible. He

raised his hands and backed up a step. "Look—"

Celia's eyes narrowed and he switched to a different tactic.

"First," he ticked off with his forefinger, "I know about chemotherapy because my mother went through it."

Celia eyed him like he'd just approached her in a parking lot asking for gas money. Before she could clarify, he supplied her answer.

"Breast cancer." He didn't elaborate, but Celia saw the change in his face. Breast cancer was a bad memory. He stared at his forefinger, still in the air, as if working hard to remember why it was there.

Celia's irritation faded and the lines across her forehead softened.

"Oh, yes. Second—" Two fingers now. "You looked like you were in distress." He cocked his eyebrows. "I'm good at helping damsels in distress."

Celia rolled her eyes, but her lips lifted for just a moment.

"And third—" he stepped closer and his voice lowered to a level that sent warmth flooding down Celia's spine and stole her breath. "—you're a beautiful woman and I was hoping to get to know you better."

He held her gaze for a long moment before giving her some space, and Celia slowly let the air out of her lungs.

"Now, could we try this again?" He held out his hand. "Hi, I'm Brad. Or Braden, if you prefer the formal version."

"C-Celia."

"Now that wasn't so hard, was it?"

Celia's smile won the war. "No."

"Where are you headed?"

She realized she'd made it all the way to the store. There was something to be said for distraction. "I'm here." She indicated the small corner grocery behind her.

"Good. Would you like me to walk back with you? You know, in case you end up in distress again?"

She gulped. "Um, no. I only need a couple of things. I'll be fine." *As long as I keep my distance from you and don't try skipping again.*

Brad pulled a business card out of his back pocket, handing it to her. "I meant what I said. I'd like to get to know you better. However, in order to satisfy your cautious nature, check me out." He spread his arms wide. "And, if you find me worthy, call me. I'd love to cook you dinner."

"I'm not sure I can—"

Brad reached for her hand. "No ring. No husband?"

"Just an ex." Reluctance kept her hand in his for several moments longer than necessary.

"Boyfriend?"

She pointed to her scarf. "Who wants to date a woman with no hair?"

"I do," he said. "Call me." He moved off, resuming his run. Several strides away, he pulled the t-shirt over his head to carry it.

Celia watched the muscled back bunch and release and felt weak all over again. *That was not playing fair.* Still, her step was lighter as she entered the store. She stopped in the middle of an aisle and stared at the shelves.

What the heck did I come here for?

Once she remembered, Celia grabbed what she needed and walked home at a much more sedate pace so she wouldn't get too tired. It didn't stop her from glancing over her shoulder a couple of times to see if her knight might be at the ready.

With the groceries stored in the fridge, Celia wandered into her bedroom, pulling off her scarf as she went. She had just enough time for a shower before Nicci got home.

That guy, Brad, had sure been nice. Celia wondered if that happy attitude was normal for him. He'd seemed genuinely concerned for her welfare. But what kind of guy tried to pick up someone they knew was in chemotherapy?

Before stepping in the shower, Celia turned to her full length mirror. For the first time since she'd started chemotherapy, she took a good look at herself. She'd lost quite a bit of weight and was more gaunt than fleshed out. She tapped her collarbone. Everything stood out more than before. And her breasts were smaller. That was just rude, considering how small they'd been to start with. Time would change the weight issues, though. She'd already gained five pounds back.

She ran a hand along the bikini incision from her surgery, and over the small scar from her port catheter, which had been removed shortly after her last chemo. Roadmaps of her disease. She'd worked hard to stay in shape before getting sick. The doctor said that was helping her recover so well now.

Still, this wasn't a body she was ready to share. As if someone would want to. Celia turned away from the mirror, the happiness of the afternoon dimmed by yet another recognition. Her disease may well have robbed her of any opportunity for another relationship.

She turned the water on and let the spray work on her tightened muscles. Who would want to date her?

Sure, Brad has said he did. But that was during a momentary chance encounter. He couldn't have meant it.

Could he have?

A week later Celia sat at Seattle's annual Relay For Life walk waiting for her cue and wondering how she'd ever been talked into this. Nicci had come home from school two months ago all agog about a bunch of the teachers who had formed a team and were fund-raising for cancer research. She'd gotten it into her head that she wanted to form her own team. Her animation was what had sealed Celia's fate. Nicci was happy. And Nicci deserved that happiness.

So here Celia sat, waiting for her turn to walk the track.

"Hey, teammate!" Jen said, walking up to the team tent hauling a refrigerator-sized cooler and two very large canvas bags behind her.

"Good gravy, what is all this?"

"Well, Keith has to close at the restaurant tonight. So lucky me, he's bringing the kids here around nine. Hence the tent, bedding, and very large supply of snacks. We all get to camp out together."

"Oooh," Celia laughed. "I don't envy you the night shift."

"Well, I'm not sitting through it alone. You're staying, partner."

"I don't know."

"You cannot leave me here with—" Jen laughed and waved her hands in the air, "—all this. And my boys, too."

"I'm not trying to ditch you."

"Oh, and what would you call it?" The gleam in

Jen's eyes belied the fierceness of her voice.

Celia didn't answer right away. She hated that she wasn't one hundred percent. That she didn't have the energy, the fortitude she used to. And that she still had to say "I can't" sometimes, even when her friend needed her. Celia glanced at the track. She should have said that to Nicci about walking today.

"Are you okay?" Jen asked, dropping the bags underneath the tent.

"I'm not sure," Celia answered.

Jen's eyes widened as she gripped Celia's arm. "What's up?"

"I just don't know if I can make it all the way around the track."

Celia watched Jen's shoulders droop with relieved stress and immediately realized her error. "Jen, I'm *so* sorry. I didn't mean to make you think I was feeling sick again. I didn't realize... I guess I got so wrapped up in my own worry, I didn't think about what I was saying."

"It's okay," Jen waved her off. "I think we're all a little over the top with our worry these days."

"Yeah. Me, most of all." Celia got up and gave her best friend a hug. "What did I ever do to deserve a friend like you?"

"Well, now that you mention it, you could do a little more to show your appreciation."

"Just ask."

"Stay the night and help me corral these kids of mine."

Both of them stared at each other stone-faced. Celia gave in first, bursting out with a guffaw of laughter. Jen followed quickly behind.

"You win. I'll try, at least." Celia said.

"So where's the brat who got us into this mess?" Jen asked.

"Over there." Celia pointed to the local news station van. "You're not going to believe this. She's doing a television interview, of all things. Apparently, she's become the darling of the community. They love her."

"As do we all," Jen chuckled.

Celia hoped that Nicci was telling them about how much effort she'd put into this event. She had asked for Celia's address book and called people all by herself to "invite" them to join the team or to donate. It must be hard to turn down a nine-year-old, because Team Nicci was thirty members strong and those that weren't walking had contributed, and handsomely. Team Nicci had raised over $10,000 for the cause. Celia smiled. Nicci Wallman was a better salesperson than she herself was.

Nicci bounded over to the tent. "Guess what, Mom! I told them all about your being a survivor and now they want you in the first row of walkers."

Celia groaned.

"Isn't that cool?" Nicci was shining with pride, so Celia buried her anxiety and smiled her acceptance. She gulped as she looked out at the track and wondered for the umpteenth time if she could actually make it around the whole thing.

A siren went off, startling Celia out of her thoughts.

"C'mon, Mom!" Nicci said, pulling her up. "It's time for the survivors' walk."

Oh, joy. Celia rolled her eyes, but allowed her daughter to pull her to the starting position.

After a speech that was, thankfully, short, a buzzer sounded and the group started off. Celia felt strong, especially with Nicci at her side. She started off with a good stride. A quarter of the way around the track, her speed began to fall off.

"I don't know if I can do this, Babydoll."

"Sure you can. Look. Everyone is cheering for you."

Celia noticed then. The stands were filled with people clapping and cheering. It was the same on the sidelines. Cheering for the hundred or so people who were here to say they beat cancer. It bolstered Celia's courage and she picked up her step.

By the halfway mark, she and Nicci had fallen to the middle of the pack. Sweat trickled down Celia's back as her whole world became focused on putting one foot in front of the other.

Out of the blue, a strong arm supported her elbow. She looked up to see green eyes smiling down at her. "Are you all right, miss?"

Celia's mouth gaped open. "Brad?"

"In the flesh."

"What are you doing here?"

"Well, rumor has it I'm good with damsels in distress."

Celia laughed.

"And you are looking decidedly distressed." He leaned in closer. "I thought I might be of help."

Celia leaned on his arm. "You're assistance is most appreciated, sir. I'm wiped out."

"Should I carry you the rest of the way then?"

Celia's eyes widened. "Don't you dare!"

"Okay, then. Lean on me and the two of us will make it to the finish line."

"No, thanks," piped Nicci from Celia's other side. She didn't look pleased. "I can take care of my mom all by myself."

Brad tried to disarm her with a smile. "I'm sure you

can."

He looked at Celia.

"My daughter, Nicci," she said. "Nicci, this is Braden Worth, a...an acquaintance of mine."

"Nicci? As in Team Nicci?"

"Yup," Nicci glared at him.

He winked at Celia as he spoke to her daughter. "This is the first time in the five years I've been doing this that my team got beat out for the most money raised. Not an easy feat." He raised an eyebrow. "We were topped by Team Nicci."

Celia watched the smile blossom on her daughter's face. Braden Worth, it seemed, could charm the snake out of a basket. And Nicci was falling under his spell.

"So, Nicci, you okay if I help you two get around to the finish line?"

"Sure. You can help. Mom's getting heavy."

Braden Worth let out a bellow as Celia scowled. Her scowl didn't last long, though. Nicci was right. She knew she needed help.

By the time they finished, Celia was leaning heavily on Brad's arm. Nicci kept going, having set herself up to walk the first hour. As soon as they were off the track, Brad picked her up in his arms and headed for the tent that was headquarters for Team Nicci. She tried to protest.

"You're beat," he said. "Besides, contrary to popular belief, you really aren't that heavy."

Celia socked him in the shoulder. Then, deciding that her arms felt rather good around his neck, she left them there. Turning to the tent, she groaned as she saw the wide smile on her mother's face. Even Jen was grinning from ear to ear. There would be hell to pay later for this. She hid her face in his chest and smelled his aftershave. Right now, in this moment, though, it seemed pretty darn nice to be here.

Two days later, Celia stood in front of her closet, considering outfits. Jen, arrived and joined Nicci on the bed in an attempt to support Celia. Some support. Mostly they giggled at her noticeable case of nerves.

"How about this blue dress?"

"You're not going to a wedding, Mom," Nicci said, rolling over onto her stomach.

"I guess you're right. Too dressy. Okay, slacks and, um, the yellow top?"

Jen answered. "Sorry. You need more color in your cheeks before you can carry that shade off."

Celia turned to the mirror and put a hand to her cheek. Food tasted good again. And she'd put on some more weight. But Jen was right. She was still too pale.

"Why not just wear jeans?" Jen asked.

"Because I don't know where he's taking me or what he's wearing."

"What did he say?"

"He just said to dress casual." She dug through her closet again and came out with a pair of khaki pants. "How about these?"

"Yes. That'll work." Jen got up and began rummaging, coming up with a white long-sleeve t-shirt and a navy sweater. "This should complete the outfit," she said. "And Celia?"

Celia stood in front of her full length mirror. "Hmmm?"

"Wear the wig tonight. Not a scarf."

The white of the T-shirt was just the right shade. Not too bright, not too faded. It managed to mute her washed-out skin tone. When Nicci added the navy sweater, she almost looked healthy.

She ran a hand over her head, which had an interesting fuzz growing from it. Almost healthy. Not quite.

Celia dropped Nicci off at her grandmother's and Nicci raced through the kitchen waving yet another *Girl Meets World* DVD in her hand. "Hi, Gramma!"

"You get back here, young lady," Celia said with a laugh, "and give your Grandmother a proper hello!"

Nicci came back into the kitchen and hugged her grandmother tightly. "I was just setting my stuff down," she said with a face full of oops. "Can I watch my show?"

"Sure, hon—"

But she was already gone. Celia and her mother waited and it was only moments before they heard the voice of Nicci's idol.

Chuckling, Celia also hugged her mother. "Thanks for babysitting tonight." She set Nicci's overnight bag on a kitchen chair.

"It's my pleasure, dear." Patricia's eyes glowed. "I'm so happy to see you have some fun for a change."

"It's only one date, Mom. With a man I barely know. Don't go marrying us off now, okay?"

"I'm not," her mother said. She touched Celia's cheek. "I want to see you happy again."

"As happy as Mack makes you?"

Patricia blushed. "Yes. I wish that for you."

Celia covered her mother's hand. "We've all earned that right, haven't we?"

"You most of all. Now here," Patricia handed her the keys to the Mercedes. "You go have fun."

"Oooh," Celia grinned. "I really do rate, getting to take the convertible." She gave her mother a peck on the cheek, tore her daughter away from the movie long enough for a goodbye that was more tickle than hug, and was out the door.

She backed the car up the slanted driveway and, since evening hadn't taken full root and the sun still took the chill out of the air, she parked and put the top down.

Sitting for a moment, Celia breathed deeply. The air smelled like freedom and the peace that settled in her heart as she pulled away reflected it. It was her first time driving since chemotherapy had taken all her strength. She didn't have much hair. But she had a date. And right now, at this moment, it was enough.

As she neared the address Brad had given, her hands tightened on the steering wheel to keep them from scratching the hives creeping up her neck. *What am I doing?* The man was a stranger. Granted, she could stare at him for hours and not be bored. But he was still a stranger. She'd checked him out on the web and, since he had suggested she be thorough, also with the Better Business Bureau. She knew that he was the CEO of some sort of holding company with a good rating. She had no idea what a holding company did, but it seemed to have a lot of assets. And they had been in business for forty years.

Hmmm. A family business? Was the man rich? Somehow, that intimidated her even more.

The French restaurant she pulled up in front of was one she'd eyed for a long time from a distance. She should have recognized the address. Only A-listers could afford this place. She glanced at her khaki pants and scratched her neck. The blue dress still hanging in her closet was looking better and better. She'd only be a little late if she hurried home for a quick change.

The valet opened her door, effectively shutting down

any avenue of retreat. Celia handed over her keys and stepped into the restaurant. No one waited in the foyer. She frowned. People made reservations months in advance for this place. She'd only called Brad yesterday. How had he managed to get them in here?

She gave her name to the maitre d', and craned her neck to view the interior.

"Ah," he beamed, "Mademoiselle Milbourne. Monsieur Braden has left the strictest orders. He's been delayed but hopes that you would join him. Please," the maitre d' came around the pedestal, "come with me. I will take you to him."

Celia looked about with interest at the cozy décor. It was different from any other restaurant she'd ever been to. No tables filled the room. In fact, there really was no room. Just a hallway passing what looked like individual eating rooms. Dark wood tables and plush chairs made it all feel very cozy.

They rounded two more corners and passed several more of the eating nooks before she began to hear a muffled noise.

Ah. That was how he'd gotten a reservation for dinner. They were sitting next to the kitchen. Probably on a card table. A friend must work here.

Her escort surprised her by pushing through the doors into the kitchen. "Come, come. I will take you to Monsieur." He motioned with his hand for her to follow.

Celia stood immobile just inside the doors. This was a completely foreign world to her. Where quiet and order reigned on the other side of the swinging doors, the kitchen side seemed to be in chaos. The cacophony of noise was almost overwhelming. She glanced behind her. How did this noise not carry through to the other side?

There were people everywhere and meals in various stages of preparation. While she stared, the walk-in refrigerator door opened and out stepped—Brad! In a chef's hat. With his arms full of produce.

"Celia!" He handed off his armload to a young woman, gave her some sort of instruction, and took Celia's hands.

"I'm so glad you made it." He glanced at the clock on the wall. "And right on time. I had hoped you would be one of those 'fashionably late' women. At least for tonight."

"What..." she gestured around the kitchen with her hands.

"I'm very sorry about this. The chef came down ill and our other chef is out of town."

"Your other chef?"

"Yes. I've called around and managed to find a replacement for the evening, but he won't be here for another hour. Do you mind waiting?"

Still in a minor state of shock, Celia shrugged her shoulders. "No."

"Bien," he said, putting a hand on the maitre d's shoulder. "Anton, please find a seat here in the kitchen for my lady friend." He turned to Celia. "Can you have wine?"

"Yes."

"Bring Miss Milbourne—" He addressed Celia again. "Red or white?"

"Red, preferably."

"—the Chateau Montrose, I think," he said to Anton.

"Chef Braden?" the young woman stopped beside him.

"I'm so sorry about this, Celia. I really have to go."

He kissed her gently on the cheek. "I'll be with you as soon as I am able."

"Go. It's no problem." She waved him away but his focus had already returned to the meals he needed to prepare.

Celia spent the next hour or so learning more about her date than any conversation over a meal would have divulged.

That he was a chef was obvious. And a complete surprise. He enjoyed it, too. He tossed orders like a mixed salad and bantered with the other workers like they were old friends. It was apparent they liked him and, more importantly, felt comfortable enough with him to tease back, even though he was their boss. As orders came in, he prepared dishes she'd never heard of with the same effortlessness she'd seen in his jogging. A momentary flash of bare torso disappearing down the street made her shiver all the way to her toes.

Celia took a sip and watched the wine settle in her glass. There was a hint of sweetness to the cabernet. Some sort of berry, maybe? She took another sip and sighed at the superb taste. She bit into an hors d'oeuvre from the plate Anton set in front of her. Some sort of mini-quiche. The flavor was unlike anything she could identify, but very, very good.

"How are you holding up over here in the corner?"

She jumped as Brad's deep voice claimed her attention. Her eyes crinkled with delight. "This isn't at all what I expected when I accepted your invitation. I feel like the Queen of England. Anton has taken very good care of me."

Brad leaned over. "I think," he whispered, "Anton has a crush on you already." He held out a hand. "I've officially handed over my hat to the replacement chef."

He grabbed the open bottle and two fresh glasses. "Come on. Let's get out of here."

She moved toward the swinging doors, surprised when he tugged her the other way. "If I go out there, we'll end up speaking to patrons all evening. I want you all to myself for a while."

Celia's eyes glowed as she followed him. Down a dark, nondescript hallway, past metal doors labeled storage or office and straight out the back door.

The flash of evening sun on its way to the horizon arced down the alleyway and blinded her momentarily. When her eyes adjusted, Celia found herself transported. Here in the back of this four-star restaurant was a tiny verandah that made you believe you were on a street corner in France. Trellised walls of greenery hid the normal alley accoutrement on two sides. The wall directly in front was filled with a true to life mural of what had to be a Parisian street. A see-through roof let what remained of the sunshine light the little area.

She ran her hand over the vines. They were real! "This is amazing. I feel like I'm in Paris," she said.

"That's the idea." The flash of white teeth showed his pleasure at the compliment as he seated her at one of four bistro tables.

"Did you do this?"

"Yes. And it must stay our little secret," he said. "I designed it for my employees. They get paid well, but they also work very hard. I wanted to give them a place to relax on their break and, being a French restaurant, Paris seemed to be the right choice."

"You've certainly captured the essence here."

He poured the wine like a seasoned veteran. "You're the first non-employee I've brought back here." His eyes darkened, daring her to look away, to deny the attraction between them. He held out her glass and his hand lingered as she wrapped hers around the stem. It felt like an electrical arc coursed through Celia's body and her hand shook so she set the glass on the table to avoid spilling it.

"Thank you. I'm honored." She touched her wig, making sure it was in place.

Braden sat back. "You don't need the wig, you know."

"I—"

"You really don't know how beautiful you are, do you?"

Celia shifted in her seat. It was hard to agree when only light fuzz covered your head where there had once been long, thick, luxurious hair. A moment's regret was all she allowed before mentally shaking herself to clear the thought.

"Do you know what your name means?" Brad said.

"I do."

"Heaven. And that's what you look like. Light-colored eyes and perfect symmetry are only part of it, though. Even with what you must have gone through, your face radiates a gentleness and compassion most people suppress."

He leaned forward and lightly traced her lips, making her sigh happily. "And these lips. Well, I'd better not talk too much about them. At least not on the first date."

Celia laughed self-consciously. "Thank you, but I'm not sure you're seeing the real me. I do have a mean streak, you know."

"Oh, yes. I was on the receiving end of that, wasn't I? Well, I'll chalk that up to exhaustion." He frowned. "How are you feeling tonight?"

"Better than ever at the moment."

"Good. How long since your last chemo appointment?"

The question startled her and she felt the rush of heat hit her face. It was still hard. She didn't feel prepared to answer questions about her condition. The social worker, Laura, had asked if she'd be willing to talk to newly diagnosed candidates. She'd said yes, but had delayed putting her name on the roster. She hesitated now for the same reason. Would she ever feel ready?

"Four weeks."

"That's not very long. You have strength in you, Celia Milbourne." He took her hand in his. "I like that."

Whether it was the wine or his way, Celia relaxed, truly relaxed, for the first time in months. So his next question hit her like a brick.

"What type of cancer did you have?"

She yanked her hand away and sat up straight in her chair. "Um..."

"I apologize. We barely know each other and I asked too soon."

"It's just that I haven't talked about it. At all. Except to those who needed to know. It's...hard."

"My mother said the same thing. Forget I asked."

"I know very little about you," she said in an effort to get back on an even keel.

The look in his eyes told her he knew she was diverting his attention. Thankfully, he played along. "Ah, well, I am a fairly open book. Thirty-eight years old, single," he held up his ring finger as proof, "and, since I never did well taking orders from others, I took the entrepreneurial road and started my own business."

"The web said you've been in business for forty years. I assumed it was family money."

His smile faded as he swirled the wine in his glass. "It was a family business until my father all but ran it into the ground. I searched out the capital and resurrected it from the ashes, changed the direction of the company and it now flourishes."

Celia sensed this was a sore subject and searched for a change of topic. "So, where does the restaurant fit in?"

Braden leaned back in his chair as he answered.

"This is the first business I bought into when I took over the company. As it turns out, it allows me to feed my soul. I actually enjoy cooking."

"That was evident tonight. You're good at it, too. And well-liked by your people."

"I like them, so it's easy to be liked back."

At that moment, the assistant arrived with a tray laden with food.

"I can't eat this much," Celia said, eyeing all the dishes.

"I know. But I wanted you to have the chance to taste whatever you wished. Now come. Eat what you can."

It turned into more of a buffet than a sit-down dinner. Celia tasted dishes she'd never imagined. And liked, well, some of them. As they ate, the sun set completely and their Parisian street corner was subtly lit by well-placed lighting.

Now, though, even coffee could not keep weariness at bay. Her eyelids were very close to winning the battle. She tried to pick up her coffee cup, but her hand dropped to her lap instead.

"I think I've kept you out too late," Brad said.

Celia shrugged. "I guess I'm still not back to normal."

"Come on, fairy princess," Brad held out his hand. "Let's get you home."

How long had it been? How long since a man had offered her his hand. Daniel seemed ages ago. And this little thing—this helping her up, made her want to cry like nothing else.

She felt normal.

She felt human.

She felt like a woman.

And she liked it. She smiled at Brad. "Thank you," she said. It didn't seem like enough, but it was all she could think of to say.

"My pleasure."

They strolled to the front of the now quiet restaurant where her car waited under the watchful eye of one of the valets. Brad tipped him and sent him on his way. Then he put the top up for her. He paused before opening her door.

"Are you alert enough to drive home?"

Celia smiled. "I believe so. I don't have far to go anyhow."

He leaned down and touched his lips to hers. The kiss was short, light, and full of promise and Celia didn't want it to stop.

She sighed. "I had...an amazing time tonight."

Now it was Brad's turn to smile. "Good enough to give me your phone number?"

Celia laughed as she remembered. She had called him, not vice versa. "Yes. Good enough for that."

Later, at home, a melancholy settled over Celia. Something felt different. She ran her hand along the top of the couch as she walked by. Everything seemed to be in place. Still, the feeling persisted as she wandered through the house, checking it. It was almost like the subdued ache of homesickness. Only not for home. It felt as if a part of her was missing.

She shook her head. Nicci was spending the night at her grandmother's house. She missed Nicci. That had to be it.

The gloom dissipated when Celia realized that, except for the deflected questions from Brad, she hadn't thought about cancer once in the last few hours. She'd only had room in her mind for one thing. A jogger turned entrepreneur turned chef turned knight-in-shining-armor.

And that felt very, very good.

Seth had to agree with Braden, even if the man was where he himself wanted to be. Celia was a beautiful woman. It ached to watch them together, yet he was grateful. For several hours she had been nothing but happy.

Seth could make her forget—for a moment or even a short while. What he could not give her was the immediateness, the warmth of tactile contact. He couldn't touch her in a way she could *feel*.

He watched the front door shut behind her, knowing each stair was an effort and that, right now, she didn't care. He couldn't bear to go in. To see the reflective smile show her joy as she relived the evening. He was happy for her. She deserved this contentment. He just wasn't sure he could watch it.

He knew that they would not meet in her dreams tonight. Instead, her dreams would be filled with a certain dark-haired chef.

He hung his head for a long moment, then stared again at her bedroom window. "Pleasant dreams, Celia," he said as the light went out.

"Happy birthday to you."

"Happy birthday to you."

"Happy birthday, dear Nicci."

"Happy birthday to you!"

Nicci's new puppy, Chocolate, a.k.a. Latte, nipped at her heels with his tongue hanging out the side of his mouth. He was a present from Brad with Celia's blessing. Just like her own childhood puppy, Maxey, it had been love at first sight.

The group sang robustly, if a little off key. When they were done, Nicci's glanced her way for a long moment and then she blew out the candles on her cake.

Celia bent over to her mother. "That was rather obvious. What do you think she wished for me?"

Patricia Milbourne, flanked by Mack, patted her daughter's hand. "She's still your little mom. I think she wished for continued good health."

"I think she wished me for you," the masculine voice behind them said. Strong, tanned arms wrapped around Celia and she leaned back against Brad's steady presence, feeling a warmth that went way beyond the late summer sun.

It had only been three months, but she couldn't imagine life without him. He had wooed her for six weeks before she invited him over to the house. Once he and Nicci re-introduced themselves, there had been no turning back. The two of them had sensed a kindred purpose and were like book covers protecting precious pages.

Celia tapped his arms and turned around in them. "She's going to wish for something else if you don't get that ice cream served up before it melts."

"Yes, Ma'am!" He saluted, brushed his hand over

her short hair and drew her close for a kiss before rushing off. "Whatever Nicci wants," he said as his laughter drifted back to surround Celia with happiness.

"I'll help," Mack said, following Brad.

"He's good for you," her mother said.

"As good as Mack is for you."

"I'm so happy you found him."

"Actually," Celia's smile widened, "I think he found me. And I'm very glad he did."

She ran her hand over her head. Her thick, auburn hair had begun to grow back. She'd kept it short to give it a chance to fill in and thicken. Now it was about two inches long—and pure white. She'd been shocked when it grew in with no color. But now it seemed sort of cool. It certainly made her stand out in a crowd.

Celia let the late afternoon sun bathe her face and sent a thank you out to the heavens for how things had turned out. Even her lab tests were holding steady. No change was good.

Life was good.

10

HOLIDAYS ROCK!

"I hope he's being careful up there." Celia craned her neck, trying to see the top of the ladder from the window. December had brought with it an unusual cold for this area. She was worried he'd slip. All she could see was feet, though. "Maybe I should go out and spot him or something."

"Mo-om, stop it. Brad can handle putting a few lights on the house."

"He's been out there for hours."

Celia caught her daughter's head shake in her peripheral vision. "Don't shake your head at me, young lady." Mock sternness gave way to laughter as she recognized the reversal of their positions. A very temporary reversal.

"He wouldn't be out there so long if you hadn't bought so many lights," Nicci said.

Celia settled back onto the sofa to sort more holiday decorations. "I just wanted..."

"I know," Nicci said, hooking the last of their four stockings onto the mantle and plopping next to Celia. Latte gleefully joined her, upending Christmas cartons and creating chaos with his wagging tail.

"Latte!" they both yelled.

"I just got those sorted out," Celia said. It was hard to be mad, though. Dog and girl had become inseparable since Brad had given him to Nicci. He moped all day when she was gone to school, perking up about ten minutes before the bus dropped her off.

Laughing as they picked everything up, Celia set the box aside for the moment as the pup took the center half of the couch, demanding attention which they both happily gave him.

"You don't have to try to make up for last year, you know," Nicci said.

Celia shrugged. "I didn't feel well. I want this Christmas to be, well, two year's worth of special."

"It already is," her daughter said. "You're feeling good."

The lump in Celia's throat stole her breath for a long moment. She did feel good. And Nicci deserved to celebrate more than anyone else. No matter how hard they'd all tried, Nicci had lost over a year of her childhood to worry. These days, the shadows in her daughter's eyes rarely showed up. She enjoyed a healthy, happy balance of school, friends, and family. Celia was more than grateful that they'd been able to reclaim this important time in her daughter's life. Even her own life had pretty much returned to normal. She was back at work, and she and Tana had opted to split the territory in two. Now they both earned commissions and both assisted each other as needed. It was a win-win for everyone.

Celia hugged Nicci tight. "I am feeling good. In fact, I feel amazing."

"Good. Then you can string the garland on the

mantle. It's too tall for me."

With another worried glance out the window, Celia stood and grabbed the garland, taking a big whiff of the fragrant cedar, a gift from Brad.

"You really love him, don't you, Mom?" Nicci said quietly, scratching Latte behind the ears.

Celia hugged the garland to her chest. "Maybe. It's not something we've talked about yet."

"It's okay with me, you know. You loving him, I mean."

Where the heck had this come from? Celia stared at her daughter for a long moment, then burst out laughing again. "You do remember I'm the mom and you're the daughter, right?"

Nicci laughed, too. "Yeah. I know. I just...wanted you to know I was cool with it. I mean, Brad's pretty awesome."

"I think he's pretty awesome, too," Celia whispered, then busied herself settling the garland along the mantle to hide the emotion this conversation had evoked. She and Brad hadn't gone there yet—hadn't discussed their feelings in depth. They'd simply been enjoying their time together. And Brad always included Nicci in their plans. It was one of the things she loved most about him. Maybe they could have a future. Who knew. For now she needed to get Nicci off this topic until she and Brad had a chance to discuss it between themselves.

Celia touched her daughter's shoulder, turning her from the candles she'd arranged on the coffee table. "Brad and I need to figure things out between ourselves. You know that, right?"

"Oh, sure. I know. No worries. I just wanted you to know I approve."

"That means the world to me, Babydoll." Celia

hugged her daughter. "Love you bunches."

"Love you back."

"What's all this love talk I'm hearing in here?" Brad walked into the room rubbing his hands. "You're supposed to be decorating, not having some girly-chat. If I have to be out there in this cold damp hanging those darn lights, you'd better be working in here."

"Aye-aye, Sir." Both Celia and Nicci gave him mock-salutes, then Celia went to help him warm his cold hands, encircling them with hers. "We've got cider all warmed and ready. Want some?"

"You bet," he said, kissing Celia, taking her breath away for too quick a moment.

"Geesh," Nicci said, rolling her eyes. "You two have got it bad."

Laughing, they all settled in the living room as Celia poured the cinnamon-instilled cider. "Did you get the lights done? Can we go and look?"

"Yes, Ma'am," he told her. "I think you'll be pleased, but you can't see them until it's dark. I want it to be a surprise."

Celia had never done well with surprises. She'd become adept at sniffing out gifts at a young age and it had been very difficult for anyone to catch her off-guard. However, Brad seemed so pleased with himself that she stifled the urge to go out the back door and spy his decorations. She'd wait until he was ready to unveil what he'd done.

She frowned. "Speaking of surprises, tomorrow..."

"Is nothing you need to know about yet."

"You do know that surprises drive me pretty much crazy, right?"

"Yes, I do."

"And you are still going to keep this a secret?"

Brad nodded.

"Even from me?" Nicci asked.

"Especially from you. You can't keep a secret from your mother. At all."

"Hey, wait a minute—" Nicci and Celia said at the same time. They tackled Brad, trying to tickle him, but he managed to hold them both at bay.

"I don't care what you do to me, you won't find out a thing until tomorrow."

"Arggghhhh." Celia laughed. "We don't even know how to dress or what to bring."

"Dress warm, in layers. And bring nothing. I've got it covered."

"Well," Celia said, turning to Nicci. "I suggest we try very hard to get it out of him no matter what he says."

"I agree," Nicci said as they both pounced on Brad again.

The ticklefest that followed didn't take long. Celia got winded and Brad had turned the tables on Nicci until she was screaming with laughter. She got free and jumped away from him.

"All right, all right," Celia said, huffing to catch her breath. "We'll wait. Not happily, but we'll wait."

Brad pulled her into his arms, his lips close to her ears. "It'll be worth the wait. I promise."

Once full dark had descended, Celia put Latte on his leash and she and Nicci went outside to view Brad's handiwork. Once he'd situated them in front of the house, Brad disappeared to flip the switch.

The houses on either side of hers were already decorated for Christmas. When Brad's lights came on, they filled a dark hole with light. Lots of light. Celia and Nicci's "ahh's" came at the same time. It seemed like every line of the house was lit up. Icicle lights dripped from the gutters and sparkles of white outlined her house, door, and windows.

It was magical.

Nicci beat Celia to Brad, rushing to hug him, Latte dancing around their feet. "This is awesome. Better than any house on the street!" She skipped away, checking the house from one side to the other.

"She's right," Celia said as she linked arms with Brad. "You outdid yourself."

Brad grinned and cocked his head. "You said you wanted an extra special Christmas this year."

"I didn't expect this, though. Wow. Thank you."

"You're very welcome." He rubbed his hands together. "Any more of that hot cider inside? It feels colder than it should out here."

Laughing, they all linked arms and headed inside, Latte leading the way, pulling on the leash.

Winter in Seattle was generally a dreary affair. Cold and damp and gray. Snow rarely fell in the city and even more rarely near Christmas. So the Christmas spirit came mostly from within the people who lived there.

Unless you got out of the city, Celia thought, as the magical snow all around them mesmerized her. She held out her hand and a flake the size of a half dollar settled there, slowly melting into memory. When she looked up, there was nothing but dusky white broken by thousands of flakes as the snow fell. Celia was in awe of the sheer beauty Mother Nature provided them with, with a lot of help from the amazing man in her life.

He'd bundled them into the car at nine a.m. with nary a word of their destination. They'd headed east on

I-90 and hadn't stopped until reaching Cle Elum. After lunch at a local hole-in-the-wall with superb burgers, they'd gone a few more miles, ending up at a ranch whose fields were covered in white.

Pulling up, seeing the large sleigh wagon hitched to two gorgeous draft horses, Celia had clapped a hand over her mouth.

"Surprise," Brad said. "Today we're picking out a Christmas tree the old fashioned way."

Celia would have thrown her arms around him in gratitude, but Nicci beat her to it, whooping and hollering so much the horses both turned their heads at the ruckus.

Now, plodding slowly through the lower hills in search of the perfect tree, the silence was broken only by the huffing of horses' breath, the soft step of their hooves in the snow, and the whoosh of the sleigh rails as they created paths in the white wonderland. Trees drooped with new fallen snow.

Nicci sat as close to the front as she could, near the driver and horses. Even she'd grown quiet, although her interest in the horses was very apparent by the way she craned her neck this way and that as she watched them move.

"She really seems to like the horses," Celia whispered to Brad.

"I noticed. Maybe horse camp would be a good Christmas gift for her?"

"That's a great idea. Let's do it." Celia leaned her head on his shoulder as he pulled her in close. "Thank you, Brad. Again. This is truly wonderful."

"I'm having as much fun as you are," he said.

"Just one question. How are we going to pick a tree when they are so covered with snow?"

Brad chuckled. "Well, not to spoil the surprise, but they have a tree farm up ahead and the snow has been knocked off most of the trees. So we'll find one pretty easily."

They rounded a bend and a well-maintained shack painted deep red was backed by neat rows of trees beckoning to find a home for Christmas. The sleigh pulled up beside the outbuilding and the driver turned to them. "Feel free to wander through the trees. Pick the one you want and either cut it down or tag it and we'll do the work for you. Afterwards, there's cocoa and cider inside to warm you up before we head back to the ranch."

"Thanks, Paul," Brad said, shaking the man's hand. He jumped to the ground, then helped Nicci down. By the time he'd helped Celia, Nicci was quizzing Paul about the horses and walking around them with an innate respect and an enormous curiosity.

"Oh, yeah, definitely horse camp," Celia said. "It's nice to have an idea for her because she could only come up with one this year."

"What's that?" Brad bundled her coat tighter around her neck, leaning down for a lingering kiss.

Celia sighed. He had the most distracting kisses. Inviting, warm, sexy, hot...all at the same time. "Hmm?"

Brad chuckled. "Nicci. What did she ask for for Christmas?"

"A college fund. She plans to become a doctor and eradicate cancer."

"Oh."

"Yeah. Oh. Way too serious a request from a ten-year-old. Noble, and I love her for it. But she needs more fun in her life before she starts thinking about all that."

"Agreed." He smiled. "I like her drive, though. That's what got me where I am today."

"She's driven, all right."

"Mom, Brad, c'mon! It's time to go find our tree."

"Let the fun commence," Brad said with a laugh, grabbing Celia's gloved hand and heading out after Nicci, who'd already managed to cross about ten trees off the perfect list.

On the way home that night, with their tree tied to the top of Brad's SUV and Nicci sound asleep in the back seat, Celia felt wrapped in contentment. Today had been absolute perfection. Nicci had been completely enamored with the horses. Celia managed to get a brochure about horse camp for kids from Paul without Nicci seeing. The cost would be a stretch, but it was worth it to see Nicci this happy.

No, there wasn't much that could top a day like this. "I love you for doing this, Brad." There. She'd said it. Maybe in a roundabout way, but she'd said it. She loved him. Celia was certain of it. And he returned her feelings, or at least, felt strongly about her. Sometimes, Celia had a hard time figuring out why—what she brought to the relationship. She cooked more than he did, but the man was capable of dinner creations much more enticing than hers. She gave him a sounding board, not that he used it often. And in bed, well, he doted on her.

When Brad didn't respond, Celia turned in her seat to gauge his reaction. His hands looked relaxed on the steering wheel and his posture didn't indicate any stress. Had he heard her?

"I heard you," Brad said. "I don't take those words lightly."

"I don't say them lightly either."

He nodded. "I know. I feel very strongly about you, Celia. Nicci, too. I think you know that."

"I do." And she did.

"I've rarely said the word love to another person. Never found a person I wanted to say it to, besides my mom. So I want to be careful about using it here."

"I can understand that. I just...well, I'm not fishing for compliments or anything, but I'm not sure what I bring to this relationship of ours. I...you do so much for us, for Nicci and me. I'm not sure why you even like me."

Brad glanced at her long enough that Celia was complimented by the surprise in his face. "Are you serious?" he asked, his eyes back on the road as they topped Snoqualmie Pass and started down the west side.

"Yes. I mean, it's not like I hate myself or anything. I just worry that I don't feed your soul as much as you feed mine. Plus I've been sick, and there's no guarantee..."

Brad gripped the steering wheel for a moment, then reached for her hand, settling it on his thigh as he drove. "When I first saw you, you were laughing and dancing, a ray of sunshine even with your low energy level. You have a positive outlook that I admire and respect. And you've given me something I haven't had for a long time, Celia. A family. Do you know how precious that is? You know my mom died a few years ago. Well, my dad has been gone since I was a teenager. I have no siblings, so it was just the Mom and Me Show. You've reminded me what that kind of closeness is like. Plus, you're generous, you're beautiful, and when I've got my arms around you, I feel like there's nothing I can't accomplish."

"Wow," she said quietly. "I—"

He gripped her hand tighter. "Don't ever say you don't bring anything to this relationship. You bring more than you can ever imagine. I'm humbled to be part of your life."

His words warmed her soul better than a thousand "I love you's." Celia tightened her hand around his. "Thank you for that."

"So we're done with this conversation?"

"I believe so."

"Good. And if you think you don't bring anything to the table, just wait until we get home and get Nicci to bed."

"Then you'd better drive faster," she said.

Christmas dinner at Celia's house turned out to be a grand affair. Celia had refused any help from Brad or Nicci. This was her present to them. The kitchen lights caught the diamond bracelet on her wrist. Brad had placed it there this morning, saying he wanted to compliment her delicate, shapely wrist. Smiling as she fingered it, she knew he treasured the Wusthof Chef's knife she'd given him as much as she did this. He'd handed the requisite penny back to her to keep the superstitions happy.

Brad had taken her start-up investment for Nicci's college fund to his broker, who set things up. Celia set up an automatic deposit to the account so it would continue to grow. Danny did the same thing, joking that Celia had better make certain he couldn't access the money. She'd silently agreed with him.

Brad chipped in, too, but not as much as he would have liked. Celia held him to an equal of what she could afford. She didn't want to short Nicci, but by the time she got to college age, this would still be a nice little nest egg to go with the scholarships her straight A's would get her.

Opening her gifts, Nicci's excitement over both the fund and the horse camp had been infectious, making this Christmas morning one to always be remembered. Nicci was at her Dad's now. She'd told Celia that Dan had started dating someone, Kate, and that she'd never seen her father so smitten. Celia was truly happy for Dan. It seemed everyone got their Christmas wishes this year.

Now her mother and Mack were due here soon. Celia realized she'd been daydreaming almost too long and got to work. The turkey, perfectly browned, came out to cool. She heated the potatoes she'd mashed earlier and made the gravy. The table was set with her mother's china.

Nicci, having returned home from her father's with an armful of gifts, poked her head around the corner. "Gramma and Mack are here. Anything I can do to help?"

"Yes. Have Brad open the wine to aerate, and you can open two of the sparkling cider bottles."

"'Kay," Nicci said and disappeared as her mother entered the kitchen.

"Hi, honey," Patricia Milbourne said. She eyed Celia, giving her the once over, something that had become her habit since Celia's illness. "How are you? You look flushed."

"I'm tired but happy. This cooking thing is hard work."

Her mother laughed. "Well, maybe I can distract you for just a moment then and give you a rest. We, uh, we'd..."

Mack joined them, wrapping his arms around Celia's mom. "What your mother is trying so hard to say is that we'd like your blessing."

"My blessing?" Celia stared at them, waiting for an explanation. The glint of light from her mother's hand caught her eye. "A ring?" She stared at the ring, then at her mother and Mack, then back at the ring. "You gave her a ring?"

Patricia nodded. "I accepted conditionally."

Filled with such love she couldn't possibly define it with words, Celia wrapped her arms around both of them. "You have my blessing. You always had it and never needed to ask. I'm so, so happy for you both."

By the time she pulled away, tears trickled down Celia's face. Her mother's cheeks weren't dry either and there was a suspicious sheen in Mack's eyes.

Dinner was a joyous occasion, with good food and lots to celebrate. Mack and Patricia were opting for a small civil ceremony, but hadn't yet talked about a date. It would be soon, though.

"At our age," Mack said, "waiting isn't a good idea."

Everyone laughed at that, but Celia agreed completely. She watched her mother, saw the happiness in her smile, in her eyes. Nicci, having everything around her she loved. Brad, so comfortable and such a big part of their family, sat at the head of the table carving the turkey. Celia watched it all, making a memory picture no camera could rival. Grateful for these people in her life. Grateful for her health.

Grateful for everything.

11

THEM'S FIGHTIN' WORDS

"Hi, Dr. Ted," Celia said as she walked into his office with a skip in her step.

Ted Jamison stretched for a hug and she gladly stepped into it. Then he held her at arm's length. "You look good, honey."

"I feel good," she laughed. "Life is good."

"Physically?"

"I feel like my old self."

"Emotionally?"

"Brad and Nicci make sure I'm on top of the world."

"Good." He shrugged, then stuck his hands in the lab coat he wore to see patients. Celia noticed that his smile didn't quite reach his eyes, like he was posed for a photograph, working hard to smile without blinking.

The room cooled all of a sudden and she stifled a shudder as it hit her. He looked like he knew something she didn't. Celia gripped the back of the chair as her brain started screaming at her.

Run.

She could leave if she did it fast. Pretend there'd been no call asking her to stop by. Pretend she was out shopping. She didn't want to ask why she was here. And she was pretty darn sure she didn't want to hear the answer. She stared for a long moment at the dull gray January winter outside. Noticed that the drizzle that could seep into your bones had stopped. That the office across the way had already taken down their Christmas decorations.

Celia took a deep breath and turned to Dr. Ted. "So, why did you need me to come down here?"

"Have a seat, honey. We need to talk."

That's when the gaping maw opened up in the floor beneath Celia and swallowed every last vestige of her joy. It gutted her peace and set fire to her future. "No." The room started to waver. "No," Celia repeated. The waver changed to a whirlpool of wood and light as the room spun around her. "Not now. No." She tried to draw a deep breath, but couldn't get more than a trickle of air down her throat. Celia forced shaking legs to move, stumbled the two steps to the chair and fell into it.

Dr. Ted nudged her head down. "Breathe, honey. Try to take nice, deep breaths. You're breathing too shallow. You'll hyperventilate." She could hear him. Hear the soothing tones in his voice, but the words made no sense. She struggled to sit up. Strained to slow her breathing. To listen to what he said.

"That's it. Nice deep breaths. Get some oxygen into those lungs."

Her body still shook, but her breathing calmed. She closed her eyes, listened to Dr. Ted, and forced air slowly into her lungs. In. Out. In. Out. Peace. Calm. It took several long moments, but she composed herself and sat up.

"I'm sorry, Celia," Dr. Ted said, placing a

comforting hand on her shoulder. "I wish I had better news."

Another deep breath. "It's okay. I appreciate that it's you." she gulped. "What's happened?"

"Dr. Mason called this morning as a courtesy. She thought..." He paused.

"The bad news would be better coming from you?"

Dr. Ted nodded. "There's been a change in your labs."

"How bad?"

"Not a big jump. But enough of one to tell us certain things."

"I don't understand. There's been no change for months."

"That's a good sign. You know it is. It means the chemotherapy did its job."

"But it's not a cure." The words tumbled through her mind, an echo of what Janice Mason had told her at the very beginning of her treatment.

"No, I'm afraid it isn't."

She stared in front of her, not seeing anything except visions of her life. How different it was from a year earlier. How much stronger, more focused, and happier she was now.

She pushed Dr. Ted's hand away. "This sucks."

"Yes. It does."

Celia got up and walked around the desk to stare again at the dreary gray outside. So the cancer had started to grow again. She had the routine memorized. More surgery, and more chemotherapy. Maybe this time it wouldn't work as well, and she'd have to look at some of the experimental options.

She'd have to tell Brad. And her mother. And Nicci. Damn. Nicci had just started acting like a kid again. She no longer had to push her out the door to play with her friends. Too many months spent looking over her shoulder, making sure her mother was there, had taken its toll.

And now the ghost of her cancer had returned. Not a ghost, she corrected. The real thing had returned to attack her anew.

She wiped her cheek and felt the wetness. She had shed so many tears early in this process. And now she would be starting all over again. Not all over. She knew what to expect. She knew how to fight.

So be it. If this was her lot in life, she'd take it on. She didn't have much of a choice. *Just remember, cancer, I don't like to lose.*

She turned around. "Okay. Let's see the test results."

That night Celia lingered as she put Nicci to bed, talking about inconsequential things. Anything to delay having to go downstairs and have *the talk* with Brad. He'd come over wiped out from a long, frustrating day and was still on the phone putting out fires. She was about to add fodder to his belief that this was a day to just power through and be done with.

She found him lying on her couch, one arm covering his eyes.

"Hey," she said.

"Hey, yourself," he answered as he scooted over to make room for her.

Celia snuggled in his arms, enjoying the hint of expensive cologne. Until Brad, she'd never thought twice about the price of cologne. Now she knew. There was a huge difference. She inhaled again, with visions of sultry evenings in the tropics, low lights, and Braden Worth walking slowly toward her clothed in nothing but a towel.

Unsure if it was the cologne or some commercial image, she took another whiff. Who cared?

"Did you get the rest of your business taken care of?" she asked.

"For now. I'll have to go in early tomorrow to finish."

"Ah."

He shifted so he could see her better. "You've been quiet ever since I got here."

"You noticed? I kind of hoped you were too involved with work to see."

He kissed the top of her head. "I see everything where you are concerned. You're worried."

"Yes."

"Is it Nicci?"

She smiled as images of her daughter's face skipped across her mind. "No. Nicci's fine. It's—"

He stiffened. "—the cancer's back, isn't it?"

"Yes. I'm afraid so. At least, my labs are up." Celia lay there waiting for him to relax. Praying for him to relax. Needing his ability to roll with the punches more than anything right now.

He didn't. Instead, he sat up. She'd give him credit. He didn't move away and he pulled her arm into his as she straightened. But he didn't look at her. "How bad is it?"

She sighed. "It's not a significant jump. But this is a tough cancer to beat and, since it was caught in a later stage... Well, I've got a fight ahead of me. I'll know more when I see Dr. Mason, my oncologist, the day after tomorrow. I expect it will mean more chemotherapy. And more surgery may also have to be considered."

Braden extricated himself and raked his hands

through his hair.

That simple motion increased Celia's sadness tenfold as the weight of her renewed illness hit her. The calendar filled with medical appointments. Shifting her work load back to Tana. Another port catheter. More chemotherapy.

She would lose her hair all over again.

"Brad?"

He stood abruptly. "I think I'll sleep at my place tonight. I have a very early day tomorrow and you need your rest, especially now. I don't want to disturb you."

Celia's gut filled with heavy rocks as she searched his face. "What's wrong?"

He folded her into his embrace. "I'm...sorry. It's just a lot to take in. I need some time to digest it."

"I know what that's like."

"Look, let's get some sleep and talk about this tomorrow, okay? Damn," he separated from her. "I've got the day from hell tomorrow and Friday I leave for France."

"I know." Celia's heart felt like it would stop beating as she let him off the hook. "Go take care of business. We can talk after you get back."

He kept her close to him as they walked to the door and kissed her as if she was a doll about to break. "I'm sorry. I'll call you later, okay?"

"Sure," Celia said, pulling away. "Call me."

He pulled her chin up gently to look at him. "I will call you."

Tears swam in her eyes. "I know you will."

Seth watched as Celia locked the door behind Brad and drifted into her kitchen. She walked over to the sink, picked up a dirty dish and just held it, staring out at the darkness beyond the window.

She'd been so content for so long. Nine months of being able to focus on living. It wasn't enough. Seth's shoulders stooped under the weight of his knowledge. It didn't seem fair. And he had no way to warn her how drastically things would change.

Smack! His hands connected fist to palm at the same time the plate in her hands shattered on the floor.

Celia crouched down to pick up the pieces. Instead, she fell to the floor and wrapped her arms around her knees to cushion her head.

Her quiet sobs shredded his heart.

He joined her on the floor, encircling her in arms she could not see. God forgive him, it felt good to hold her again. He'd left her alone these past months. She hadn't needed him. And he was sorry beyond reason that his presence was necessary now. He'd never wish any of this pain on her. He tightened his imaginary grip on her shoulders.

Celia cried herself out, wiped her face, and tossed the pieces of plate in the trash like an automaton. Leaving the dishes, she went to bed and curled up into a tight ball, wishing Brad was here. But he wasn't. And it was selfish of her to want his strong arms to comfort her. He'd looked stunned when he left. Celia knew she'd have to give him time to get used to the news.

But a part of her, deep down in her churning stomach, got angry. He should be here. With her.

Damn him.

Damn her cancer.

Damn it all to hell!

Patricia had not let go of Celia's hand since they sat down in the oncologist's office. Celia understood why. They were all pretty much in a state of shock since the news. Now, two days later, Janice Mason was about to outline the next phase of treatment. Dr. Ted had come along and Celia was grateful for his support.

Celia closed her eyes for a moment and wished for the umpteenth time that Brad was here. She hadn't seen him since the night she'd told him. Had it only been two days ago? He had called her yesterday in a rush between meetings. She didn't know if the distance in his voice was work-related or due to her news. And this morning he flew out to France for several days of work at a prestigious cooking academy. He hadn't needed to go. His chefs could learn what they needed without him. But it was one of his passions and he had been looking forward to it for quite a while.

A part of her wondered if she was still one of his passions or if the relationship was another thing forfeited to cancer. He should be here, damn it.

The office door opened and Janice Mason walked in, Dr. Ted following close behind. Celia sat ramrod straight, as if she was the teenage daughter of a parent from historical times.

"Hello, Celia."

"Hi, Dr. Mason. You remember my mother, Patricia."

"Yes." Dr. Mason reached for Patricia's hand, but Celia's mother wouldn't let go of Celia's for even a moment. So Janice Mason did a very un-doctor-like thing. She put her arm around Patricia Milbourne's shoulders. Tightly. Patricia's eyes widened, then misted over. Finally, she released her daughter's hand long enough to squeeze Dr. Mason's arm in gratitude.

"It's important," Janice started, "that we all heal from this latest news. It has taken a toll on each of you, both mentally and physically." She looked at Patricia. "Your energy is gone."

Patricia nodded.

Celia inclined her head.

"You can't concentrate?"

Another nod. And another silent agreement.

"And you don't care what's happening anywhere except in the pool of misery in which you currently reside?"

Patricia teared up, but she straightened and sniffed them back.

Janice looked at Celia. "You are affected the most, but everyone around you helps you bear the burden."

God, she'd give anything to not have to put her mother through this. Celia placed a hand on her mother's arm. "I know."

"Good. That strength will be your solace in the coming months."

"So," Celia said, "it's back to chemo."

"Yes."

"The same regimen?"

"Similar. We need to determine the best approach."

"Surgery?" Celia asked.

"I'm not sure. I'd like some more tests before we consider that," the oncologist answered.

Celia's steel-straight back melted a little. "I just got back into the swing of things with my job."

Dr. Ted hugged her. "We'll help, honey." He reached a hand over to Patricia.

"I know." Celia wanted to cry. She'd wanted to so many times since Dr. Ted had told her. It was strange that no tears would come anymore. As if her body had decided to stop mourning. Now if only her heart and head could catch up.

Dr. Mason picked up the medical thread. "The first thing is to get some additional blood work and a CT scan. You can do the lab draw on your way out today. The CT scan," she consulted Celia's chart, "is scheduled for tomorrow at five o'clock." She looked up. "Will that work for you?"

No-o-o-o-o! Celia's scream sounded to her like an echo through the Grand Canyon. All that the others heard, though, was a rigid "yes."

"I'll have the nurse give you the specifics."

"I know the routine," Celia said in a monotone. All over again. She was going to do this all over again. How much time would it buy her this time? How long...

She looked at her mother who stared down at the notepad on her lap.

"Could I have a minute with you, Dr. Mason?"

"You've got it."

Celia implored Dr. Ted with her eyes. "Alone?"

He took the hint. "Come on, Patricia. Let's go see if we can find that information the nurse has for us." He ushered her out of the oncologist's office with a wink over his shoulder.

Celia's first question shot out as soon as the door closed.

"Chemo is less and less effective the further into treatment you get, right?"

"I wouldn't say that exactly."

"We've had this conversation before. I don't want sugar-coating, remember? I have a daughter. And plans that need to be made. What's the bottom line here, Dr. Mason?"

The oncologist settled on the stool next to her. It did

nothing to enhance Dr. Mason's petite stature, but somehow, her close proximity comforted Celia.

"All right. In survival terms, we consider your first go-round of chemotherapy to have been highly successful."

"Yeah. It bought me another, what? Nine months?"

"Yes, it did. You were diagnosed with advanced ovarian cancer. You already know the cure rate for that."

Celia blinked. Several times. "Yes. So this round won't be as effective as the last?"

"Probably not. It will, however, buy you more time."

"At what expense?"

Janice Mason placed her hand over Celia's. "I agree that there may come a time when we need to discuss quality of life."

Celia struggled to keep her gaze on the oncologist— to view this head on.

"We're not there yet. I think you still have a lot of valuable time left. Time when you won't feel so sick. Time to spend with your daughter."

"Time to plan."

"And yes, I think. Time to plan."

Barely able to nod her head, Celia's mind screamed the question she was having so much trouble asking. "How much time?"

"I don't believe we should be thinking in those terms yet."

"How much time?"

Dr. Mason stared at Celia for a long moment. "There's no pat answer for that. A year? Six months? Five years? This is only your second round of chemotherapy. We have to see how the cancer reacts— and how your body tolerates it. After that, ask me this question. Right now, we're still in the stage of trying to figure out how to destroy this disease."

Celia stared at the wall, the window, her hands, wherever she could for several long seconds before she answered. "You're right. It's not time."

"That's good to hear. I need you fighting."

"I will be. One favor, though?"

"Certainly."

"When it is time? Be honest with me, okay?"

"I will."

That night Celia had the hardest conversation of her life. She told Nicci about her visit to the oncologist and that she would be returning to chemotherapy. She watched with overwhelming sadness as ghosts dimmed her daughter's happy-go-lucky attitude. And it broke Celia's heart. She lay down with Nicci and Latte until her daughter fell asleep, then crept out, carefully closing the door.

"Mom?"

"Yeah, Babydoll?"

"Could you leave the door open."

"Sure, honey." Celia almost wept at the request. Once again, cancer would claim her daughter's childhood.

Celia tapped her stomach. *Damn this cancer. Damn it to hell for robbing my daughter of fun.*

She tapped harder and thought of Brad somewhere in France. *And for stealing my own happiness.*

Turning into her own bedroom, she threw herself down on the bed and beat her pillow until feathers covered her bed and there was nothing left to pummel but the casing.

Where the hell are you, Brad? I need you here! Now!
Exhausted from killing her pillow, she was

unprepared for the quiet chime of her cell phone and jumped.

"H-hello?"

"Hi," Brad said.

Breathing heavy, Celia barely managed to rasp out his name. "Brad."

After a pause, he responded. "Are you all right?"

"Yes," she looked around at the feathery mess. "Just a little working out."

"Really? That's great. Then you got good news from the doctor today?" His words all rushed together.

"No. Not good." *Not by any definition.* "I'm to have a CT scan tomorrow and as soon as they decide what and how much, I'm back in chemotherapy."

The pause on the other end of the line felt like a rubber band stretched to the breaking point. Finally, Celia could take it no more. "Brad?"

"I'm so sorry, Celia."

About chemo or something else? "Well, we pretty much knew a couple days ago this would be necessary."

"Yes, but I'd hoped—" Another long pause, only this time a deep breath on his end, too. Her mind's eye saw him run his free hand through his hair. "I mean, we all hoped that maybe it wouldn't be necessary."

"Are you okay, Brad?"

"I don't know. I just...think I'm having trouble with this whole thing."

"You think I'm not?"

"I am fully cognizant of the fact that this is hardest on you." The edge of steel in his voice was like a slap to Celia's face.

"What's going on, Brad? You're acting spooked."

"I...am."

Again, she had the vision of him raking fingers

through his manicured hair. The explosive sigh he expelled reverberated through the phone and plucked the wrong chord in Celia.

"Fine," she said. "Just let me know when you get over seeing ghosts, okay?" She didn't wait for an answer as she flipped her cell phone shut and stared at it. It just wasn't the same. Slamming a receiver on the cradle would have been much more satisfying. She tested the weight of the phone as she stared at her bedroom wall. Better yet... But common sense overrode emotion and she set the phone back on her night stand.

Damn it! Wasn't it enough that this cancer was back? Was she going to lose her boyfriend because of it? It was not fair. Not in the least.

Her cell phone chimed, startling Celia again. Instead of picking it up, she ignored it and went to get the vacuum. She had some feathers to clean up, after which she took a tank-draining shower.

And felt no better.

The tiny light of her cell phone blinked like a Vegas sign.

She turned it off. Crawled into bed. And begged for a respite from her misery as she drifted off to whispered words.

Join me.

"Hello."

The warm voice came from behind her and Celia turned, an unfamiliar swish following her. A glance down revealed that she was dressed in yards and yards of a deep-green fabric, an elaborate dress, complete with a hooped skirt, that would make a bride envious.

And a low cut bodice that showed a bosom Celia hadn't seen in many years. She exercised regularly, or had until she'd gotten sick. She even did those dreaded isometrics that were sworn to keep things from falling. Still, at thirty-five years old, gravity had started pulling ahead in the fight. But somehow, at this moment, in this time, she had a shelf.

She tried to draw a deep breath but a vise tightened around her.. She felt her ribs. Or tried to, at least. They were confined by a very restrictive corset.

"Ouch!"

"Are you all right?" The voice was deep. And smooth enough to talk a cat out of a tree.

Celia's head rose as her jaw dropped. The solicitous man in front of her looked like he'd been formed from the golden roads of heaven. White-gold hair was haloed by the setting sun. A face that was both angular and soft smiled at her. A fluffy white shirt peeked out from a long, tight, fitted jacket. He looked as if he'd just returned from a Halloween party.

She glanced down at her own attire again. The same could be said of her.

"Have I died?"

He blanched and his eyes widened first, then squinted. Furrowed brows followed. "No. No. Not at all." His voice lowered even further, as if imparting a deeply hidden secret. "You're dreaming."

Celia opened her mouth to speak, but nothing came out. She stared down at her own garb in disbelief. "Dreaming," she repeated.

"Yes." He smiled then and the sunshine brightened even more. "Would you care to take a stroll around the grounds?"

This can't be happening. She felt the yards of material that comprised her skirt. It felt like cloth. It even looked like cloth. Bunches of it.

Celia turned in a circle. She stood on a sprawling, well-manicured lawn. One direction led to what seemed to be an immense garden. Another showed a gravel—no, strike that. A cobblestone road leading up to a stone and brick mansion. She'd seen buildings like this before, but always in a state of disrepair and covered in ivy. This home was pristine. Like a country home described in one of those historical romance novels.

She leaned down to touch the grass, but her corset stopped her short. *Okay, so we'll assume the grass is real.*

As she straightened, a dark auburn ringlet stroked her cheek. Celia froze. She lifted her hand slowly, afraid to break the spell. Then she felt it.

Hair. All woven into some sort of intricate concoction, but hair, nonetheless. She pulled on a curl and felt the follicle tighten. It was real, too.

She looked around her again. As real as things could be—in a dream.

"Where am I?" she asked.

"This is my...home," the man said, although the wonder in his voice didn't lend much credence to the statement.

"Your home?"

"Yes." He seemed much more certain now. "These are our family estates. Welcome."

"So you live here?"

"When I'm not in the city, yes."

"And which city would that be?" Celia spoke as if he were a child standing by a broken lamp, denying any involvement.

"London, of course." The man cleared his throat. "I know we haven't been formally introduced and I should look for a relative or some sort, but," he waved an arm in a wide, sweeping gesture, "there seems to be no one else about. So please allow me to introduce myself. My name is Seth Margrave." He tilted his head in a bow as he spoke. A note of surprise crept into his voice as he said his name.

Celia couldn't quite shake the nagging feeling that she knew him from somewhere.

"And you are?" he asked.

"Um. I'm Celia. Celia Milbourne."

"Miss Milbourne. It's a pleasure to finally meet you."

Delight melted any remaining resistance in Celia as he said her name, warming her right down to her toes. His voice sounded like that of an old friend. Yet she couldn't remember ever meeting him.

"Do I know you?"

"Most certainly, since we've just been introduced. Would you care for a walk through the gardens?"

Celia was still in the throes of confusion. She'd been here before. Or met him before? Or maybe she'd dreamed about him before?

That was it. This is a recurrent dream. That had to be the explanation. Celia reached up and felt the thick auburn curls.

She could definitely live with that.

"Certainly, sir," she smiled, taking his proffered arm. "I would love to see the gardens.

When Celia woke, her legs were all tangled up in her skirts, except when she kicked them off, it turned out to be the covers of her own bed. She was back in her bedroom, her oasis. Right now it seemed dull in comparison. She'd been having the loveliest, most vivid dream about a walk in the gardens on the arm of a tow-headed Renaissance man. She stretched and remembered. A very handsome man at that. She'd been wearing the prettiest green dress. And her hair had been—

She sat up abruptly and reached for her head.

It was gone.

All that glorious, thick, dark hair. Gone!

All she felt were short spikes, probably going in all different directions from a night of tossing and turning.

She climbed out of bed and checked the mirror, certain of what she would see. Short hair, completely white. She had to clamp a hand over her mouth to keep from crying out. She'd lost her hair all over again. And somehow, even though it had only been a dream, it felt even worse this time.

"Mom? Are you all right?"

Her daughter's hushed voice pulled Celia out of her woe-is-me reverie and back to the real world. She had cancer. And a CT scan to get through. Plus a daughter who deserved her focus. It had been a nice dream. She smiled as she thought of the man on whose arm she had spent the afternoon. She couldn't even remember his name.

It didn't really matter. After all, it had only been a dream.

12

SETTLING IN

Here she was again. The familiar, understated furnishings of Dr. Ted's office had changed little. Celia picked up one of the frames beside his stethoscope and realized it was a photo of her taken the day she got her job as a pharmaceutical rep. Nostalgia tugged at the corners of her mouth. Dr. Ted had been like a proud father when they received the official word she'd been hired. Definitely a high point in her life.

The smile disappeared as she set the frame down and wandered a slow circle around the office. Normally, this room brought her comfort. Ever since her diagnosis, her visits had been for medical reasons. It no longer felt like a sanctuary. And right now, it felt...heavy. Like air laden with the weight of doom.

Her scan results were in. That Dr. Mason had agreed to meet here couldn't be good. Celia could feel it in her bones.

The world was starting to close in around her and she wished for the thousandth time that Brad was here. Not that he wasn't trying to be supportive. He'd called daily from France. There was so much to learn, he had opted to stay another week. He said all the right things. He was sorry. He wished he could be here for her. But the words sounded too smooth. Rehearsed. He was covering something up. She would bet her...well, she was just sure he wasn't telling her something.

Chemotherapy would start soon. She'd once again lose her hair. She felt ready for that. As ready as anyone could be.

It was the bigger picture that had her as weak and limp as a ragdoll. Fear shredded her insides and the only thing that kept her from shaking apart was a barely adequate level of control.

She might die.

Her breath came out in chopped up little wisps and she tried hard to get them to coalesce into some sort of normal pattern.

Breathe in. Be at peace.

Breath out. Be calm.

Breathe in.

Breath out.

The office door opened and she whirled around. Marilyn, Dr. Ted's nurse, came in with herbal tea. Dr. Ted followed behind, pulling Celia into a hug so big it sent fear flying. He held her there for a long moment. Celia's body, stiff from refusing to lose control, could not resist. Slowly, inch by inch, she relaxed into Dr. Ted. And hugged him back just as tightly.

"I can't help it," she said. "I'm scared." Her muffled voice sounded frail even to her. Stray tears escaped and she clung to him as she fought to regain her composure.

"I know, honey. I know." He held her until she found the strength to push away.

"I'm sorry. I appear to be a blubbering idiot today."

He led her over to the chairs and sat opposite her.

"No, you're not. You've got a serious situation here and it doesn't help if you keep it all in. You need to have a good cry once in a while."

"Yes, but it seems like I'm way over my quota."

"You have a lot of strength in you, my dear. You've shown that over and over this past year or so. Give yourself a little credit. And a little down time. You'll bounce back to fighting form when you need to."

His office door opened then, and Marilyn ushered Dr. Mason in, along with Laura, the counselor. Dr. Mason has suggested Laura attend and Celia had jumped at the opportunity to see her friend again. Extra chairs were brought in and everyone was given coffee or tea as desired.

Once all the settling in was done, everything went silent for a moment. Not long. Celia doubted anyone else noticed but her. She'd felt the pause, heavy and weighing on her. The desire to run rushed to her heart and she almost got up from her chair. But running wouldn't fix this. Nothing would. At least that was what she suspected she was about to hear.

"Celia," Dr. Mason started. "We have the results from your CT scan."

"And the cancer is growing again."

"Yes. New tumors showed up in the abdominal cavity."

Sighing like it was the last breath she would ever take, Celia whispered her thought. "That's not all."

"No. I'm afraid it's not. There is evidence of tumor growth on one of your kidneys."

There it was. The final diagnosis. Celia knew from living with her cancer that as long as it was contained, she had a shot of remission. If it was spreading to other organs, though...

She shook her head. It appeared she would have no more time to feel sorry for herself. There was an even larger fight to begin. And she would need all of her strength for that. She had to fight. For as long and as hard as she could.

She straightened in her chair. "What do we do now?"

Laura smiled and grasped her hand. "Good girl."

"We start by taking a closer look. It means another surgery, but I'd like to make sure exactly what, and where, we are fighting."

Celia nodded. "Okay. Then back to chemotherapy?"

"Yes. Surgery will once again help us to design the best therapy. You remember," Janice Mason paused, "that, statistically, a second round of chemotherapy is not as effective?"

"Yes. I know that."

"We may need to look at some alternative treatments. I see some real promise in a study being done right here at Fred Hutch. I'll contact them and get some preliminary information for you to review."

"Thanks. I appreciate that." She looked around the small group. "Any other options on the table?"

Laura answered. "The most important thing is to take care of yourself as you have been." She pointed to the hot beverage sitting untouched next to Celia. "Healthy fluids, a good diet. Are you still doing yoga?"

"I was until about a week ago. I—" Celia waved her hand half-heartedly, "let this all get to me."

"I can understand that. How do you feel about resuming?"

"I can do that."

"Good. It gives you a measure of control to help when things feel like they are spiraling out of your hands. Also, let's start to talk on a more regular basis."

Celia smiled. She'd come to respect Laura's advice. "I'd like that."

A week later, Celia waited as the elevator took them up to the surgical unit. The doors opened and the memory of her last time here flooded her mind. A lot had happened since then. A lot of fighting against a foe she could not control. And today the next battle would begin.

She would fight.

And she would win.

She had to. For Nicci.

She walked resolutely to the admitting desk, ready for the fight.

Once she'd settled into the pre-op alcove, Dr. Mason stopped by in her surgical greens. "How are you feeling?"

"Like I'm having a déjà vu moment. Any chance that's all this is?"

"Sorry," she smiled. "I leave the surreal stuff for the shrinks and stick to reality."

Celia huffed. "Yeah. Some reality, eh?"

"It will be over before you know it." Dr. Mason looked around. "Where's your shadow?"

"Nicci's in school. I didn't want her to miss anything she didn't have to. But she gave me quite a fight."

The oncologist nodded. "I bet she did. So, here by yourself then?"

Celia thought of Brad, due back late last night. She had left a message on his answering machine that surgery was this afternoon.

He hadn't called.

"By myself, yes," she said. "Mom will be here with Nicci when school gets out."

Dr. Mason patted her hand. "We're almost ready, so it won't be long."

The nurse walked in with an orderly behind her.

"It looks like we're ready to go now," Celia said.

The nurse nodded.

"I'll see you in the O.R., Celia."

"Oh, joy." The attempted sarcasm was feeble and Celia knew it. The repressed dread returned with a vengeance as her empty stomach threw globules of acid at her throat. She clasped the rails tightly as the orderly started to wheel her out.

"Stop!" The male voice carried down the hall.

Celia turned to see a man wearing jeans and a crumpled, white dress shirt and carrying a suitcase, rush down the hall.

Brad! It was Brad. The acid churning in her stomach mellowed as he reached her side.

The orderly backed off as Brad leaned over the rail and cupped her cheek. "I didn't think I would make it."

"Where—"

"—plane was late." He kissed her forehead. "Missed my connection." He kissed her lips. "Got here as fast as I could. I'm so, so sorry."

Calm replaced the nerves jangling in Celia's brain. She took a deep breath and smiled. "I'm glad you're here."

Brad grinned. "Me, too." He wouldn't stop staring at her. And she was lost in his eyes as everything else faded, including time.

A cough reminded them they had an audience. "I'm sorry, Ms. Milbourne, but it's time to go."

She let go of his hand reluctantly as they started to move her toward the surgical suite.

"I'll be here waiting," Brad called after her as she

rounded the door.

Brad looked around the pre-op room, unsure what to do now. He'd been so focused on getting here in time, he hadn't considered what he would do once Celia went to surgery. He heaved a huge sigh of relief that he had, in fact, made it. Frowning, he thought of how pale and small she looked, swaddled in blankets on that gurney. He looked at the ceiling. *Please, God, wherever or whoever you are... Please let this take care of it. Let this heal her. It's too much to bear. For her. And for me.*

"Sir," the nurse said. "Can I show you the waiting room?"

"Yes. Thank you." He picked up his bag and, with one last look down the hall, followed the nurse.

Hours later, coming out of the anesthetic, Celia groaned. Memory returned slowly through the haze. Recollection of what post-op felt like. She tried to lick her lips and even that was an effort.

"Hello, princess."

Brad? She tried to open her eyes but they wouldn't cooperate. "Bra—"

"Shhh. Don't try to talk. Not yet."

"How—"

"They've allowed one of us to sit here as long as we behave ourselves."

"Nicci?" Celia croaked.

"Asleep on the couch in the waiting room."

Celia's brows knit together.

"She wouldn't go home. We tried. You know how stubborn your daughter can be." He laughed softly. "So your mom and I have been trading back and forth between you two. Trust me, she's sound asleep."

"Don't. Wake. Her."

She could hear the smile in his voice. "We won't. Now you lay still. I'm going to get the nurse."

"Mmm-mmn." Celia opened her eyes successfully this time, only to find her world blurry beyond recognition.

"Don't worry. They said you'd have a tough time coming out of the anesthetic this time." He paused. "You were under longer than they expected."

"How did it go?"

Brad's face filled her clearing vision as he leaned over. "The surgeon said it went fine and she would be here in the morning to explain more."

His eyes were drawn, with enhanced lines surrounding them and a blue-black shadow hinting at his lack of sleep. His smile, though, seemed relaxed and genuine. Celia let it wash over and calm her. His normally perfect hair was sticking out in ways she'd only seen in the mornings. The man was fastidious about being groomed in public.

"You look like hell," she said, then drifted off to the sound of his warm chuckle.

"We found what we expected to find," Dr. Mason said.

Celia was seated in the chair next to her bed, having roused the nurses to help her up before they could ask her if she wanted to. Seth could see her determination. She wanted out of this hospital. He smiled as he watched. Her mother sat on the bed beside her chair. Then he looked at Brad, standing behind Celia with a hand on her shoulder, and his eyes narrowed.

What color she'd managed to recover in the few hours since surgery fled in the wake of Dr. Mason's comment. Celia's body straightened a touch. Seth doubted anyone noticed how hard she was working to shore up her courage. "Go ahead, Doctor."

"We knew there were masses in the abdominal cavity. We believed, and were proven right, that some of the lymph nodes also had cancer cells." Dr. Mason hesitated. "We also found a mass on your kidney so we removed the kidney."

Celia gripped the arms of the chair. "How much of the tumors were you able to remove?"

"We believe we got all of them."

Patricia expelled a whoosh of pent-up stress. "Thank God."

Brad grinned at the news.

But Celia closed her eyes briefly. And Seth dipped his head in acknowledgement. She knew what he knew. It still wasn't good news.

"The problem is that these types of growths tend to return. And multiply."

Celia nodded her head as she settled a hand over her mother's arm. Brad ran hands through his hair, the shake barely noticeable. The furrowed brow was easy to spot, though. Seth was glad the man was behind Celia where she couldn't see him. She had enough to worry about.

"I am aware of that," Celia answered the doctor.

"So you know we need to get started with chemotherapy as soon as possible."

Celia took a deep breath. "Yes."

"It will be an even more aggressive regimen this time—"

Patricia started to argue, but Dr. Mason held up her

hands. "I know chemotherapy was hard before. We don't have a choice now. We need to keep these tumors from growing again. We need to destroy as many of the cancer cells as we can."

But you won't be able to kill all of them, Seth thought. By the stoic look on Celia's face, she knew the unspoken truth also.

Dr. Mason stood up and patted Celia's hand on her mother's arm. "For now, you need to get your strength back. As quickly as you can. I'll discharge you tomorrow and I want to see how you are doing in one week. We'll decide then when to start."

Celia's pressed-together lips tried to lift into a smile. It ended up looking more like an upside down clam shell. "Thank you, Doctor Mason. I'll work on it."

After the oncologist left, Brad helped Celia back to bed, then went to stand at the window. He stood straight. Too straight.

Seth watched Celia's eyes focus on his back. Her mother picked up her crocheting, but it lay untouched in her hands. Seth moved beside Celia, whose hands rested on her stomach. His hands covered hers as he sat beside her. She turned in his direction, eyes filled with too many emotions to name. Fear, regret, resolve. All at war within her. He knew strength would win. She would see this through with a dignity she was not aware she was capable of.

Seth looked at Brad, who hadn't moved. She would weather these next few weeks and months much better than some others.

Still staring at Brad, Seth renewed his vow to stay and help her.

13

EXCUSE ME IF I THROW UP ALL OVER YOUR DREAMS

The spasms clutched Celia like a vice and the acrid smell of chemo's aftermath disgusted her. As the waves of nausea subsided, she flushed it all away, but the smell of sour bile remained.

Latte, Nicci's dog, scratched at the door, wanting in. Knowing better than to move too far away, Celia let him scratch, collapsed to the floor, and leaned against the shower door. The side-effects seemed worse this time. Or was it that she had pounded the prior episodes to a pulp and buried them deep in her mind? The pattern, however, was achingly familiar. A slow loss of energy until the third day and then—<u>Pow</u>!

She would spend the next week recovering her strength. After that, one good week to spend with Nicci then back to the beginning again. For eight treatments. Six months worth. She lost two weeks out of every three to the symptoms of the medicine that held her cancer at bay—

Celia felt the familiar tightening in her throat as the nausea gripped her and she grabbed the bowl like a frat boy after a binge, letting loose with a guttural wail. Long moments later, she settled back once again to wait for the next wave, using a cool, damp washcloth to soothe her face. Nicci was at school and Celia closed her eyes in a moment of gratitude. Her daughter had handed her this cloth way too many times.

She wondered how Brad's day was going. He was at work, but had promised to stop by later. Ever since surgery, he'd spent as much time as possible at her side, doing much of his work from a laptop. But things were different. She shivered as the deep, penetrating ache wound its way to her heart. Personal discussions had disappeared from their relationship, replaced by medical issues and calendar organization. Celia snugged the blanket around her shoulders tighter. She missed the closeness they had shared more than she thought possible.

He was scared. That was pretty darn apparent. She couldn't fault him. The question was, how scared? Celia's throat constricted and she swallowed, managing to keep the nausea at bay. For the moment.

She smacked the washcloth down on the floor. She'd weathered chemotherapy without his help before and could do it again if she had to. If Brad couldn't handle her being sick, he had no business being here. And he sure as hell shouldn't have initiated a relationship with her in the first place. He'd known from the outset. What the hell was he doing, anyway?

"Hello?"

Brad. It figured. Celia groaned and ran a hand through her hair, quite certain she looked like crap. She tried to look at herself in the metal corner of the shower door, but couldn't see enough.

Well, there was nothing like trial by fire, right? The

man was about to see her at her absolute worst. As if things weren't bad enough.

"In the bathroom. Come on in." she called, staring at the door to gauge his reaction when he entered.

After listening to a brief scuffle as he tried to keep the dog out of the bathroom, Brad opened the door. To his credit, he didn't flinch. And he didn't run. Two points in his favor. He stopped, though. And stared for a long moment, nullifying the points she'd given him.

"Do you need anything?" His voice remained hushed, like speaking normally would bring on another battle with the toilet bowl.

"A new body would be nice." She tried to smile but knew it pretty much fell flat.

Then Brad wiped out all the bad points she'd given him. All he did to manage that was to sit down on the bathroom floor next to her. Celia had been throwing up for the past couple of hours. Even with the constant flushing, the room had to reek like a sewer. He had on one of his best suits, too.

He didn't leave. And that felt like a very good sign.

"I've missed you," he said, reaching for her hand and drawing it to his lips.

"Mmm, me, too." The sensation of his warm hand holding her cold one was a definite distraction from the reality of her day. The warmth traveled up her arm and infused her body with good news. She liked it. She leaned against him and he raised her expectations even further when he pulled her tighter against his side and wrapped the blanket snugly around her.

"Just warn me if—" he waved in the direction of the toilet.

"Definitely."

They sat that way for several long moments. And

there, in the middle of her bathroom floor, Celia once again felt a little bit like a princess, having just bagged the prince. She could deal with anything as long as these arms were around her.

"Did I ever tell you about my mother?" Brad broke the stillness.

"Mmm. Just that she had breast cancer and you knew about chemotherapy from her experience."

"Yes. First hand. I helped her through all of it." He paused a long moment. "In the end, the drugs couldn't save her."

Compassion and sorrow mingled with self-centered fear and twisted her heart like a wet, wrung towel. He'd never told her the whole story. She couldn't speak, couldn't ask the questions she wanted to. "I-I'm so sorry, Brad."

"I've always considered myself to be a strong person. Or did up to that point. Watching her slowly deteriorate and being unable to help...it was the worst point in my life. I couldn't fix this for her. Just as bad, and this is very selfish of me, I couldn't acknowledge how terrible I felt. I had to be outwardly strong for her."

"Didn't you have friends you could confide in?"

"Not any I could talk with about this." He drummed his fingers along Celia's shoulder and she stayed quiet, letting him work through the memories.

"It's been a few years," Brad said. "I thought I had learned to cope with it."

"Why didn't you ever tell me the whole story? I know you and your mother were close."

"Yes. We were. Considering what you had been through, I didn't think telling you was a good idea."

Celia frowned. "Why now?"

"Because...I haven't been myself lately. And you

deserve to know the reason why."

Celia gave a gentle nod and waited for him to continue.

"You have to understand. It took my mother four years to die. Four years of treatment, then recovery, then having her hopes dashed. I was her only child, so I was there for all of it. The chemotherapy, the surgeries. I saw her body and spirit waste away until there was nothing left."

Celia's nausea settled like a large rock at the bottom of her stomach. All of her empathy and emotion became a pool of black bile surrounding that rock.

"Where was your father?"

Brad's voice went all edgy and bitter. "They'd divorced years earlier. I don't have much to do with him, especially when he all but ran the company into the ground." He took a deep breath and turned her to face him. "I don't know how else to say this except to just come out with it. I'm not sure I can do this again."

And there it was. The punch line. Only it wasn't very funny. The stone in her stomach rumbled. Celia ignored it and did her best to build a hasty wall around her heart. It didn't work. His arms tightened their hold on her as if begging her to understand. She could feel his pulse racing. It felt as if her heartbeat matched his. Both were pounding, but for entirely different reasons.

She stiffened and pulled away from him. "Can't do what?"

"Watch you,"—he waved an arm at the room—"go through this."

She grabbed hold of the toilet and used it to pull herself up. Brad reached to help her but she shoved his hand away. "Fine," she said. "I can do it myself."

Once on her feet, she turned on him. "You knew I

was sick when you met me."

"Yes."

"And that stage III ovarian cancer has a markedly high incidence of death."

"Yes. I did my own research, beyond what you told me."

"And still you asked me out. Again and again. You ingratiated yourself in my family."

"Yes."

"Why?"

"I think—" he ran both hands through his hair, then reached to take hold of her shoulders. "I fell in love with you the first time I saw you, exhausted and trying to catch your breath on the way to the market."

She raised her chin a fraction higher. "You don't need to remind me. I have that day seared in my mind. And my heart."

Brad rushed on. "I thought I was over it. You were doing so well. I convinced myself that you would be fine. And that, even if you weren't, I could see it through. I thought I could be there for you." He shook her slightly, then realized what he was doing and stepped back.

"When you told me about the relapse, I couldn't breathe. I couldn't think. It was happening all over again. I saw my mother. What she went through. I panicked and...well, I ran to France."

"I noticed."

"Please understand, Celia. I am in love with you. Truly and deeply. But...I'm not sure I can do this again. I...just can't watch..."

"Watch me die?"

The agony in his face showed in deeply etched lines, and the sparkle had disappeared from his eyes. Celia didn't care. She couldn't. She didn't have time for weakness in her life. She needed strength to fight this thing.

"Then leave."

"Celia, I—"

"Just go, Brad. I need strong people around me. People who believe I'm going to beat this." She closed the distance between them, her voice more like a drill sergeant as the words rushed out in a staccato rhythm. "Make no bones about it. I *am* going to beat this."

She gulped air in ragged breaths and Brad took full advantage of the pause, pulling her into his chest. "I'm not leaving."

"Then what the hell is this about?" Celia shoved away, coming to stand in front of the bathroom mirror. "In case you haven't noticed, there's a lot going on in my life. And your mixed messages sure as hell aren't making it any easier!"

"I know. You deserve a lot better than what you are getting. Which is why—" He moved behind her and wrapped his arms around her, but she stiffened, so he let them drop.

"Which is why we are talking about it now. I don't want to leave. And I'm not planning to. I want to help you fight the fight." He paused and turned her toward him.

"But you're not sure if you can hack the whole thing. Is that what you're trying to tell me?"

"Yes."

Celia sank down onto the only seat in the bathroom and tried to figure out what it was like to watch someone waste away like Brad had his mother. It was different from being the one who was sick. She thought of her dad. He'd probably been in pain for a long time before he finally called the doctor. By the time they diagnosed the cancer, he was in the hospital and only made it another couple of days. It was a blessing of sorts, at least for her and her mother. She tried to envision him wasting away over a period of years. How hard would it be to watch?

Horribly hard. She recognized the truth.

She studied Brad's face. Anguish pulled his mouth tight and etched deep lines in his forehead. He was being honest with her. And it was a tough concession for him to make, staying.

She'd asked for honesty from her doctor. Celia appreciated honesty, and Brad's went a long way toward closing the wound in her heart. She got up and crossed the short distance between them. "I understand. And appreciate what it took for you to have this conversation with me." She sighed and laid her head on his chest. "I guess, well, I get so wrapped up in my own issues, I forget how hard this is on the people around me."

She reached up to cup his face in her hands. "Especially, the ones I love the most."

His hands covered hers. "I do love you."

"And I love you." Celia smiled. "So I guess we take it one day at a time, eh?"

"Yes."

"I'm going to ask a favor of you, though."

"Anything."

"When you reach that point...when you can't handle it anymore, don't close yourself off. I don't think I could bear that again. Talk to me."

He kissed both her hands and held them to his chest. "That's an agreement I think I can keep."

"Good. Now if you'll get out of here, I think I can

finally freshen up and go lay down."

Brad dropped a quick kiss on her forehead. "I'll wait in the bedroom."

When Celia joined him, he was shoeless and in slacks and crumpled white shirt. He sat back against the pillows with his laptop open. When he saw her, he patted the bed beside him.

"Come on, princess. Time for a nap."

She curled up under the covers and felt the additional warmth. Brad had turned the electric blanket on, a Christmas gift that she very much appreciated. She snuggled in next to him.

"Will you sleep if I work here or should I go downstairs?"

"Here is fine," she said. "In fact, here is perfect."

As he tapped away on his laptop, Celia's thoughts drifted to Nicci and her heart ached when she realized that her daughter was going through with her what Brad had endured with his mother. Nicci had slipped back into the role of little mother. Brad cooked and did what he could. Nicci's father also helped. Or rather, his girlfriend did. Kate and Dan had moved in together. Nicci seemed happy with the situation. Celia had only met Kate once, but she regularly sent dinners home with Nicci to save Celia from having to cook.

Still, Nicci had taken on the role of self-appointed gopher. Water, medicine, cool washcloths—whatever her mother needed. Nicci even read books to her. And there had been more nights than Celia cared to remember when Nicci had been awakened by the ravages of chemotherapy.

Brad thought he had come through his mother's ordeal unscathed, but there were still deep scars to contend with. And he'd been an adult. How could Nicci possibly survive this intact?

She curled up into a tight ball as she tried to figure out some way to make this easier for Nicci. The thought crossed her mind so quickly, it took her breath away.

She could go live with her Dad.

The reaction was just as quick. *No!*

Before the misery could fully engulf her, she heard the voice. Not Brad's. But gentle and comforting and somehow familiar.

"Nicci is strong."

Yes. She is.

"Nicci will be fine."

Will she?

"Yes. And she is where she wants to be."

I wish...I don't know what I wish.

"Then show me," the voice said.

Celia's mirror reflected a vision she had dreamed of her whole life. The white dress with simple lines, capped sleeves, and a full skirt, was exactly as she'd imagined. Her thick auburn, unveiled hair had been tamed into a relaxed and slightly more modern version of Victorian curls adorned with small pearls. Her mother's necklace and the matching two-pearl droplet earrings were the only jewelry she wore. Besides her engagement ring which Celia currently twisted as if it was worry beads.

"Where is he?" she muttered. The most important day of their lives and Daniel was late. Again. Exasperation, tinged with a sliver of fear, made her heart start to pound. She knew her Daniel. He would show up.

He *would* show up.

Behind her the door to the church library, which

doubled as a dressing room, opened. Her father, gray-haired and resplendent in his tuxedo, walked in, his hand raised to still her questions. Seeing him, Celia felt a swell of love override her worry. He'd always made things better.

"He's here." He looked like he had just tried one of her mother's failed culinary experiments. "He's changing now."

Placing a hand on her chest, Celia willed her heart to slow. "Where—"

"At the bank, finalizing paperwork for his new business."

On our wedding day? Her lips disappeared into thin lines, then puckered as she remembered the lipstick she wasn't used to. A glance in the mirror verified her teeth were color-free. It also showed flushed cheeks and a suspicious sheen to her eyes.

I will not cry. Celia took a deep breath, letting the worry go as she did. He was here. He hadn't abandoned her. She swatted at the little red-suited guy on her shoulder who'd been screaming in her ear for half an hour about Daniel's inability to maintain any sort of schedule.

Celia took another deep breath in and held it for a few seconds. Daniel was late, but he was here.

To marry her.

Recovering her emotional equilibrium, she blew out one last calming breath and shook her head. "That's my Daniel. Always marching to a tune and time clock that no one else can hear or see."

Her father settled a hand on her shoulder. "Are you sure you want this? You two have had issues with this type of thing before. It's not too late to walk away."

"Dad!" Celia laughed.

"It was worth a try," he said with a shrug.

Celia placed a hand over his and looked directly at him. "I love him, Dad. I think I've loved him my entire life."

He smiled and patted her cheek lightly. "Ah, Ceelie. How did you manage to grow up so fast?" His eyes misted as he took her hand and twirled her in a dance spin. "Somehow, without my notice, you turned into a beautiful young woman."

Celia blinked quickly and started to fan herself, a smile working valiantly to stop the tears from spilling over. "Don't make me cry, Daddy. I've made it all the way through until now."

Jen popped her head around the door. "We're ready."

Those two words sent little shards of panic straight through Celia and she leaned on her father for momentary support.

He looked at her. "Are you sure you're all right?"

Am I okay? Months spent making sure every detail was perfect, from the bridesmaid's gifts to the lavender entwined hearts adorning her cake. Last minute fires dealt with, like finding someone to light the candles.

How could she ever have forgotten to do that?

Three days of final frenzied preparation and whirlwind parties. And very little sleep.

Am I okay?

"We can slip out the back way—"

"No, Dad." Celia straightened. "I won't back out. I love Danny and I know we're destined to spend our lives together." She reached for her bridal bouquet. "My only worry is that something will go wrong. I want this day to be perfect."

"It already is." He touched her cheek, then held out

his hand. "Shall we?"

As the music began, they watched the flower girls start down the aisle, followed by the bridesmaids.

Celia kept shifting her weight from foot to foot as each attendant walked at what seemed like the pace of a turtle.

Then Jen was there and Celia beamed. Her best friend and maid of honor. Jen squeezed Celia's hand and grinned as she started out.

Finally, it was Celia's turn. Moving into position, she took a long moment to sear a picture in her mind of what all their hard work looked like. The lavender tulle that looped its way down the aisle, held up by flowers on each pew. The candles that all cast a warm glow on the small vestibule. And there, at the front, brushing his unruly hair back with one hand and looking elegant in his black tuxedo, was Danny.

Her soul mate.

Her love.

Her life.

Celia realized at that moment that nothing else mattered. Keeping her eyes on the man who had stolen her heart that day at the mall so many years ago, she moved, taking her first step forward into her new life.

She awoke alone in her bedroom, feeling as if hours had passed. By her clock she'd only slept for about an hour. She felt better somehow. Refreshed.

The she remembered the dream. Her wedding day. Seeing her father!

"You are beautiful, Ceelie."

The words echoed through Celia's mind as she curled into a tight ball at the memory. It had been so long.

"Ah, Daddy. I miss you so much."

And she remembered how happy she had been. Life with Danny, while no picnic, held most of her best memories. He was an easy man to love. And, except for the money issues and the occasional scheduling snafu, an easy man to live with.

Now, everything was harder. The pile of unpaid bills grew daily. She'd given her boss notice, although it was more a formality than anything. She had little or no income and had all but exhausted her trust fund.

Celia looked around at the bedroom she had decorated so carefully only a couple of years ago. All light earthy colors, simple lines, and natural woods. She loved this room, but it was time to re-evaluate what was important. She punched her pillow. It was time to dig deep for some more of that determination. This was going to hurt.

"Hi, sleepyhead," Brad said. He sat down on the bed and kissed her. His kisses always made her world a sunnier place to live in, even in the darkest winter.

Celia smiled. "I've been thinking..."

"Uh oh. That usually means trouble."

He ran his fingers along her back, massaging muscles sore from throwing up and making it very hard for Celia to concentrate. "Ha ha," she said, then took a long moment to let the pampered sensation pour over her. "Seriously, I think Nicci and I need to move in with Mom."

Brad's hand stilled. "Wow. That's a left field maneuver. What brought that on?"

"It's hard to pay the bills when there's no money coming in."

"I knew you were struggling, but did not realize it was getting that bad."

Celia hung her head. She'd been as guilty of keeping her struggles from him as he was in keeping his from her. "I'm sorry. I should have told you. I just thought I'd figure something out."

"Let me—"

"No."

"But I have some money."

Celia sat up. "And I'm not going to borrow something I may or may not be able to repay."

"You don't—"

"I'm not a charity case, Brad. That's not what our relationship is all about."

He was quiet for a long time, running his hand up and down her arm as if he didn't notice.

When Celia made a move to get up, he stopped. "Move in with me, then."

She sat back down, floored. "Brad—"

"I'm serious," he smiled. "You and Nicci can come live with me. Okay, and that mangy mutt of hers, too."

Celia looked at Brad's face. His eyes had a haunted, what-am-I-doing look that contradicted the dazzling smile.

"Moving in with you is not a good idea," she said.

"It's a sound decision."

"Maybe financially, but not in any other way."

"We can make it work."

"No, Brad." Celia covered his hand with hers. "I love you too much to do that to you." She paused. "When you need to leave, I want you to be able to do it without complications."

He ran his free hand back and forth across hers several times before he spoke. "I'm not saying it won't be difficult."

"Then why make it any harder than it has to be?

Moving in with Mom makes more sense."

"I don't know what to do," he said. "I want to whisk you away to my place. But there's a small part of me, and it is small, that feels...relief."

Celia smiled. "It's okay. See. My choice is right."

"Maybe," Brad said. "But it still doesn't *feel* right." He looked at the bedside clock and rose from the bed. "I'd better get some dinner going."

"One more favor, Brad?"

He leaned down and kissed her. "What's that?"

"Will you still cook for us, at least occasionally, after we move home?"

He laughed. "Now that might have to be at my place. I can't see your mom letting me have free reign in her kitchen."

Celia laughed, too. "Yeah, I guess you're right about that."

After Brad headed downstairs, Celia reached for the phone and dialed. "Mom?"

"Hi, honey. I was just thinking about you," her mother said with a voice filled with comforting sunshine.

"You're always thinking about me," Celia chuckled.

"Of course. You're my daughter."

"Mom, back when I was starting chemo for the first go around, you asked me if I wanted to move back home."

"I thought it would be best for you and Nicci, yes."

"Is that offer still on the table?"

"Of course it is. I would love nothing better than to have my two favorite girls under my roof again."

"And a dog?" Celia couldn't ask Nicci to give up Latte. He'd been her solace night after night.

"Of course."

Celia took a deep breath, pushed regret to the back of her mind, and plunged ahead. "Then, if you're sure, I'd like to take you up on it."

"Ah, honey. You've made my day. My entire year, too, I think."

"You see, it's just too hard right now. I can't work, so I can't pay my bills."

"You don't have to give me reasons."

"Yes, Mom. I do. It's also Nicci. She's dealing with too much, even with Brad's help. I need her to be reassured that, when I'm at my worst, she's not the only one looking after me. I-I'd like her to have a childhood."

"Our little girl is having a childhood."

"Not enough of one."

"Then come on home. We'll settle you two and make sure she has some fun. You can have the extra bedroom and we'll put Nicci in the little sewing room."

"No. I'll take the sewing room."

"But you need more space."

Celia's eyes wandered slowly around her roomy haven, then shut her eyes. "No, I don't. I'd rather Nicci had the room to grow."

"Well, all right. If you think that's the right way to go."

"I do. Mom?"

"What, dear?"

"I-I don't know for how long this will be."

"You can stay for as long as you want to or need to. This is your home."

The damn tears started to well up all over again. Sniffing them back, Celia tried to sound happy. "T-thanks, Mom. I don't know what I would do without you."

"Oh, you'd be just fine. You're a survivor. Always were. Always will be."

"Yes." Celia sat up in her bed. "I am."

After finalizing the details, Celia hung up the phone and took a moment to let the weight of a thousand worries slide off her shoulders. She ran her hands over the coverlet she'd saved six months for. *At least,* she thought, *you can come with me.* Most of her furniture would have to go into storage.

She'd managed to lose her house, but had also reforged a relationship with her boyfriend all in the same day. Talk about a roller coaster ride.

Celia sniffed the air. Mmm. Tacos. Her and Nicci's favorite! Maybe she could dredge up a bit of an appetite. She stood up and waited to get her balance back, then headed down to the kitchen.

14

THE CALM BEFORE THE STORM

Mother Nature graced them with an unusually warm March day for moving and just about everyone they'd put the call out to showed up. Celia had enough helpers to move the Library of Congress. It was a good thing, too. She was amazed at how much she had accumulated.

Her best friend, Jen, came up behind her and enveloped her in a big hug. As big a hug as she could, anyhow, being about due to have baby number three. Celia turned and placed her hand on Jen's stomach.

"How are you feeling?"

"My back hurts." Jen laughed. "And I'm basically useless. No one will let me do *anything*."

"Good. We can be useless together." Celia looked at the rooms that were emptying out much faster than she had filled them. She walked over and ran her hand along a bookcase. She'd scrounged for most of her furniture. This had come from college row the evening of graduation. Seems all the departing seniors put anything they didn't want outside for the general public to pick through. Her office chair had come from the same place.

The only piece of new furniture in the entire house was Nicci's bed. A four poster with an eyelet lace canopy. The one splurge she'd allowed herself when they moved in here. And the reason she'd been so adamant about Nicci having the bigger bedroom. She could sleep on anything. But her daughter loved, and deserved, this bed.

She turned as Keith, Jen's husband, came down carrying part of it.

"This goes—"

"—in Nicci's bedroom at Mom's," Celia said.

A steady stream of parts came down the stairs, followed by mattresses, box springs, and dressers. Celia had labeled everything she possibly could as to what went to her mother's and what went to storage. There just wasn't enough room for everything.

She was even selling her car. Or rather, Brad was selling it for her. She would drive her father's for now. She thought of the little red sportster and smiled. At least that wouldn't be a hardship.

Armload by armload, Celia watched her belongings get loaded onto trucks. Jen had been here each day for hours helping her and Nicci pack up things. Finally, the trucks were all loaded and they headed out in separate directions, Mack driving the one headed to her mom's and Brad taking the other one to storage. Celia followed Brad, needing to be at the storage facility. She prayed she'd labeled things well enough for the unloaders at her mother's house.

After cramming everything into a small storage unit, everyone headed to Patricia's to help there. Nicci was already there. Celia drove back to the old house to grab a jacket she'd left. It was an excuse, but it worked. She wanted a moment to herself. Brad seemed to understand and said he'd get over to her mother's and make sure Nicci wasn't ordering the movers around too badly. Celia smiled at the thought.

"Oh, hi, Celia." The realtor stood in the front yard. "How are you doing?"

"Hi, Debby. I'm fine." She looked at the house critically, as if she were a prospective buyer. The paint was only two years old and the well-manicured flowerbeds showed her tender care. It was a cute little house. And the only one she'd ever bought on her own.

She would miss it.

Debby patted her arm. "I don't think we'll have any trouble getting your asking price for this little gem. It's obvious you took good care of the place. It will be the perfect starter house for some newly married couple."

Celia smiled. "I like that idea."

"Good." Debby pounded the For Sale sign into the yard and turned to go. "I'll let you know as soon as I get a bite."

"Thanks." Celia let herself in and quickly found her jacket. She took a final walk around the place. Her mother and Mack's moving gift, besides feeding the whole brood of helpers, was a cleaning service. They would be in tomorrow to prep the house for sale.

A twinge of sorrow threaded its way through Celia as she locked the door behind her. She walked to her car and turned for one last look, then headed for her mother's house.

When she arrived, her friends had not only unloaded the truck, they had all the furniture in place where she wanted it. Thank goodness for post-it notes. Nicci's bed was together and Jen was helping her dig out sheets and bedding from a large box. Celia peeked into her new room and found her bed set up, complete with sheets, comforter, and pillows. The room had been pink, her mother's favorite color. They'd painted it last week at her mother's insistence so everything would match Celia's own choices.

It looked good. Different, but good.

"Mo-o-m-m!" Nicci hollered.

She walked back into Nicci's room and laughed. All she could see of her daughter were two legs sticking out of the box.

Tickling the back of one of the captive knees, Celia asked what was up.

"I can't find the top sheet."

"That's because you spilled milk on it. This morning. Remember?"

Nicci pulled herself back out of the box. "Oh, yeah."

"It's in a bag I have downstairs to wash."

Your mom already found it, I think," Jen answered. "I bet your sheet is about done. Want to go see?"

"Yeah!" Nicci bounded off.

Jen laced arms with Celia and walked back to her bedroom.

"It's a bit small in here, isn't it?"

The queen-size bed took up most of the room. A dresser with a television on top took up the rest. She could open and access the closet and had a small table next to her bed. And a...hall tree? Celia inspected it closer. Additional hooks had been added and all of her scarves and hats were settled in. And, on the top, the one wig she owned sat like the star on top of a Christmas tree.

"Your mom found it at a garage sale and thought it would be a nice touch," Jen said.

Tugging her scarf du jour down a bit further, Celia

tried to act flip, but the reality of the situation was beginning to hit her. "It's nice. I know she had my interests at heart."

"Yep. That's your mom. Always thinking of others." Jen cradled Celia's shoulder. "It'll be all right, my friend. You'll make it work. I know you will."

"Yeah. I will, won't I?" Celia straightened her shoulders.

"Now," Jen said. "Let's go see what the cooks have cooked up for us. It smells awesome."

The cooks had indeed prepared a feast in honor of the movers. It felt like they were in the kitchen of a noisy family restaurant. Jen's in-laws, who owned an Italian place, dropped by with a huge pot of their award-winning spaghetti sauce. The smell of garlic permeated the room as Patricia's homemade bread was slathered with seasoned butter, then broiled to perfection.

A salad kept things marginally healthy and, of course, the Chianti was there for the anti-oxidants.

The hungry crew all dug in without breaking stride in the myriad of discussions being held. Celia ate a little and sipped at a glass of the contraband wine, more interested in enjoying the moment.

Everyone was there. Everyone had come to help when the call went out. It was humbling. Brad, Jenn and her family, even her old boss, Tom, and Tana, along with her husband, had come over to help with the move. Danny and Kate, too. Celia had made a point of inviting them for the dinner portion because they'd both been so helpful. They'd turned up for the work portion of the day, too.

Nicci's eyes sparkled with happiness as she bounced around the table. Under the watchful eye of Grandma, she'd spent the day babysitting Jen's two little boys and had earned her first significant money—a whole forty dollars. Celia watched as she pulled the money out of her jeans pocket for about the tenth time and counted it again.

Oh, yeah. The girl is hooked. Celia made a mental note to enroll her in babysitting class, even though she wasn't old enough yet. Her Babydoll was growing up fast.

She looked around the table at her friends and felt humbled at all they had done to help her. It would have taken her weeks to do what they did in hours. She tapped her glass lightly with a spoon to get their attention.

"I don't know how to tell you all how grateful I am for your help today with Nicci's and my move." She started to get choked up and Brad covered her hand. Nicci stepped behind her mother and put her arms around Celia's neck.

"We couldn't have done it without you," her daughter finished.

Murmured "no-problem's" and "hey, we had nothing to do today anyway" noises made the rounds of the table.

"It's...it's been a long road for us already and there's more to go. But friends and family like you make it much easier to tolerate." Celia raised her glass to them. "It's not enough, but I thank you from the bottom of my heart."

"Here, here!" they cheered as they raised their glasses.

Her mother called for Nicci then and they disappeared briefly into the pantry and returned with two pies each, all different and all homemade.

"Anybody for some pie?"

Jen's husband groaned, grabbing his stomach with one hand and a fork with the other. "Well, if you insist," he said with a sly smile on his face.

"I'll get the ice cream," Jen said getting up. She returned from the pantry with a face filled with mischievousness. "Hey, Ceelie, remember the time when we were teenagers and we stayed up late studying for that biology test?"

Celia shook her head vehemently, trying to clue Jen in. "No. I. Do. Not. Remember."

"Sure you do. After your folks went to bed, we got into your mom's Harvey Wallbanger mix. You've *got* to remember that!"

Celia groaned and glanced askance at her mom. "I never told mom," she said below her breath. "Thanks a lot, friend."

"No problem at all." Jen answered with a grin.

"You only had one drink each. Besides, you were seventeen. I'd rather you experimented with that at home than at some wild party."

Both Celia and Jen stared with mouths agape at her mother, who settled at the table next to Mack.

"You knew?" Celia asked.

"Of course, I knew," Patricia said, continuing to serve up pie. "We parents are not as dumb as teenagers think, you know."

With that, the entire table broke out in tear-making laughter and it was a long moment before anyone realized that Jen had stopped laughing and was clutching her belly.

Keith was the first to see the signs. "Now?" he said calmly.

"I think," Jen answered, "baby number three wants

to join the party. My water just broke."

A flurry of activity started then as everyone tried to help at once. Soon seated back at the table, Jen spoke calmly with the hospital.

"I guess," she said as she hung up, "it's time to go. They are worried that things will progress quickly since this is our third child." She grimaced. "They may be right. That back pain I was having seems to be coming in stronger waves now. Geesh, you'd think I'd know labor by now."

As her husband helped her up from the chair, Jen turned to Celia. "Come with us."

"Oh, no. This is your time," Celia balked.

"You're my best friend." Jen saw the mock expression of hurt on Keith's face. "You're my husband," she said to him. "It's different." Turning back to Jen. "Come on. Keith's a gem, but he's no good in the pain department. Help me—" she grimaced again, "bring this baby into the world."

Celia looked at her mom.

"Go," Patricia said. "We've got Nicci."

"And I'll clean up the kitchen," Brad chimed in, kissing her cheek. "Go."

"All right," Celia gave in. "You go on ahead," she told Keith. "I'll meet you there."

Several long hours and a few happy tears later, Jen and Keith welcomed their little baby girl into the world. Celia kept her hand on Jen's shoulder as they placed the baby on her belly. "She's beautiful."

"I agree completely," Keith said from the other side of the bed.

"We finally have our little girl," Jen said. She and Keith exchanged glances and he nodded.

"Go ahead. Tell her," he said.

"Tell me what?"

"The name we've chosen. With your permission, we'd like to name her Elizabeth Celia."

Celia eyes misted over and she touched little Elizabeth's tiny hand, totally smitten when her fingers curled around Celia's. "I-I would be honored."

In the wee hours of the morning, Celia drove home, weak, tired, and happier than she had been in some time. Her body was calm, but her mind was going one hundred miles an hour, replaying the events of the past twenty four hours.

She crawled into bed with a satisfied grin on her face and gave herself up to the world of dreams.

Show me.

"What do you mean, I can't?" Dan sounded like an off-key soprano as he shrilled the question.

Celia rubbed a hand across her brow. "You can't pour our savings into another one of your business ideas, Dan. That's our house money. You've been promising me we would start looking."

With a retort obviously fighting for release, Dan paused. He sat down next to Celia and placed his hands over her crossed ones on the table. "Ceelie, honey, you have to understand. This is a once-in-a-lifetime opportunity. All I need is a little stake money and we'll be off and running. Then we can afford the house of our dreams. We won't have to settle for some second-hand shack."

"How would you know what we have to settle for? You won't even go looking at houses with me."

"Honey, baby. I've been busy. After all, we have to be able to pay the bills."

"Something we are barely managing with my job at

the restaurant," she retorted. "Your *businesses* haven't paid one damn bill since we got married."

Dan rubbed the back of his neck. "I've tried to explain this to you, Celia. It takes time and money to get a business off the ground—"

"The problem, Daniel, is that you keep switching businesses. If you'd just stick to one—"

"I'm trying to do the best I can to provide for our family."

Celia stood like her chair was on fire and paced the kitchen.

"That's another thing. We were going to start a family shortly after getting married. It's been four years now."

Dan moved to her and enfolded her in one of his "everything's-going-to-be-all-right hugs. "We will, honey. We will. I just need a little more time to get settled with this new business."

"You don't have any more time."

He pulled away. "W-what?"

"I said time's up."

"What do you—are you pregnant?"

Celia placed a hand over her stomach and smiled. "Yes."

Dan started to pace and with each step Celia's heart broke just a little bit further.

"How did it happen?" he asked, his voice shaking.

"How do you think babies happen, Daniel?"

"I know that part. I mean, aren't you on the pill?"

Was there a hint of suspicion in his voice? Celia couldn't tell, but his response so far was less than desired. "Yes. The doctor switched me to another type of contraceptive pill. I never missed a day taking them, but it happened anyway." Celia reached out and touched his arm. "This baby wants to be born."

"Yes, but—"

"But what?" she said in the same voice her mother used when she expected no further argument.

Dan sat down, looking like he'd just been tossed into the Roman arena with two hungry lions. If Celia weren't so hurt, she'd laugh.

She watched him for a moment. He was the sweetest, gentlest husband and lover. At times, she had difficulty equating him with the inept businessman who seemed bent on running their finances into the ground. She knew him. Fear of failure drove him. That's why he kept switching business ventures. Quit before you fail. That seemed to be his motto.

She sat down and covered his hands with her own. "Daniel, this is a happy thing."

"But a baby. I don't know what to do with a baby."

"You'll learn."

"I suppose so."

"However," Celia looked around at their small apartment. "We can't raise a baby here. There isn't enough room."

He stared blankly around.

"We need to buy a house now. Not down the road sometime."

"Yeah. I guess maybe we do," he admitted.

"Good, because there's a house I'd like you to see."

The suspicion stole back into his eyes. "Are you setting me up?"

Celia laughed. "No."

He was starting to get angry. "You get pregnant without my knowledge. You find a house to buy without my knowing. What would you call it?"

"First of all, you were there when this baby was

made, so don't tell me I did that by myself. Second, I've been asking you for weeks to go look at houses. You were always too busy. This one couldn't wait. It's a great price but they need to move this month. So *we* have to act quickly. Which is why you can't tap the savings. It's enough for a down payment and any renovating we'll need to do. You know—" She punched him in the arm. "For the baby's room."

"Yeah," Daniel said with a weak smile. "For the baby's room."

Celia woke in the morning and smiled in spite of the remembered argument. Daniel had always been so scared about doing anything permanent. It had taken her a long time to convince him they could spend a lifetime together. He loved her. He just couldn't think that far ahead.

Still—Celia's smile disappeared. That argument had been the beginning of the end for them.

15

FAILURE APPARENTLY *IS* AN OPTION

"I'm sorry, Celia. The cancer cells seem to be resistant to chemotherapy. The remaining tumors decreased some at the beginning, but now...well, you've seen your cancer markers. They are climbing. And this—" Janice Mason pointed to the CT scan pictures, "is definitive growth."

Growth.

The word echoed through Celia's mind like an electrical charge frying all her circuits.

Growth.

She tried to take a breath, but found her lungs frozen, unable to expand.

Her cancer was growing.

She placed a fist over her chest and tapped until air infiltrated and she could expel it. Once. Twice. A third long breath.

She knew she'd started to shiver, but it was as if she were watching from the outside. She clutched her arms. "I-I c-can't seem to s-stop shaking."

Janice Mason wrapped her in a warm blanket and held her, rubbing her arms, speaking soothing words

Celia's brain couldn't translate. But the mellow tone of Dr. Mason's voice finally got through and Celia began to calm.

After several more long moments, Celia pulled back and reached for a tissue, then asked the question that had been flashing like a neon sign in her mind. "Is that it, then? There's nothing else we can do?"

"I wouldn't say that. There's a promising research program here at Fred Hutch. I think I mentioned it before."

"I remember."

"I've taken the liberty of contacting them on your behalf. I've got a packet of information here for you to take home and read through tonight. I'd like to have you back in here tomorrow to discuss it further."

"That quickly?"

"I don't think we should waste any time. If you choose to try this, the sooner the better."

"Are there any other options out there?"

"A few. But none that I would recommend."

"Why not?"

"There are a lot of reasons to recommend a program. There's really only one reason not to. If there are no studies to back up at least the possibility of the trial working, it's not worth putting you through all the testing and everything. So I don't like to steer my patients in those directions."

"I can understand that. Um, Janice?"

"Yes."

"What—" Celia's voice choked. She tried again, but it came out more as a whisper. "What will happen if I do nothing?"

Janice Mason reached for Celia's hands. "Things can happen slowly or quickly. It's hard to tell for sure. But you will begin to feel more effects from the cancer. Primarily pain, which we have gotten pretty good at controlling these days."

"I'll get weaker, too, right?"

"Yes. And...if you don't have your affairs in order, this would be the time to do it. As this disease progresses, the combination of the toxins in your body and the medication to control your pain will cause confusion, which will worsen."

Celia thought of her mother and daughter, sitting out in the waiting room, anxious but unknowing. Some sixth sense had told Celia to be by herself for today's news.

"How do I tell Nicci this? She's not old enough to understand."

"I've seen your daughter deal with some significant changes in her life and yours. She's handled each one with a maturity unusual for someone her age. I think you need to trust her. Tell her when you feel it's right. It won't be easy for her. But she can handle it. Plus, from everything you tell me, she seems to have a lot of support in your mother and your friends."

Hope turned the corners of Celia's mouth up. "That she does."

"Good. Let me get the nurse to find you a slot of time tomorrow when we can talk. I've given you three packets. I suggest you give one to your mother and also have Ted read one over. It might help you make a decision.

A little while later, when Celia walked out to the waiting room, her mother looked up from the book she and Nicci were reading. Patricia's face filled with worry lines for a brief moment, then she shook her head in a we'll-talk-later way and told Nicci it was time to go. As they walked toward the door, her mother stumbled and barely caught herself before falling. "Silly me," she joked. "I must have tripped over my own feet." But the strain in her voice belied the lightness of her comment.

Later that day, while Celia lay in a hammock in the small backyard with Latte settled beside her, her mother tended to her prize-winning rose bushes, getting them ready for the blooming season. This is how her mother coped when life handed her lemons. She made beautiful flowers. It soothed Celia to watch her snipping a blighted leaf here, removing a petal there. Nicci had gone to her friend's house to play for the afternoon, giving the two of them time to go over options. Sadly, that hadn't taken long. So now, relaxing was the best thing she could do for herself.

Celia felt the gentle touch on her cheek. It felt like a caress. Fleeting, but powerful. She closed her eyes as she heard the words she'd come to know in her darkest hours.

Show me.

"Push, Celia. One more. You can do it."

Celia felt like she'd just pulled a twenty-four hour stint at the restaurant carrying a twenty pound steak with spikes in it. Covered in sweat, her hands were all but slipping out of the death grip she had on Dan as the contractions kept coming one right after another. And the doctor wanted one more push?

Fine.

Grunt.

She'd give him...

Grunt.

One...more...damn...push.

"Argggggghhhhhhhhhhhhhhhh!"

Just like that, the hardest work was over and they were placing her tiny baby girl in Celia's arms.

"Nicole," Celia whispered.

Her wet hair was dark and her red, chubby cheeks made her look like a little cherub, even with nothing but a quick wipe to clean her. Celia touched her little fingers and they latched on to hers. Her heart broke wide open and mended itself with threads swathed with love. She had never seen anything more beautiful than this little girl. She looked up at Daniel, whose arm lay over her pillow to get a closer look. Shed tears were proof the happiness in his expression was real.

"She's beautiful, isn't she?" Celia whispered.

He gulped. "Yeah."

"Do you want to hold her?"

Daniel nodded. "Yeah."

Pressure being applied to her stomach got her immediate attention. "Ouch!"

"I'm sorry, Celia. We need to get the bleeding to stop."

Celia handed Nicci to Daniel. He picked her up like a precious piece of porcelain and froze as if afraid to move. With a tired but contented smile, Celia watched the awe on his face. Everything was going to be fine. He loved their little Nicci as much as she did.

"Celia," her doctor said, "you're bleeding heavier than we'd like and we need to get it under control. We're going to have to do a D&C."

"Now?" Celia turned her gaze from their new baby to the doctor.

"Now."

Hating to be separated from this new joy for even a short time, she couldn't take her eyes off baby Nicole.

Daniel looked up as they wheeled Celia away, panicked surprise on his face. He started toward her.

"I'm all right," she said. "You take care of Nicci, okay?"

He stopped at the door as she was moved down the hall.

"Stay with Nicci," Celia said. She watched her family until her gurney rounded a corner and she couldn't see them anymore. The word—*family*—warmed her even as they gave her anesthesia and the world went fuzzy.

Everything still seemed fuzzy when Celia opened her eyes. It took several blinks for her sight to clear. She felt...groggy. Like she'd been asleep for hours. Last she remembered, the nurse had wheeled her into an operating room and they'd given her anesthesia.

She ran her tongue over teeth that needed a good brushing. How long had she been out? Her hand felt heavy and she looked to see Daniel with a double-handed lock on it, his head resting atop their hands as he slept.

Celia wiggled her fingers and he shot up.

"Ceelie. Oh, Ceelie. You're awake!"

"Um, yes. How long—"

"I've been so worried about you. You've been asleep for so long."

"Where's Nicole?" she asked.

But Daniel went on as if he hadn't heard. "The doctor said you'd wake up. I wasn't sure I believed her."

"Where's the baby?" Celia said with more force.

Daniel was really rolling up to a full case of hysteria. "They had to do more than they thought to get the bleeding stopped. You lost a lot of blood. Oh, God! I thought I was going to lose you." He hung his head until it touched their entwined hands.

Celia pried her hand loose and pulled his face up by the chin. "Daniel. Where. Is. Our. Daughter?"

"Nicci's right here." He moved so Celia could see the bassinet beside the bed. "They had to feed her formula since you've been out for so long. I fed her," he puffed. "She took to the bottle like a champ."

Lifting up to get a look inside the crib, Celia felt a wave of dizziness hit her.

A gentle hand on her shoulder guided her to relax. Her mother smiled at her. "It's good to see you awake, sweetheart. Don't worry. My granddaughter," she looked up at Daniel, "and your husband are doing just fine."

Daniel had once again secured her hand in his and she saw the intense worry in his face.

"What happened? Do I... Am I..." Celia couldn't voice her worst fears—that something serious had happened and they'd taken her uterus. She wanted her daughter to have siblings...to not be an only child like she'd been.

She felt her stomach. No tell-tale bulges or bandages. *Thank goodness.*

"They couldn't get the bleeding stopped after Nicole was delivered, so they had to take you to the O.R.," her mother said. "But don't worry. They got things under control." Patricia placed her own hand over Celia's, still resting on her stomach. "You can still have children."

"Oh, thank you," Celia said, relief flooding her. "I was afraid..."

" I know," Patricia said. "You can let that go now, though. You've got a daughter to enjoy."

Nicci made little waking sounds in her bassinet. Her

mother picked the baby up and handed her to Celia. She watched in wonder as this new little life started automatically rooting for food. The baby latched on to Celia as if she'd never been given a bottle and a thrill shot through Celia along with the initial shock of learning to breast feed. She felt all the pain and concern melt away as love suffused her whole body.

Right there and then, as she held little Nicole Elizabeth Wallman, the world was in perfect order. Nothing else mattered. Nothing at all.

Celia knew she was still in her mother's back yard. She could hear the clippers as her mother worked in the flower beds. But she didn't open her eyes. She wasn't ready. She wanted to remain in the past. To feel again the euphoria of seeing Nicole for the first time. To have her latch on to a breast with a trust that filled Celia with love and emotion.

She wanted to see her baby smile for the first time— again. To see her take those first hesitant steps. Watch again as she learned to run. Then to ride. And finally, to grow into the wonderful child she'd become.

Would she see Nicci's eleventh birthday? The question came out of nowhere and hit Celia like a lightning bolt. She was not going to see her daughter grow up. Celia curled into herself and the finality of that knowledge made her shake, as if the late afternoon sun had disappeared behind a cloud.

Even with an experimental program, it was likely she would not survive much longer. And there were things she needed to accomplish. Decisions to make. Celia needed to think about what she wanted to do with the time she had left.

Just in case.

Resolved, she got up and joined her mother in the rose garden. The fragrance of the spring roses surrounded her. This was a scent she'd grown up with and one that could always relax her. As a child, she'd hidden in her mother's rose garden on multiple occasions. Sometimes because she'd done something she shouldn't have. Other times she'd needed consoling. Her mother had always found her here, always encouraged her, as they sat amongst the roses, to be honest and forthright. These roses were the smell of home.

"Did you get enough rest, honey?"

"Enough for now. Mom?"

"Hmmm?" Patricia clipped a Double Delight Tea Rose, Celia's personal favorite, and handed it to her.

Celia took a long sniff and admired the yellow and rose colors in the flower. "Have you and Mack talked about when you plan to get married?"

Sliding her clippers into the pruning apron she wore, Patricia turned to Celia. "We would prefer it to be soon, but haven't talked about specific dates. Why?"

"I'm fighting this thing, Mom. I really am. But...I'm not sure how long I'll feel this good. Things might get worse, you know?"

She saw the struggle in her mother's face. Saw denial fighting the tears that filled her eyes, but wouldn't fall. Saw the slight shake of her head, the eventual acceptance that nothing she said could change the reality. Celia hugged her mother. Tight. And felt those unshed tears dampen her shoulder. Knew that her own tears fell unchecked, too.

Long moments passed before Patricia straightened. "I know you're right. I haven't wanted to think about it. I don't want to imagine your health declining any more...or worse. But..." She sighed, long and deep. "I guess we need to."

Celia nodded. "Which is why I was wondering if maybe you'd consider tying the knot while I'm feeling pretty good. You know, in between chemo treatments and before...well, soon anyhow. I know it's selfish, but I'd like to feel good and help you celebrate."

Patricia's smile wasn't forced. She took Celia's arm and moved them toward the house. "I think that's a lovely idea. In fact, I'm going to call Mack and ask him right now." She paused and turned Celia to face her. "One more thing. I'd like you and Nicci both to stand up for me. Would that be all right?"

"Oh, Mom, that would be more than all right. It would be awesome. And Nicci, I'm sure, will say the exact same thing."

"Good. Then let's go call Mack. And we'll ask Nicci as soon as she gets home from school."

16

CELEBRATIONS AND DECISIONS

Two weeks later, timed to fall in between Celia's chemotherapy treatments when she felt her best, the small group waited in the vestibule of the little church that Patricia had attended for over forty years. Happiness floated everywhere, from Mack's wide grin to Nicci's barely contained enthusiasm for the wedding. Patricia smoothed the simple ivory dress, wondering again why she'd bought it for this one occasion. Neither she nor Mack had wanted any fuss. The important thing was being together. She glanced at Celia, who sat with a smile on her face as she watched Nicci bouncing around, and Patricia knew exactly why she'd purchased the dress. Because Celia and Nicci had been excited to make this fuss over her.

Shopping that day had worn Celia out, but the look on her face when Patricia had walked out in this dress...well, Patricia would hold that expression in her heart for a long time to come.

Celia sat resting with Brad while they waited. The chemo took such a toll on Celia's body, Patricia didn't know how she stood it. Her own heart was breaking over what her daughter had gone through...would go through. It wasn't fair. It shouldn't be Celia. It should be her. Yes, they were still fighting the good fight, but with each successive treatment, Celia got weaker, sicker. And Patricia could do nothing to stop it. Nothing at all, except pray and be strong. Or try to.

It wasn't easy. Especially on a day like today. She shouldn't be happy. She didn't have a right to be when her daughter was so sick.

"What's the frown for, pretty lady," Mack whispered in her ear, encircling her shoulders with his always comforting arm. His kiss against her temple did more to soothe Patricia than anything.

Patricia turned into his arms. "What did I ever do to be so lucky to find you?"

"I think I got luckier," he said. "You were worrying about Celia, weren't you?"

Patricia sighed. "Yes. It's so hard to see her go through this. To know how it might end."

"You know," Mack said, hugging her tight. "Things will happen as they happen. We can't change that. And Celia's strong. For now we have to be content with the fact that she's still fighting. And you," he leaned back to lift her chin so she could look him in the eyes, "are one of the strongest women I've ever met. You, too, will handle whatever you have to. I'll be here to help you. Today is for happy thoughts. I'm about to marry the woman of my dreams."

He kissed her, replacing all the worry and pain in her heart with gentle happiness.

Patricia took a deep breath, letting all the residual negativity go, at least for today. "You're right, Mack. Today is a happy day."

Perfect timing, too, since the pastor joined them at

that moment to let them know he was ready. The hastily organized wedding had happened thanks to the man's understanding and willingness to work with them. He'd squeezed this wedding in between two baptisms.

Patricia glanced at her daughter, standing next to her, a wide smile on her pale face. And Nicci, holding her own bouquet, had calmed down to watch the ceremony with rapt interest on her face.

In moments too few to count, Patricia was Mrs. Mack Thomas and the pastor was blessing their union. Mack's kiss before they left the church reminded her she wasn't an old lady yet. She still had some playing around to do.

She would love being married again. For Mack. For Celia. For herself. Patricia looked over at her daughter. Today they would celebrate everything good in this world. Tomorrow would take care of itself.

Patricia and Mack led the small procession outside. "Okay, time to eat," Mack said. "I'm starving!"

"You're always starving," she said.

"I know. That's why I married such a good cook," he answered, pulling her tight to his side for another kiss.

Everyone laughed as they headed out the door to the restaurant they'd reserved for a group dinner.

For the next two nights, she and Mack would have the house to themselves. Celia's wedding gift to them was to vacate for a while. She and Nicci would stay with Brad. Patricia had told her there was no need, but her daughter had insisted.

Mack's house was bigger, and maybe sometime down the road they'd move in there. For now, status quo was all she could handle. Mack had been happy to do whatever she wanted, so they planned to rent his house out for now and make decisions later.

Patricia looked around the restaurant table at her family, focusing most on Celia. She was so blessed to have such a wonderful daughter. Even though today was only for happiness, Patricia Thomas couldn't keep herself from sending one more plea heavenward on her daughter's behalf.

Yesterday had filled Celia with a profound happiness she hadn't felt in a very long time. She'd loved the short ceremony, loved seeing her mother so happy. It had been a good day physically, too, as if the gods gave everyone, herself included, the day off. Today, though, the real world returned with a vengeance. Exhaustion kept her on the couch at Brad's. Apparently, she'd overdone it the day before. Brad had dropped Nicci off at a friend's house on his way to the office, so it seemed the perfect time to talk to Dan about the future. She called him and he managed to get there within an hour.

"We don't have to discuss this now," Dan said with a wildness in his eyes.

Celia sighed. This wasn't going to be easy by any definition. "Yes, Daniel. We do."

"No. I was on the internet this morning and there are a lot of other options out there. Treatments that the medical community calls quack medicine, but you don't know. One of them might work."

"I've researched them, too. Medicines, both herbal and foreign, with no proof to back up their claims that they cure diseases. I'm not about to take that kind of route."

"You're quitting!"

"I'm not quitting, Daniel. I'm still in chemotherapy. Still trying to keep the cancer at bay for as long as I can. And I am under consideration for the one research program that my doctor finds promising."

"So we wait for that to come through."

"We are waiting, Daniel," Celia said. "The problem is, I don't know how long I have to wait."

"The chemotherapy—" Dan said.

"—can only do so much now." Celia cut him off. He needed to understand. "It cannot stop or reverse the growth. It only slows it down."

Daniel knelt in front of her and clasped both of her hands. "Celie, we've got to do something. We can't just give up. I won't let you give up."

Celia puckered her lips as she tried to find a way to get through to him. He loved her still. She knew that. And he was dealing with his own demons, just as she had hers. Her lips softened and she tried to smile. "Daniel, I know this is hard." She glanced away. "I just...I want everything in place in case something goes wrong. Is that so hard to understand?"

He touched her cheek. "That's my Ceelie. Always organizing everything."

She leapt on the idea. "Yes. So, please, Daniel, let me organize this. Let's talk about the possibilities so that I can stop worrying about them." She covered his hand with her own. "The only thing I can do for Nicci now is make sure she's well provided for."

"I'll take good care of her."

"I know. You always do. Have I told you lately how much I appreciate all you've done to help her through this? Not just you. Kate, too."

He waved a hand. "It's nothing. Besides, she's my daughter."

"It's not nothing. Thank you."

"You're welcome."

"Daniel, I think I know the answer to this, but I have to ask, especially since you and Kate live together. Do you want Nicci to live with you...if something happens to me?"

"Of course I do. We do. What kind of question is that?" Dan stood and started to pace. "I can't even believe you had to ask me."

"I didn't *have* to ask you. But I needed to hear you say it, so I'm glad I did. Honestly, being with you will be best for Nicci. You can always make her smile. I love that about you."

Dan clutched her hands. "Ceelie, you know I love you, don't you? I'll always love you."

"And I, you. You were my first love." She touched his cheek. "But love changes sometimes, morphs into different shades of emotion. I'm really glad we get along. It's the best thing for Nicci. And I know we both had to work pretty hard at that initially."

Dan chuckled. "Yeah, but we got past it."

"For Nicci's sake."

"And for our own." He took a deep breath. "Okay, make your plans. Organize things. Let me know how Kate and I can help."

"Thank you, Danny. I really appreciate it."

After he left, Celia sat quietly, doing some yoga breathing to center herself. The conversation with Dan hadn't gone as bad as she'd thought it would. But he was only the first person she needed to talk to. Celia reached for her phone, beyond ready to get this organization thing over with.

Celia took a deep breath of the fresh outdoor air. Interlaken Park was full of people enjoying the warmth of late May. She chose a bench in the sun as her best friend's kids ran toward the playground equipment.

"Jen?"

"Mn-hmm?" Jen's focus remained on the play equipment, where her young boys were busy finding trouble.

"I need to talk about arrangements for Nicci."

Jen's head whipped around, her mouth opening and closing in slow motion. Her eyes screamed the protest her lips would not utter. She shook her head. When she did speak, her words all came out in a rush. "I'm not ready to discuss this. We don't have to do this. Not yet. Hopefully never!"

"I need to be realistic, Jen."

"Not about this. Not about..."

The word not spoken hung out there between them. Death.

"Jen, I need to have this settled. Look at it this way. It reduces my stress if I know Nicci will be well cared for if I don't make it through this."

"Of course she will! Keith and I will take her."

"That's very sweet of you," Celia said, patting Jen's hand. "But unnecessary. Daniel has first dibs."

"Pu-lease," Jen moaned. "He's such a scatterbrain."

"He may be, but he's her father and she adores him. Plus, he's got Kate now, and she seems to make him tow the rope. Even has him doing a monthly budget with her." Celia chuckled. "I also know he will rely heavily on my mom. And she'll let him. That's where I could use your help. I need you to make sure she doesn't take on too much."

"Soo-o-o-o," Jen said with mock horror written all over her face. "Let me get this straight. You get to go play hopscotch with all the other angels on the paths of heaven and I'm stuck babysitting your ex-husband?"

Celia stared at her for one lengthy frozen moment. Then they both burst out laughing, long and heartily.

"I cannot believe you said that!" Celia said between deep, gulping gasps for air.

"Neither can I."

With tears streaming down both their faces, Celia reached over to wipe them from her friend's cheek. Jen clutched her hand. "Seriously, Celie. Nicci's my goddaughter. I'll always be involved in her life. I'll make sure of that."

"Thank you."

"Anytime. You're my best friend."

"And you're mine."

"I'd better be," Jen muttered, chuckling. She reached to the stroller and fussed with the blankets over baby Beth, then checked on the boys. "Mikey! Jonathan!" she said in her best don't-argue-with-me voice. "Stop throwing rocks up the slide!" Then she turned back to Celia. "I don't like to think about this. None of us do. But I want you to know something. *If* something happens to you, now or ever, Nicci will know who you were. She'll hear the stories she doesn't remember, from me and from others. You won't be forgotten."

"Thank you," Celia whispered, tears filling her eyes. Her friend knew her so well. Knew that this until now unspoken wish scared Celia more than anything. That Nicci would eventually embrace life after Celia was important. But she didn't want her daughter to forget everything. Just the bad stuff.

Her heart hurt, thinking she wouldn't see her baby grow up. There was so much she'd miss. She might not see Nicci grow into her teen years. Or go to dances. Or be able to help Nicci know how special that first kiss can be.

She wouldn't see her graduate from school and dive into whatever field she chose for a career. Or be there when she married.

Celia gulped. Nicci would have children who wouldn't know their grandmother.

Oh, God. This was worse than any physical pain. Celia stared at the playground seeing nothing but the misery her heart wallowed in.

That's when it happened again. She recognized it and, in fact, wanted it. "Take me away," she whispered to the gentle caress of her cheek. "Please."

Show me.

"What do you mean there's nothing there?" Celia asked with a hard-earned calm.

"I mean exactly what I said. We have no money in savings," Dan answered. "It's all gone. Where did it go?"

"That's exactly what I would like to know. Where *did* it all go, Daniel?"

"You're blaming me?"

"Who else? I haven't tapped it. In fact, I've been putting every penny I could scrounge *into* that account. My car is all but dead. That money was for a new car." Her voice choked on the last words and she gulped air to steady herself, glaring at him. "If I'm not taking money out, who is?"

"I've barely withdrawn anything. Just a little bit here and there to bolster the business."

"What's this thousand dollar withdrawal two days ago?" she asked.

" I had bills to pay."

"And the fifteen hundred two weeks earlier?"

"Look," he said, slapping the table as he stood.

"That money isn't just yours. We're a team, remember? I have a right to use it just as much as you do."

"Yes." Celia said sadly. "You do. The problem is that you access those funds on a regular basis." Celia rested her elbow on the table and began to rub her forehead, tired of this same old argument. "I've had enough of living hand-to-mouth, Daniel. I can't do it anymore."

"Ceelie, come on." Daniel rounded the table to kneel beside her, turning her to him and pulling both her hands into his. "Don't say that. If you don't want me to touch our money, I won't touch our money. We can work this out."

"No, Daniel. I don't think we can."

Celia watched the flash of anger cross Daniel's face and he pushed off and stood up. "So what are you saying?"

"I think that Nicci and I should go stay with Mom and Dad. Until we can sort everything out."

"Great. I've got a big business dinner next week. They are expecting my wife to be there. Instead, you're deserting me. And taking my daughter with you."

"I'm not deserting you. I'll go to the dinner and you can see Nicci whenever you want."

"You're going to ruin our daughter's life."

"No, I'm trying to salvage it. She doesn't need to hear us fighting anymore." It was Celia's turn to stand. She placed a hand on her husband's shoulder. "There's a lot of good in you. And you have a lot of things you want to do in your life. I'll only hold you back."

A grunt was the only answer she got.

"Daniel, think about it. Without me around you'll be in charge of your own finances."

Daniel's brow furrowed. If it weren't so sad, Celia

would laugh. He was so predictable. Put dollar signs in front of his eyes and everything else faded.

"Dear, dear Daniel. I still love you. I always will. You know that, right?"

"Yeah." He was back to grumbling. "You just can't live with me anymore." He walked away then, out the back door.

Later that night Celia heard him return. Tired from packing, she didn't go downstairs. And he didn't come up. In the morning she saw the rumpled blankets on the couch. And wanted to cry at having hurt him. Still, it was the best decision she could make for herself and Nicci and in time, for Daniel.

"Ceelie, are you all right?"

Celia opened her eyes. She was back at the park. Or, most likely, still at the park.

"Ceelie?"

"Huh?" Celia remained distracted by the memories. "Yes, I'm fine," she said more confidently. "Sorry. I must have dozed off."

"Well, it's probably time to get these kids home before they totally tear up the place. You still look tired, too. Ready to go?"

"Sure."

"Great. Watch Beth, okay? While I go round up the boys."

"Sure." Celia peeked in at the sleeping baby and thought about her own family.

It had taken six months of ironing out details and giving in to financial pleas before her divorce could be finalized. Even then, she'd felt the tug of regret. Nicci had complained bitterly, had hated living at her Grandmother's house those first months, and most of all, had hated Celia for quite some time, swearing on multiple occasions that she was going to go live with Daddy. Still, Nicci had gotten over it. Their relationship became stronger than ever. And Celia had been forced to search for a different type of job, a better paying one and one that she'd ended up loving. Finding a house close to her mother's had also been good for all of them. In time, Daniel had come around. He still spent at least part of every weekend with Nicci. And it was obvious the adoration between those two was mutual.

He'd take good care of their daughter, especially with occasional nudges from her mother and her best friend. This would be the best situation for Nicci. She'd be happy afterwards. Celia felt that in her heart and her relief was palpable.

17

QUITTING TIME

"The new drugs aren't helping," Janice Mason said. "We knew it was a slim possibility at the outset. I thought the research showed promise, but in your case I'm afraid it hasn't worked."

Patricia clenched Celia's hands in response to the news. Celia didn't move. She couldn't. Numbness had invaded her, holding her captive. She'd just been given the final sentence. Nothing would stop the cancer now. Shouldn't she be screaming? Or crying? Or shaking with emotions too strong to voice? She'd cried a lot of tears over the past two years. Maybe she didn't have any left.

Even knowing this was coming, hearing the final possibility go down in flames should affect her in some way, shouldn't it? All Celia felt was tired. Tired of fighting. Of getting good news, then bad, then more bad. At least this would be the last of the bad news. Wouldn't it?

"So it's time to get comfortable and make sure everything's in order, then?" Celia asked the doctor.

Janice reached for her other hand. "You said no

withholding information, right?"

"Right," Celia answered through tight lips.

"There's not much more we can do except make you comfortable. We could continue chemotherapy. That might buy some more time."

"How much?"

"A couple months, maybe longer. You never know for certain."

"Anything that prolongs my daughter's life is worth it," Patricia said with force behind her voice.

Celia turned to her mother. "I'm not as sure of that as you are, Mom."

"What do you mean? We have to keep fighting."

Celia reached for her mother's hand. "You've shared this fight with me, been there through the good and the bad, most of which was bad... You have a voice in this decision. However, you have to know that I've come to terms with the fact that I have a limited time left on this earth. I think we've all been thinking about that a lot lately."

The numbness that had infused Celia fled, and Celia's gut tumbled when her mother started to cry.

"I'm sorry, Mom. I can't see myself spending what's left taking meds that make me so sick. I think our time together—" She stopped to clear her throat when her voice broke. "Our time now is so precious that I don't want to spend it throwing up in the bathroom. Can you understand that?"

Her mother grasped Celia's hands in hers. "I know it's been hard. You've been so brave through all of this. I just..." She turned to the doctor. "Can Celia take some time to think about this?"

"Certainly. At this point I suggest we discontinue the experimental drugs. You don't have chemo again for another week, so you have that time to consider your options."

"Then take that time, Celia," her mother said. "Take time to make sure."

Celia didn't want to think anymore. She just wanted to be. To enjoy time with Nicci. But her mother was right. It was important enough to mull over. She nodded, even though she knew she wouldn't change her mind.

That night, curled up on the couch with Brad and Nicci watching television, Celia felt a true sense of peace come over her. This was what she wanted. This kind of time. Not chats while sitting on the bathroom floor, or conversations from an outpatient recliner while drugs dripped into her body. She wanted to feel well enough to enjoy these moments for as long as she could.

After Nicci went to bed, Brad wasted no time asking her how the doctor appointment went.

Celia left the warm comfort of being snuggled up to him and sat up. She didn't want to feel the tension invade his body when she told him. "It wasn't good."

And there it was. The slight tightening of his features, his muscles. "How bad was it?"

There was no way to ease into this. "The treatment's not working. Even chemo isn't as effective anymore. The tumors are growing."

Brad stood and paced the floor for long moments, his hands shredding his hair. "There must be something else we can do. Some other treatment, another kind of chemotherapy. I should have gone with you today."

"You've been researching this as much as I have. Did you find anything else? I didn't. Neither did Dr. Mason."

"But there has to be something." Brad slapped fist to palm. "We can't just... wait a minute." He stared at Celia, then sat down, taking both her hands. "You can't quit. You have to keep fighting."

Celia tried to smile, but the deep melancholy filling her kept it from feeling real or natural. "Mom said the same thing today. But at what cost?"

"Any cost."

"Even if whatever time I have left, I spend sick instead of enjoying the people around me? Do you want me to feel that way?"

"No. Of course not. But I don't want you to—"

"Die. Say the word, Brad."

"No. I'm not ready." His hands tightened on hers. "Neither are you. You can't be ready. You need to stick around. I—we all need you to stay."

Celia pulled her hands away and cupped his cheeks. "Believe me, I wish more than anything that I could."

He kissed her, gently. They hadn't made love in months because of how the chemo affected her. She missed that, missed the closeness with him. Celia thrust those thoughts aside and rested her forehead against his.

"I'm sorry to have to bring this up, but wasn't there a time with your mother that she said enough?"

It's funny what she noticed at times like this. She could feel his forehead crease, even count the three indentations while they were skin-to-skin. Celia almost laughed at the absurdity.

Brad pulled away, looked away. When he answered her, his voice was so quiet she hardly heard him. "Yes."

She turned his head to face her and smiled a soft, gentle smile. "You argued with her, too."

"Of course."

"A part of you has to know that she was right in her

decision." She placed her hand over his heart. "And that I'm right now."

Brad covered her hand, clutched it for a moment, then set it away, back on her own lap. It was the saddest movement Celia had ever experienced, because she knew.

It was time.

"I think it's time for you to go, Brad."

"I don't—"

"Before you say anything, remember your promise to tell me when you couldn't handle it anymore. You were honest with me then. Be honest now."

He stood and walked to the window to look out on the darkness of night. He stayed that way for a long time and Celia waited, giving him the time he needed. Finally, he pushed his hands deep into his pockets and turned. There were tears in his eyes.

And so much grief that Celia almost gave in and asked him to stay.

"I don't think I can watch you...die," he whispered.

Her heart broke. For him and for herself. This was harder than just about anything she'd endured so far. Celia gulped, then straightened. "I know you can't. And I understand. I'm going to be selfish here, Brad. I need people around me who can deal with this. It's going to be hard for everyone, but mostly for Nicci. That's where my focus needs to be now."

"I know." He walked to her and pulled her up and into his arms. "You are the strongest, bravest woman I've ever met, Celia Milbourne."

She smiled into his chest. "I do believe you're right."

"I love you, you know. I've loved our time together more than I can say." His kiss was the softest, saddest, most poignant kiss she'd ever had. Celia longed for it to never end. Longed for the changes in her life to never have happened, for everything in the world to just go away for a little while longer while she stayed in his arms with his lips pressed to hers. She was safe. She was loved.

And she had cancer. Celia sighed as she ended the kiss. She touched Brad's lips with her fingers, lingering, searing this moment in her mind and heart. "I love you, too. You've been my rock when I've needed one. You took on a lot with me, even though it was eating you up inside."

Brad nodded, let out a long breath, and stepped back. "Well, then, I guess this is it."

"I guess it is."

Brad moved to where his jacket and briefcase lay. He picked them up and tried to straighten, but his shoulders didn't get the message. Slumped, they seemed to drag him back to the sofa and he sagged down onto the cushion. "Maybe..."

"No, Brad. You and I both know this is for the best." Celia held out her hand.

He took it, stood, and followed her when she walked him to the door.

"I'm sorry," he said, rubbing her arm with his free hand.

"I'm not." She held her head up high. "I've loved every moment we've had."

"Me, too."

He walked through the door and out of her life then. Celia closed the door and leaned against it, her heart shattered into a thousand pieces on the floor. She had no strength left to move. Saying goodbye had taken every last bit of it and left nothing but an aching chasm in her heart and soul. But no tears came. As much as she'd wanted to hold tight to the happiest parts of her life, some would only be memories to sustain her. All that was left now was a resolve to make sure everyone dealt with this in the best way for them. That was what she needed to be thinking about. She'd been completely honest with Brad. She needed to focus on Nicci.

"Mom?"

Celia's head whipped up. How much had her daughter heard. "Nicci! I thought you were asleep."

"He's not coming back, is he?" There were tears in Nicci's eyes.

"No, he's not." Celia held her arms out and Nicci ran down the rest of the stairs and into her embrace. They walked together like that to the couch and sat down.

"Did you hear our conversation?" Celia asked.

"Just the last part. About him not being able to watch you—"

She hugged her daughter tight to her side. Her worst fears had just become reality. Nicci knew the truth now. There could be no more smoothing it over. And at ten years old, it sucked that she had to deal with this.

"I'm so sorry you heard that, Babydoll."

"Are you going to die, Mom?"

She couldn't have this conversation. Not yet. "We all die sometime."

"That's a cop out."

"You always could see right through me." Celia took a deep breath, knowing she wasn't getting out of this. "You know I went to the doctor today, right?"

"Yep."

"Well, the news wasn't good. The treatment's not working."

"This was the last thing the doctor could think of,"

Nicci said.

"Yes, it was."

Nicci hugged her mom back. They sat there like that for several minutes, holding onto each other and processing.

"I wish I were older," Nicci whispered.

"Why?"

"Because then I'd already be working on a cure for your cancer and you could be healed."

Pride swelled in Celia's heart. "I do believe you will find a cure, Babydoll. If anyone can, it's you."

"You *bet* I will."

Her daughter sat up then and made Celia more proud of her than she'd ever been. She looked her Mom in the eye. "I'm gonna love you forever, no matter what."

"And I'm going to love you, too. You're going to weather this storm just fine. You have to. I need you to."

"And I'll help you, too, Mom."

"I'm counting on it. Right now, the best way you can help me is to get back in bed. You've got school tomorrow and need your rest."

"You need your rest, too, you know."

Celia chuckled. "You're absolutely right. We'll head upstairs together."

The next morning, after Nicci got on the bus to school, Celia called Dan. "Any chance we could talk today?"

"Sure. I can come right over." She could hear the trepidation in his voice.

"Could Kate come with you?"

"Umm, you want to talk to Kate?"

"I want to thank her for all she's done to help. And

yes, I want to talk to both of you."

"Okay. But you'll have to give me a couple hours. She's all about looking perfect before she leaves the house."

Celia laughed. "That's fine. I'll see you later, then."

"Count on it."

An uncharacteristic melancholy filled Celia as she disconnected the call. Dan seemed happy with Kate. In some ways Celia knew she'd failed him by not sticking it out for the long haul. She hadn't been patient enough, hadn't been able to harness his focus. Not like Kate. She seemed to bring out the best in him. They both had a strong entrepreneurial spirit, something that had been a difference between herself and Dan. Celia had been more focused on their home life and Dan on growing the business. It had hurt Celia every time he'd put work before their life together. But she'd come to terms with it and was glad she could still remain friends with him. In the end she knew they hadn't failed. It was more like their marriage had been a stepping stone to their future selves. And Nicci was the gift they'd given each other.

All in all, Celia was content with how things had turned out. Thanks to Kate, she wouldn't have to worry about Dan anymore. He'd be fine. And Kate would also be good for Nicci. In light of Celia's choices now, Dan's new life with Kate would turn out to be a godsend, she thought.

Seth watched them arrive. Kate looked a bit like a deer in an oncoming car's headlights. Celia tried to put her at ease right away, taking her hands and thanking her for all the food she'd sent home with Nicci.

"That was no trouble at all. I just made a little extra when I cooked."

"Well, it was appreciated by all of us and I thank you for the kindness. Come in, sit down," Celia said. She motioned them to the couch. "Can I get you any water or coffee or tea?"

"No," Dan said, keeping Kate's hand in his as they sat. "We're fine."

Seth liked how protective of Kate Dan seemed to be. Nicci'd been right when she told her mother this one seemed to be a keeper. He knew Dan had recently visited a jeweler, adding to the belief that Kate would be part of the family for a long, long time. He smiled. She'd be good for Nicci. Had been ever since she'd moved in with Dan.

"So," Celia said. "I wanted to talk to both of you about some things. Treatment has not been successful and we're at a point where plans need to be finalized."

Kate's eyes became round circles and filled with tears. There was even a sheen to Dan's eyes. "Is there nothing else that can be done?" Dan asked.

"Nothing. Except making the most of the time we have left."

"I'm so sorry, Ceelie." And his words were heartfelt. Seth could hear the sorrow.

"I know. It's time to get beyond that, though. Dan—" She looked at him and Seth could see in her expression how hard this was and how resolved she was to make this work. "I'm sorry to have to be so blunt here, but I need to be sure. I know I asked you, Dan, but I need to hear from both of you. When I'm gone, do you want Nicci with you or should I make other arrangements?"

Dan's mouth dropped open and Seth wanted to shut it for him...hard. It surprised him when Kate answered.

"There's no question. Of course we want her with

us."

Celia smiled, even if it was a bit tremulous. "Good. I had to be sure you both wanted this." She reached across for Kate's free hand. "You really have been a good, stable influence for Nicci. I—" She gulped. "I can't imagine a better...person to see her through her teenage years."

The tears in Kate's eyes lost the battle to stay put. "I will never be the mother you've been to her."

"No. You'll be a different kind of mother. But just as important." Letting go, Celia handed her a Kleenex and took one for herself.

"Hey," Dan said. "Don't I have a say in this?"

"No," they said in unison. It was the perfect moment, breaking up the sadness and adding some light to their conversation.

"Well, I'm going to have a say anyhow." Dan reached for Celia's hand. "You and me...that was all my fault, Celie."

"Dan—"

"Let me finish. I know it takes two to end a marriage, but honestly, Ceelie, I was too young, too focused on myself to be the husband you deserved. I'm sorry for that."

Celia bit her lip and Seth could see she was trying not to cry. "It wasn't just you. I could have been more patient."

"You shouldn't have had to be. But...I'm older now. I understand better. And Kate, here, well, she's making sure I stay focused on what's important."

Celia smiled. "I see that, and I truly am happy for you. For both of you."

"I'm glad," Dan said. "Because I'm about to do something very unconventional and I'd like your blessing, Celia."

Seth didn't think Dan was capable of surprising him, but when he saw the brightening of Celia's face, saw her smile and nod as Dan went down on his knee in front of his girlfriend, Seth's eyes widened.

"I'm sure this is the most unusual situation to do this in, and it wasn't what I'd planned." Dan reached into his pocket as he spoke. "But I *have* been planning this. And somehow this just seems like the right time." He opened the small case. "Kate, I've been a mess up, and I probably won't stop making mistakes. But you make me want to learn from them. You've made me tow the rope, set budgets, and stick with one business. You've been my partner in every respect. You've made our house a home and I want to be with you forever. I love you, Kate. Will you do me the great honor of becoming my wife?"

Kate, who'd covered her mouth with the hand Dan wasn't holding, whooped. "Yes, Dan. I'll marry you. Oh, yes!"

He placed the ring on Kate's finger and they kissed, then hugged. Dan turned to Celia. "You sure you're okay with this?"

Seth could see the tears on her cheeks. Tears of joy, he knew.

"I'm more than okay. I'm at peace. Congratulations to both of you," she said, hugging them both.

"Okay if we pick Nicci up after school to give her the news?"

"I think that would be spectacular."

After seeing them off, Seth watched as Celia settled on the couch and stared out the window. The smile that tugged at her lips meant she was in a good place. She really was satisfied and at peace. He settled at the end of the couch, content to just watch her be happy in this moment.

Anything else could wait.

18

HOSPICE

The hospital bed made the dining room look like something out of a bad B-movie. Not even the feminine drapes and sheers could mask the antiseptic look of the bed.

"It's ugly," Celia said.

"I know," Laura, her social worker-turned-friend, answered. "But it's functional. And you're having too much trouble navigating those." She waved a hand at the steep stairs behind them.

Mack, who was helping the tech situate the bed, nodded.

"Couldn't I just sleep on the couch?" Celia said, eyes wide open in a mock-pleading expression.

"Nice try, but this will be easier on your mother, too," Laura said.

"Now *that* is the argument that got me into this mess." Celia stared askance at the bed and sighed. Sitting on the side, she tested the mattress. "Yuck. It's soft."

"Try it for a week. If you don't sleep well, we'll get a different mattress."

"All right. I'll try it."

When Nicci came home from school that day, she stopped short. Celia tried to see the changes through her daughter's eyes. The table had been placed in storage for now. They didn't need it anyhow, since they all ate in the kitchen nook. The dining room looked like a hospital room. And Nicci had seen too many of those in her short life.

Celia struggled to keep from hitting something. This was too much for her daughter to bear. No, she corrected herself. Nicci was strong and would handle it. She knew that. But she shouldn't have to. She should be able to go out and play with her friends after school instead of rushing home to make sure Mom was okay. She'd even stopped spending any nights at her father's. He'd understood and let her make the choices for now.

Damn it. Her daughter should be able to sleep with her bedroom door shut. It totally and completely sucked. And Celia still wanted to hit something. Instead, she held out her arms. "Come here, Babydoll."

Nicci ran into them and hugged her tightly.

"You knew we were getting this today."

"Yes." Nicci's voice sounded like it was coming through one of those tin can phones every child tried at least once. "It just...makes everything look so different."

"And it makes it impossible to forget mommy's sick, doesn't it."

"Y-yes." Her voice was even smaller.

"Nicci?"

"Yeah?"

"You know I love you, right?"

"Yeah."

"I think maybe it might be better if you started

staying over at your Dad's house."

"Uh uh! No way." Nicci hugged her mother even tighter.

"That way you'd get a break from all this." Celia waved an arm around the room.

Nicci pulled back and Celia's heart broke at how grown up she looked in that moment. "When do you get a break, Mom?"

A flash of white-blonde hair crossed Celia's mind. Whoever the man was, he'd been showing up more and more when she closed her eyes. "In my dreams."

"Well, then, that's my break, too. This is our home and I'm staying right here." Her chin raised exactly the same way Daniel's did every time they disagreed.

Celia pulled her back into a tight embrace. "Ah, Babydoll. You are so much like your father." Celia smiled, then made a decision. "All right. You can stay here. But you sleep in your own bed at night. No more hunkering down on the floor by mine."

Nicci looked as if she were about to protest, so Celia used her daughter's own ploy against her. She raised her chin. And Nicci closed her mouth without argument.

Hospice would visit the following day. It wasn't that Celia was exactly ready for hospice. But she was getting weaker. And they were the ones who'd ordered the hospital bed. Laura had explained that, for now, they'd just be checking in on her every few days.

That night Celia lay in her new bed in the makeshift bedroom, and felt more exposed than she ever had in her life. There were no doors she could close. Only doorways. And only three walls, as the fourth opened into the living room. It felt...too big.

As quietly as possible, she stole out of bed and

headed for the stairs. One foot climbed, then the other joined it. One step done. She looked up. Ten more to go. Slowly she made her way to the top and paused to regain her strength. Then she wobbled down the hallway to her own room. As she passed Nicci's, she stopped to listen to her daughter's deep breathing. Nicci was sound asleep. So asleep she hadn't even heard her mother labor up the steps. Latte lifted his head, but went back to sleep without awakening Nicci.

Celia smiled, happy to see her daughter in such good slumber. She made it to her own room, grabbed an afghan, and climbed into bed, content as she, too, fell into a deep slumber.

When she woke in the morning, she stretched and then rolled to sit up, stopping short. There was Nicci, sound asleep on her bedroom floor, her faithful dog beside her.

Her daughter had been sleeping so well when she'd come upstairs, but sometime during the night she must have woken up and looked for her mother. Had Celia made noise in her sleep?

She reached for her robe and carefully slid by Nicci, trying to let her sleep. Latte lifted his head to stare at her for a moment before dropping it back down to sleep some more. At the top of the stairs, Celia stopped, working up the strength to go down. One foot started, but the other leg wobbled too much. She was definitely getting weaker. The pain was starting to become a bit of a problem, too.

In the end, she sat on her bottom and scooted down the stairs. After a moment's rest, she followed the aroma of coffee to the kitchen.

"Mmmmm. That smells good," she said, pecking her mother on the cheek as she reached for a cup.

"You don't drink coffee anymore, remember?"

"I think that, this morning, I'll make an exception. It smells heavenly."

She sipped the brew as her mother puttered, making preparations for the day's meals.

"Where's Mack?"

"He left early to take care of some things at the rental."

"Oh, good." The coffee tasted as good as it always had and Celia vowed to have coffee every morning she could. No more missing out. She prayed her daughter wasn't missing out, either. "Hey, Mom?"

"Yes, sweetheart?"

"Do I make a lot of noise when I sleep?"

Her mother turned to her. "I heard you go upstairs. Was Nicci in your room when you got up?"

Celia breathed in the tangy aroma of the Columbian blend. "Mm, huh."

Patricia shook her head. "I don't know what to do to get that girl to sleep through the night. And yes, I'm sorry, but you do make these little snuffling noises at night, like you're reaching for breath sometimes."

Celia set her cup down abruptly, knowing what had brought Nicci into her room last night. She'd slept like a log until she heard her mother breathing. Celia sighed, knowing that she was done with sleeping upstairs, if for no other reason than her daughter's well-being.

"I won't go upstairs anymore, Mom."

"That would probably be best. What made you go last night?"

"I just felt so...exposed."

Later that day Mack hung blankets between the living and dining rooms. And that was all it took for Celia to be comfortable in her new bedroom. As the days progressed, more and more of Celia's things found their way into the dining room. Nicole mysteriously disappeared with her father one afternoon and no amount of cajoling would get the "why" out of her mother.

A couple of hours later they returned, laden with many of the pictures and items from Celia's old bedroom. Things that hadn't fit upstairs now found a place in her new bedroom. The television got moved in, as well as the DVD player. Celia and Nicci spent hours watching movies. Celia could no longer go to the park with Jen, so Jen came to the house. At first she brought the kids along. Eventually, though, she came alone. It was better that way. All the chaos made Celia nervous.

Hospice now came daily instead of once a week. Celia spent most of her time in bed. Some of that time was hard to remember. Her meds had increased to help her deal with the pain.

She'd been adamant with her friends and family, though. She wanted to be wakened when they came to visit. And there were a lot of visits. Everyone stopped by. Her boss, Tana, Dan and Kate. Everyone. Well, just about. Celia missed Brad, but knew this was for the best. The missing him thing seemed to fade, just like time seemed to be fading. She had trouble figuring out the days now.

In the evenings she took less medication so she could be alert to hear about Nicci's day. It was worth a little extra pain to get that time with her daughter. Well worth it.

The pain worsened and Celia lost count of the hours and days and visitors. Always the faces, Nicci's included, showed happiness, but there was a lingering sorrow underneath.

And always in her dreams, the man with the blond hair smiled at her, helped her to be happy. She wished she'd had a chance to know him in real life.

That chance was gone now.

19

SHOW ME

Celia didn't even try to hide her sorrow. Tears sprang unbidden as she immediately recognized where she was. The hospital. Only this was another time, another place. One she didn't want to remember. What possible purpose could dredging up this memory have, except to make her miserable? She curled up into a ball and squished her eyes tightly shut.

She wouldn't watch.

She refused to see.

She didn't want to relive this.

But the voice was insistent. "Celia," he said softly. "It's all right. I'm right beside you."

"Why?" She sobbed. "Why would you make me go through this again?

"There's something you need to learn. Trust me. You'll be okay."

She felt his familiar touch like a warm blanket. It soothed her. Her muscles relaxed and she felt like she was floating. Her eyes were still shut, yet she sensed movement.

The doctor's voice intruded. She opened her eyes

and found herself still in her father's hospital room. Seven years ago, yet it seemed like yesterday.

A typical room, much like the one she inhabited now at home. A male nurse fussed with the I.V. She frowned. He was familiar, but she couldn't quite place him.

Her father was asleep in the bed. Wait, that wasn't right. He was out because of all the medications they had him on.

"Daddy," she whispered.

But no one heard. She could only watch as the doctor spoke to her mother and a younger Celia.

"If we had caught it sooner, we might have been able to do something." He glanced at the bed. "He must have been in a tremendous amount of pain."

Her mother cried softly into a hanky and Celia cocooned her in an embrace as the doctor went on.

"The cancer probably started in his colon, then spread unchecked from there. Now his body can't fight it anymore and his organs are starting to shut down."

Patricia gasped and Celia struggled to maintain some composure.

"That, uh, doesn't sound good, doctor."

"I'm afraid it's not." He paused and it felt like a thousand tornadoes had just descended on the hospital. "There's really very little time."

"Very—" Celia's voice broke. "How much—" she found it hard to get the words out.

"Hours. Maybe."

She looked at the pale white visage of her father in the bed. "Will he wake up?" she asked without turning back to the doctor.

"He's heavily medicated. We can reduce the morphine, however, that will increase his discomfort."

"N-no," her mother spoke up, moving to the bedside. "I don't want him in any pain."

"All right. I'll leave orders to be called if there is any change in his condition." He rose and placed his hand on her shoulder. "I'm really very sorry." Then he quietly left the room. The nurse followed him out the door.

As Celia watched her mother and younger self, all of the emotions rushed back. The anguish of losing her father. The worry about what she and her mother would do. And the guilt she felt at being left out. She never was, but it had seemed that way to her at the time.

The stab of aloneness hit younger Celia like a wall of pressure. Her father was dying. Oh, God. She couldn't believe it. Flashes of thought rushed her brain. Memories.

He taught her how to read before she ever went to school.

He gifted her with her first piece of jewelry ever. She fingered the tiny ring with the inscription "Love, Daddy," now worn on a chain around her neck.

When the bullies at school picked on her friends, he didn't talk to their parents. He nudged her with his own wisdom to resolve the issue herself. And she had. Because he gave her strength.

Who would be her strength now?

Celia looked on as her mother stood at the bedside of her husband. Forty-two years of marriage, one yearned-for daughter, and countless memories. All coalesced into these final moments.

How would her mother go on? How would she?

Oh, God. She couldn't stand it.

The same nurse entered. Instead of moving to the bedside, he looked up to the corner. It seemed as if...

He looked directly at her. And finally, she knew.

"It's you!" she said.

"Yes," the voice beside her said. "It's time, Celia."

"No," she turned away. "I don't want to watch this. Not again. Please," she pleaded. "Why are you doing this to me."

The hand soothed her forehead. "Trust me. Let me show you."

Compelled, she opened her eyes. She and her mother stood by the bed, unable to see the light beginning to emanate from her father. The nurse dropped all pretense of checking the I.V., sat on the bed, and took hold of his hand.

Her father's eyes opened.

Celia didn't remember her father opening his eyes. He never regained consciousness.

"He did to me," the voice said in her ear.

Her father smiled then, and she listened as he told the nurse how happy his life had been. How loved he had been as a child. How he'd tried hard to return that love for his wife and daughter. He mentioned the angst when they had endured seven years of barrenness and three miscarriages. His joy at Celia's birth. His pleasure in spending time with both her and his wife.

His pride in how well she had grown and all of her accomplishments. His feeling of peace when little Nicole was born. How gratifying the knowledge was that the family would continue and thrive.

And, finally, he spoke of his ever-present love for his soul mate. His wife. His life.

He turned then and looked at the same corner she watched from. "I will love you and your mother for forever."

The light brightened and his focus changed. His

smile of love changed to one of tranquility. His hand twitched just a little bit as her mother held it. Then it was over. The smile stayed on his lips, but what made him her father passed on.

Celia turned at the touch on her shoulder. The nurse was there. The nurse was...The nurse was the boy, the man, the gentle soul who had been guiding her through this journey.

"Your name is Seth."

"Yes."

"You've been here through everything?"

"Yes."

"You've helped me through the worst of this illness."

"I have tried."

"Why?"

"Because I love you. And it was all I could do."

Tears flowed freely down her cheeks. She knew now who he was. Knew he'd been there through everything, helping her. Her heart cracked open, filling up with all the love she'd failed to notice all this time. "I can see you. Why can I see you?"

"Because the time is close."

Tears filled her eyes. "I'm not ready."

"Yes, you are."

"I haven't finished—"

His hand caressed her cheek. "You've done all you can. Your mother knows how much you love her. You've prepared for Nicci's future and she, too, feels well-loved. It's time now to focus on you."

"It's not enough. I need more time," she whispered desperately. "I haven't accomplished everything I wanted to."

"You have accomplished more than you know. Do

you know what effect you have had on people? What an example you set for others?"

"Me? I'm not sure I believe that."

"Do you remember Bernadette?"

Celia frowned. "My friend from grade school?"

"Yes. Remember how you first became friends? How you helped her during the game of Red Rover? That incident was a pivotal point in her life. It was the first time she ever stood up for herself. It gave her the courage to do whatever she wanted. Bernadette became an attorney who fights for those who can't or won't fight for themselves."

"I-I didn't know."

"That's only one example. You have cared for and about others your entire life. And you are well-loved in return."

"But what about my mother? And Nicci. How can I leave them?"

"It's your time now. Your mother is strong. Mack will help her weather this. And Nicci will grow to be a vibrant woman. She will make you prouder even than you are right now."

"How will I know that?"

"Look..." Seth said.

Celia watched as the air around her swirled out of focus. When her vision returned, she watched an auburn-haired teenager saying goodbye to her grandmother as she headed off to college.

"I'll be good, Gramma. I'll do my studies. And I won't get into trouble." Celia's own mother, grayer now, hugged Nicci tightly. Mack, who'd lost most of his hair, stood beside her and shared her pride.

"You be sure you do behave," Nicci's grandmother admonished.

Celia watched the images shift and change. She saw Nicci graduate from university, go on to medical school, and received her degree, specializing in oncology. She watched her choose research over patient care. But she didn't isolate herself. She had many friends and was well-loved.

The scenes blurred again, refocusing on a church. The church she herself had attended all through childhood. The church she'd married Daniel in. There was Daniel now, walking the bride down the aisle. Nicci was awash in white and more beautiful than Celia ever imagined.

"Nicci will be fine," Seth said quietly beside her.

"I—" Celia couldn't speak.

She turned to Seth, beaming with pride as if the accomplishments were her own. "Thank you. Thank you *so* much. She does grow up to be a beautiful and successful woman, doesn't she?"

"Yes." He looked behind him and up for a moment. "Now it's your turn for happiness, Celia."

She glanced back one more time at the vision of her daughter and the man she was marrying. It faded and, somehow, she didn't mind.

Turning to Seth, she smiled. This was her future. This was her new life.

Seth held out his hand as the light grew brighter. With a smile filled with peace, she placed her hand in his.

Looking at the face she felt she'd known all her life, she mouthed the words that had guided her through these past few months.

"Show me."

The End

If you'd like to read more about Celia's brave daughter, Nicci, and see how she turned out, her story can be found in Healing Love, part of a two-story anthology called *Holiday Magic – The Gift of Love*. Thank you for reading *Show Me*. If you enjoyed this book, please consider leaving an honest review on Amazon, Goodreads, or wherever you prefer, and know that it would be greatly appreciated.

For new release information and news about Laurie Ryan, please sign up for her newsletter at:

laurieryanauthor.com

OTHER BOOKS BY LAURIE RYAN

Holiday Magic – The Gift of Love
Northern Lights

The TROPICAL PERSUASIONS Series

Stolen Treasures
Pirate's Promise
Dare To Love

ABOUT THE AUTHOR

Born and raised in the Pacific Northwest, Laurie Ryan writes contemporary stories about women's journeys and contemporary romance with enough spice to be fun and endings that feed her belief that this world is a happy place. When not writing, she provides freelance editing services. She also love to scrapbook and walk, when she can get time away from her handsome he-can-fix-anything hubby and their gray cat, Dude, who generally rules the entire house.

A devoted reader, Laurie has immersed herself in the diverse works of authors like Tolkien and Woodiwiss. She is passionate about every aspect of a book: beginning, middle, and end. She can't arrive to a movie five minutes late, has never been able to read the end of a book before the beginning, and is a strong believer in reading the book before seeing the movie.

62480993R00155

Made in the USA
Lexington, KY
08 April 2017